HERBERT RESNICOW

THE HOT PLACE

ST. MARTIN'S PRESS · A THOMAS DUNNE BOOK · NEW YORK

Design by Judith A. Stagnitto

Library of Congress Cataloging-in-Publication Data

Resnicow, Herbert.
    The hot place / by Herbert Resnicow.
        p.   cm.
    "A Thomas Dunne book."
    ISBN 0-312-04985-4
    I. Title.
PS3568.E69H6   1990
813'.54—dc20   90-37308
                                                    CIP

First Edition: January 1991
10 9 8 7 6 5 4 3 2 1

1

The moment I stepped into the main entry lounge of the club I saw Warren, my Warren, sitting on one of the easy chairs, surrounded by cops. One of the cops, the one doing the questioning, was Sergeant Ben Palmieri, who *owed* me from when I—all right, Warren helped—solved the Kassel murder. For which I let Palmieri take all the credit, practically.

The Oakdale Country Club is authentic imitation Georgian, inside and out—like a lot of the fancy buildings on the North Shore of Long Island—to make it look like it's been there from before the Revolution. The paneling is beautifully matched walnut—solid wood, not veneers— the floors are random-width pegged oak, and the light fixtures look like their candles had been removed just last week. Warm and comfortable and homey for people whose fathers and mothers had come over in steerage one generation ago. Like mine. Cops did not fit there.

I pushed in. Two of the cops tried to stop me. Lots of guys've tried to stop me in my day, but I don't stop so easy, especially when I'm mad. And I *was* mad. Not just about

1

the overcrowded links—it was near the beginning of the spring vacation and some of the college kids had come home instead of going to Fort Lauderdale. And not just from the lousy golf game; Iris and Marvin Guralnik beat me and Jerry Fein as usual. I could live with that. I was also sore about the needling I got from Iris, especially because I couldn't give her anything back; orders from Warren. But mainly my blood pressure was way up because I could see Palmieri was giving Warren a hard time. Anybody starts up with my son, the philosopher, he's got to deal with me first.

"What the hell's going on, Palmieri?" I asked. Very politely, sort of. I respect Palmieri—he's smart and honest and tough—but that was my son he was questioning, my only son, absolutely completely without reason. Whatever it was, Warren didn't do it. Warren's a philosopher, for Pete's sake. Or will be, now that his thesis is finished, as soon as he passes his orals. Philosophers, *real* philosophers, don't steal or sell dope or kill people or *anything*. Talk you to death? Sure. But that's not illegal. Yet.

"So it's you, Baer?" Palmieri didn't look too friendly. "Go sit down someplace; I'll talk to you after I'm finished with Warren. Not here; the dining room."

"What do you mean, 'finished with Warren'?" I turned to my tall, skinny, guaranteed-innocent son. "Don't say another word, Warren. I'll get Irv Waxman here right away. He's got to be on the ninth hole by now."

"Relax, Dad," Warren said, and smiled. It tore my heart. When he smiles it's just like seeing Thelma again, may she rest in peace. We should have had a girl too, when we were young enough, even if we couldn't afford it. "I don't need a lawyer, Dad. I'm a witness, not a suspect."

"Yeah," Palmieri broke in. "So would you kindly go away, Baer, until I finish my third degree? I promise not to break any bones or leave any marks."

"Witness to what?"

2

"The murder, Dad. I found the body."

"What murder? What body?" Why was everybody so goddamn *relaxed*? A murder is something to be relaxed about? Finding a body is ordinary? *Normal?* Maybe it is these days—in Manhattan, maybe—but not the Oakdale Country Club. I tried to think of a calm, sunny meadow, with buttercups, which usually works for me; keeps me from blowing my top. It didn't work. "Where did you find it? The body, I mean? And what were you doing in a place like that in the first place? Didn't I bring you up not to—"

"In the steam room, Dad. By accident. I went in to relax after my workout—" And that's another thing: He's too skinny. When I made him start pumping iron—no son of mine is going to weigh 140 at six feet—I figured he'd start to look like a real man soon instead of like a starving philosopher. But it didn't happen. After six months of exercise he'd put on maybe two pounds of muscle, tops. Positively hopeless. No matter how hard you try, children never turn out perfect. "—and when I cooled the room off—"

"Stop right there," Palmieri said. "Okay, Baer. Out. This is information for the police alone."

"You're throwing me out? Me? I'm a taxpayer, Palmieri; I got a right—" My last resort was to try to think of a tropical island. Which guaranteed always helps, especially if the palm trees are gently swaying. That didn't work either. That ungrateful son-of-a-bitch Palmieri, after all I did for him . . . No. Wrong attitude. With bureaucrats—I learned this when Thelma and I were in the construction business—you never let them see you get mad. They love it when you turn blue; makes their day. What you got to do is *sound* reasonable. Like you're in control. "Warren's going to tell me what he told you anyway, as soon as we get home. So what's the difference?"

Palmieri sighed wearily. "Okay. Stay. But don't discuss what you hear with anybody. *Nobody.* Got that?"

"Sure. Absolutely. Just Irv Waxman. My attorney."

"He's a member of this club?"

"Of course. One of the founders."

"Then not him too."

"Irv? Why? You mean, *he's* a suspect?" I couldn't believe this. *Irving Waxman?* "But he's a lawyer."

"Everybody in the club's a suspect."

"Everybody? In the club? You're crazy, Palmieri. Sergeant, I mean."

"Not the women."

A pity. There went a chance to get rid of Iris Guralnik so I could win a game once in a while. Not that I wanted Iris to fry, or even go up the river for an eight-to-twenty-five, but just so she could see what it feels like to *get* a hard time once in a while instead of giving one. Which Warren would never allow me to give Iris once he finally decided to marry her daughter, Lee.

Unbelievable, the things you do for your children.

2

Back when I sold my construction company, I figured that Thelma and I could live a little, make up for all the time—practically our whole married life—when we were knocking ourselves out, struggling to build up the company and meet the payroll and fight with business agents and get the lousy bureaucrats just to let us *breathe* and . . . Forget it; if you were ever in the building business, you *know*, and if you weren't, you'd never believe the kind of crap you have to go through just to . . . It's a wonder *anything* ever gets built in this country.

I got out of construction when the prime rate had already started going up but just before it took off for outer space, selling the company for half of what I could have gotten the year before, but that's life. No complaints; if I wasn't smart enough to get out earlier, I deserved what I got. Not that we were starving; I had enough money put aside to let Warren finish school and for me and Thelma to enjoy the fruits of our labor with clear heads, plus a little more laid away for a safety net. But after you've been active all your life, you can't just stop everything and do nothing. So Thelma, who was always way ahead of me—not that I'm stupid, far from it, but she was the real brains of the family—steered me into the venture capital business.

We started small—the first time you do anything, it's not going to be perfectly perfect, so you don't risk a lot—and we were lucky. The business succeeded. Not big, but I learned a lot from it. We used only our own money; gambling you can always lose, so you don't want to drag your friends down with you. I found that venture capital investing was a wide-open market. All over the country there are thousands of bright, ambitious people, hardworking people, with great ideas. All they need is a little help with money and a lot of help from an experienced businessman to carry them through the crucial first year. If you pick the right people to invest in, the ones with *character*, most of the time you're going to come out smelling like a rose.

We formed the Nassau Venture Capital Corporation, a limited partnership, with me, Edward Baer, as the general partner. The way it works is I put up half the money for each venture and take full responsibility; the limited partners put in the other half and have no responsibility. They don't have anything to say either, which is fair; all they can lose is what they put in, I could hang for everything. Of course I get extra stock for what I do. In a fairly short time we were doing very well. Not that everything we touched turned to gold—nobody bats a thousand—but on the whole, no complaints.

No complaints, that is, until that senseless accident that took Thelma, may she rest in peace. Exactly when everything was going perfect. The business was working just fine, but without Thelma my life was completely ended, so what kind of a deal was that? It should have been the other way around—money I could live without—but God didn't make me the offer.

Although he hadn't finished his dissertation, Warren

came home from school to take care of me and, like I said, he helped save one of our companies by finding the killer who . . . It's not that I'm not capable—actually, I was the one who figured out how it was done—but Warren and I think a little differently. Like night and day. I think practical and he thinks theoretical. Backwards. Like a philosopher. Which figures.

The troubles brought Warren and me closer. Partway, at least. For the first time I felt that Warren was really beginning to understand me. Not completely, but beginning to. Too bad it took a murder for it to happen, but at least some good came out of it.

Even Iris Guralnik helped. Not with the murder directly—she's a psychologist, not a detective—but in advising how I should get along with my son, the philosopher. Which is not so easy; if you're related to a philosopher you'll know what I mean. Answers they got for everything, but real-life experience?—*that* they're lacking in large quantities. Iris gave me instructions that went directly opposite to my regular personality—not that there's anything wrong with my regular personality—but it worked out okay, so maybe she's not such a bad psychologist after all, even though she's a little too . . .

A big *noodge* is what she really is; always trying to tell me how to *everything*, but that I can handle. It's only on the links that she turns into a needling, nagging pain in the ass. So, though I took up golf to relax, her attitude makes golf very *not* relaxing for me. She says it's to help me break a hundred. Hah! How would you like to have somebody always reminding you—just when you're ready to *schlomm* the ball—to swing easy and smooth? Always? Every stroke? And what's worse, she's the club's ladies' champ, consistently breaks eighty, so I can't even tell her she don't know what the hell she's talking about or that I don't need her advice. Or *want* it. One of these days, *one of these days*, I'm going to take her advice, but it ain't the ball I'm going to swing smoothly at. I swear I will. A perfect stroke, for once in my life.

That's another headache: Even if I was willing to go to jail for it, Warren won't even let me yell at Iris. I can't even *think* about doing it. Not with Warren going steady with Lee Guralnik. Lee's a terrific beauty—it's not her mother she inherited her looks from, and sure as hell not her father—and the sweetest girl you could imagine. She loves children and wants a large family. So for Warren's sake I have to bite my tongue and not say to Iris Guralnik what I *know* I should say to an Iris Guralnik. It's very unhealthy to bottle up your emotions—I never did it before in my life—and if I keep on doing it I could end up getting an ulcer.

Ulcers I'm going to get any day now anyway, knowing I'll never break a hundred, guaranteed, and fighting with Warren about how to run the business. He owns half the stock now, inherited from Thelma. When we wrote our wills, I wanted to make sure Warren would never have to depend on anyone for rent and eating money. I was sure I'd go first—the construction business guarantees a heart attack before you're fifty, and on top of that I was five years older than Thelma, may she rest in peace—so it was a good idea at the time. I wanted to make sure Thelma would have someone she could trust handling the business, and I also wanted to provide for Warren—from philosophy you don't make a living—so in our wills we each left him our halves of the company. He was such a nice kid when he was little; go know he'd turn into a philosopher.

A philosopher in the venture capital business is not the greatest thing to have, especially since I'm positive Warren would rather be a teacher or a writer than a businessman. But that we can work out. I *hope*. We better; *I'm* sure as hell not going to change. I mean, how the hell can I tell our investors we're risking our money, and theirs, on

8

a company that, *if* it succeeds, will return less than insured CDs, just because they plan to be ecologically sincere?

But business isn't the only headache I'm having with Warren; Lee Guralnik is a bigger problem. And, much as I hate to say it, it's not her fault; it's Warren's. At first I was against Lee; the girl I picked out for Warren was Jerry Fein's daughter, Judy. No beauty, but smart, and a terrific girl in every way. Make a wonderful wife. But when Iris told me that Lee and Warren liked each other, and I took a second look at Lee . . . She's an absolute doll, so nice you wouldn't believe she's related to Iris and Marvin. After I got to know her, I was willing to overlook that she's no big brain. A B+ average from Bennington—it's an arts-type school where they never even *heard* of engineering—you don't brag about in my house. She's certainly not up to Warren in IQ—even I'm not—but brains aren't everything. Everybody knows that Thelma was the brains of the family and that I never got even a bachelor's from Cooper Union, but I worked hard and we loved each other and that's what was important. I did everything I could to make Thelma happy, and she never threw up her education to me. It could be just as good with Warren and Lee.

But what's more important, even though Lee looks like an actress, she's an old-fashioned home-style girl who doesn't want a career, and she would make Warren a very good wife. Believe me, I can tell. Whatever faults Iris Guralnik has—and Marvin Guralnik especially—they didn't pass them on to Lee, thank God. So I'm depending on Lee and Warren to . . . Bad enough that someday I'll be left alone in this big house, but shouldn't I have some *naches* from my grandchildren? Six sweet, nice, beautiful, blond grandchildren who love their grandfather, is that too much to ask? Three girls and three boys. Maybe four girls and two boys, to make up for the girl Thelma and I didn't have. I'm not entitled?

So what does Warren do? He has *dates*. Dates he needs?

Lee he's known from the sixth grade: She likes him, he likes her, so what's he waiting for? To give me an ulcer? Thelma couldn't have the happiness of seeing our only child married; at least let *me* dance at his wedding. They have to wait until she graduates? So get engaged at least; make it official. But no; he wants to be sure. Sure? What kind of sure? Guarantees you don't get in this world. The moment I met Thelma, I knew she was for me, and at Warren's age, I was already a father. Certain things you don't have to think about; you *know*. In the old days, the parents picked who you should marry, and the kids listened to the parents, and we had a lot less divorcing in those days. So today is better, with a 50 percent divorce rate? Not by me, it isn't. But whenever I barely bring up the subject, Warren gives me a smart-ass quotation from some dead philosopher who was wrong even when he was alive.

And on top of everything, Warren's a witness to a murder. That I needed yet too?

3

"Why'd you go in the steam room so early?" Sergeant Palmieri asked Warren. So I hadn't missed too much by letting my mind go back to when, for the first time, Warren and I got really close. Which hadn't happened again since then; why I can't imagine. God knows, *I* tried my best. "You go for a steam after work, Mr. Baer, to relax, not to start the day."

"I have to exercise before I go to the office, Sergeant," Warren said. "After work I study for my orals; it's the only time I have. My father insists I be in the office at nine—" Insists? Me? Ed Baer *never* insists; what I do is *inform*. Educate. As often as I have to until the message gets across, that is. A couple of times I quietly explained to Warren that the best fertilizer on a farm is the foot of the farmer, so he has to be in the office on time. Period. We have investments in fourteen businesses, and four new ones under consideration right now, and if anyone thinks all that can be handled part time . . . "And he also says," Warren went on, "I have to do muscle building three times a week, so . . ." Have to? It's for his own good, isn't

11

it? The Greeks said it a long time ago: a healthy mind in a healthy body, right? What else don't they teach them in a college that costs like you wouldn't believe?

"So I come here on Mondays, Wednesdays, and Fridays at ten to seven, just before the gym opens, change, work out until five to eight, five minutes in the steam room to sweat and relax, shower—start hot, because I just came from the steam room, and go down to body temperature—and I'm in the office at eight-thirty." I never told Warren he had to come that early, but I'm glad he takes such an interest. One minute to nine is okay by me; same time as I come in.

"You just said you had to be in the office at nine." Palmieri had caught it too. "Why go in at eight-thirty?"

"That's when I'm finished here. Violet, our house-keeper, makes me eat breakfast at home; she's afraid I won't eat right in the club coffeeshop, so where else can I go for a half hour? If I'm not in the steam room by five to eight, I can't go in there at all. Mr. Brodsky went in at exactly eight every day, and he stayed in there a full hour so, from eight to nine, nobody else could go in."

"He didn't allow anybody else in?" Palmieri looked very concentrated at Warren. "Nobody at all? He owned the club?"

"Just about. He was chairman of the board of directors and very influential, but that isn't why. You see, the rule is you can't change the thermostat in the steam room unless whoever's in there at the time agrees. Which is reasonable, unless you have somebody like Mr. Brodsky who turns the thermostat up to maximum. It gets so hot and steamy in there that no one else can stand it."

"He stood it for an hour and he was an old man." Again *was*? Brodsky was the one who was killed? Barney Brodsky?

"Mr. Brodsky was very skinny; always complaining about the cold. He liked it very hot, even tried to have the heat turned up all over the club last year. The board turned that down, but in the steam room he could do what he liked, even though nobody else could use the room while he was in it."

"*You* went in."

"I didn't really go in until . . . I lost track of the time while I was working out. It was only a couple of minutes after eight and I thought if I could beat Mr. Brodsky into the steam room, I could get my five minutes of steam and relax."

"You said you found the room all steamed up," Palmieri pressed, "so why did you go in?"

"When I opened the door—the room was so hot, so full of steam I couldn't see or breathe—I thought I'd check, just in case. Maybe Mr. Brodsky wanted to warm up the room first, or he had forgotten his towel or something, and once I was in there alone I could set the temperature to normal. I yelled in, 'Anyone in here? Mind if I lower the thermostat?' There was no answer, so I yelled again. Still no answer, so I figured Mr. Brodsky had left for a minute and I could lower the temperature; it wouldn't kill him to wait five minutes for me to finish." Warren caught himself. "I didn't mean it the way it sounds, Sergeant; just a figure of speech. I reached in with my towel—the handle gets as hot as the room—and turned the thermostat to OFF. Then I leaned in and pulled the chain of the shower. There's a cold shower inside for anybody who wants to . . . I know it sounds crazy, but there are people who like the shock; in Finland, they roll naked in the snow after a sauna. The shower lowered the temperature of the room so I could go in before Mr. Brodsky came back."

"How long did that take?"

"At least a minute. That room was *hot*."

"So it was five after eight when you went into the room?"

"About; I wasn't timing it. I spread my towel on the tile shelf nearest the door, the lowest bench—that's the coolest place, and even that's hot—and sat down."

"When did you see Mr. Brodsky?"

13

"Just when I was ready to leave. About five minutes. There was still lots of steam, but it had thinned. He was lying on his back on the top shelf, on his towel, right under the steam inlet. The hottest place. Where he usually was."

"So you went over to him?"

"I was pretty sure he was dead; he was lying so still. He hadn't responded when I yelled twice loudly, and he didn't say anything when I turned down the steam and turned on the shower. He used to yell when anything didn't go exactly his way. If he'd been alive, I'm sure he would have—"

"Did you touch him? Go close to him?"

"I stood in the corner, in front of him, at the bottom of the tile shelves—there are three tiers—and just looked."

"Maybe he was sleeping? Or having a heart attack?"

"His chest wasn't moving and it wouldn't have helped to touch him; I don't know CPR. So I went to the nearest phone—the one in the quiet lounge—and called Mrs. Dauber, the office manager, and told her to get an ambulance, fast."

"She said you told her it was a murder. You know what that did to her?"

"I happened to mention that it had to be, logically."

"And then you went back to the steam room?"

"Outside. She asked me not to let anyone into the steam room until she could locate Bill Carey, the spa manager."

"How long before he came?"

"About five minutes. Then I took a hot shower because I felt cold, and went into the quiet lounge to dry myself."

"With the towel you had in the steam room? Wasn't it wet?"

"Sort of, but it took off most of the water. By the time I got back to my locker to get dressed, I was completely dry. Then the ambulance crew came in."

"Why didn't you go to work after that? You did all you were supposed to do, so why'd you hang around?"

14

"I wanted to verify that I was right. It was logical that Mr. Brodsky'd been murdered."

"I don't even know that now, Warren; how could you know that then? A man in his seventies, not in good health, in a very overheated place . . . He could've had a heart attack."

"A heart attack doesn't kill instantly. If he had an attack, he would have sat up, moved, not stayed flat on his back on his towel. If he was badly stricken, he would have rolled off—fallen off—the top tile bench. Those benches are about eighteen inches wide; I don't believe he could have died a natural death and stayed in that position. Ergo, he was murdered. Wasn't he?"

"I'll know when the medical examiner tells me," Palmieri said. "We don't use guesswork."

"It's not a guess," Warren muttered stubbornly. "It's logic. He was murdered."

"We'll find out," Palmieri said grimly. "Meanwhile, for the next few days, don't go anyplace far. If it's murder, I'll want to talk to you later. And if it ain't, you got a lot of explaining to do why you told Mrs. Dauber that Mr. Brodsky'd been murdered, so she had to call us and cost the taxpayers all this dough."

So who else could it be but Warren the Philosopher who stirred up the whole *tsimmes*? I positively knew it the minute I walked into the lounge. My son, the genius, who was smart enough to figure out from such nothing clues that Barney Brodsky had been murdered, didn't have sense enough to just walk away and stay out of trouble? Warren, who knows all there is to know about what happened two thousand years ago in Greece, doesn't know that when it comes to a murder the first one the police suspect is the guy who finds the body and calls them in and sounds the most innocent. Guess who would have to take over now and save Warren's neck?

Like I didn't have enough headaches of my own.

15

4

Warren and I didn't get to work until after ten. Without saying hello to anybody, I led him directly into my office. Doris Starr, my secretary and the real brains of the outfit, followed us right in. She looked all upset and worried. Doris has been with me since day one and, just because she's a few years older than I am, she thinks she's allowed to nag me about everything. "You didn't even call," she nagged.

"We were delayed by the police," I explained. God forbid she should think I didn't come to the office at nine on the dot just to torture her. Or for some other pleasure.

"My goodness." She turned blue. "What did you do this time?"

See what I mean? "I didn't do anything." Unless you count losing a few golf balls a crime. "There was a *death* at the club."

"A murder," Warren muttered.

"Right in the club?" she asked. "Oh, that's terrible. Anyone I know?" Then it hit her. "A *murder?*"

16

"Barney Brodsky. Right in the steam room. And it's not necessarily a murder. *Warren* thinks it's a murder."

"Barnet Brodsky?" You could see the wheels turning behind her eyes, where she kept her secret data base. "That mean old lawyer we had all the trouble with last year?" I nodded. "He was murdered," she said positively. "Everybody hated him. Warren is right." She always stands up for Warren; all the women do. Because he looks so undernourished? I'd have to make him work out four times a week from now on. And take vitamins. *Suggest* it, I mean. "You still didn't have to be so late. And if you knew you were going to be late, why didn't you call? Do you know how worried I was?"

"I wanted to get away from the club fast," I explained. "Before Palmieri changed his mind about letting us go."

"Letting you go? Why should he . . . ?" Doris looked at me, horrified. "You didn't lose your temper again, did you?"

"Me?" See how her mind works? Just because, in the construction business, it sometimes happened that things got too much . . . I'm in the venture capital business now, and I hardly ever . . . Except maybe once in a while on the golf course, where it's only natural. "I was playing nine holes when it happened. It was Warren."

"Warren? *Warren* lost his temper? I don't believe it."

"Not his temper, his common sense. Warren decided he didn't have enough work to do, so he had to get involved with the police again. Palmieri."

"I didn't *get* involved, Dad," Warren pointed out. "I just happened to be there."

"Be there, yes; that could happen to anybody. But to decide there was a murder? Just on guesswork?"

"It was pure reasoning. Logic."

"It was pure *guesswork*. Very *thin* guesswork. And once you said it, Grace Dauber had to call the police. That was no 'just happened.' You *decided*. You made yourself *responsible*. By *choice*. Like with that existentialism you told me about."

"What would you have done, Dad?"

"Me? I would have called Bill Carey on the intercom phone. He's the spa manager; that's what he gets paid for. Let him decide who to call: a doctor, the police, whoever he wants. Then I would've taken a quick shower, gotten dressed fast, and been at the office before Palmieri even knew I was in the spa today."

"What about civic duty? 'To thine own self be true'?"

"Your civic duty was to inform the responsible authority, Bill Carey. If the emergency medics decided the police should be called, they would've done it."

"By then all the clues would have been washed away and all the suspects would have left the scene of the crime. The murder would never be solved."

"Who cares? Barney, may he rest in peace, was a no-good bastard that everybody hated. And what clues are you talking about? What suspects? You know something?"

"No, but there have to be clues. And the suspects are the people who were there at the time, the ones that I saw."

"Assuming that it was a murder in the first place. Which we don't know. And clues? How can there be clues? No gun, no knife, no rope, no poison in the martini . . . What clues can there be in a steam room where everybody is naked?"

"I don't know, Dad, but if there are any, it's important to get the police there fast, to make things official for the trial of the murderer. And to question the suspects."

Again with the suspects. "What suspects are you talking about?" Warren can be really irritating at times. Such as when he acts like something that's only a theory—excuse me, a hypothesis; with Warren I have to be exact—is really for real. "Palmieri said that all the club members are suspects."

"In theory, yes, Dad. But in practice, only the men who were near the steam room at the time of the murder are the actual suspects."

He's telling me about theory and practice? Me? When *I'm* the only practical one around here? Besides Doris? "You

18

know when the murder happened?" See how it works? Already I was talking like there was a murder for sure.

"Well, of course. Mr. Brodsky went into the steam room at exactly eight, give or take a minute or two. Say he took another minute to turn up the heat and settle down on his towel. I yelled in at about five after eight. He was dead at that time, because he didn't answer me. The murderer was already gone, because I was sitting on the lowest-level step right next to the door and nobody passed me."

"You told Palmieri it was still steamy when you went in."

"Sure, but after I cooled off the room it was not so thick. No one else was in the steam room and nobody passed me; I would have known."

I almost died. Warren may be intelligent, but he's still mostly book smart. What he didn't understand . . . "You told all this to Palmieri?"

"Of course. That's how we know who the suspects are."

Perfectly logical. And perfectly damn stupid. I turned to Doris; better she didn't hear what I was going to say. "Go in your office," I told her, "and call Palmieri. Find out what the medical examiner said."

"I'll call from here." She picked up the phone before I could stop her—Doris didn't want to miss a thing—and punched in the number, which she knew by heart from the last time we had a murder. "Sergeant Palmieri wants to talk to Warren," she said, holding out the phone.

I grabbed it. "Get your ass down here fast," Palmieri yelled.

"It's a murder?" I asked politely.

"None of your goddamn business," Palmieri said, very not politely. "I ain't talking to you, Baer."

"*We'll* be down in a little while," I told him, still polite. Meaning me and Irving Waxman too. Irv's a good lawyer, and he doesn't *phumphah*. If he knows, he tells you, and if he doesn't know, he finds somebody who does, fast. And he never tells you how busy he is when it's important.

"Get Waxman," I told Doris, "and tell him to meet

us at Palmieri's office." She knows when to schmooz around and when it's important, so she picked up the phone and called. I turned back to Warren, my damfool genius son. "You remember the Hamilcar Hi-Fi case? The police couldn't and we did?"

Warren nodded eagerly. "I was thinking about it, but I was afraid to suggest it to you. I know how you feel about getting involved unnecessarily, but the murder took place practically under my very eyes, so I *am* involved. Besides, it's our human obligation to see that justice is done."

"Good. Then you and I will find the killer. The police sure as hell can't, in a case like this." Human obligation, bullshit. All right, not bullshit, but I had a stronger reason. Since Warren knew he didn't do it, it never occurred to him that . . . I mean, look at it this way. We had a rough fight with Barney Brodsky last year, just a few months ago, and what Barney tried to do to us was not too straight. Warren, especially, he gave a real hard time to. Warren was very upset about it, that a human being he knew could be so lousy. Now Brodsky was alone in the steam room and Warren was the only one in there with him about the time Brodsky was murdered. Brodsky had a big, nasty mouth—a worse needler than Iris Guralnik—and could drive anyone crazy, ready to kill him, in one minute. I know, because I felt like killing him myself lots of times. Then there was the election in the club, where I was running against Brodsky for chairman of the board. From the police point of view, Warren was in the right place at the right time: opportunity. Motive he had plenty of too. As for means, since Palmieri told Warren to come down, it must have been something you could do with your bare hands. Motive, means, and opportunity; three out of three. To Palmieri, Warren wasn't just a witness; he was a suspect. And not just a plain suspect; Warren was the *prime* suspect.

20

5

The interrogation room at police headquarters was neat and clean, like everything else in Oakdale, but it was still a place where if you opened your mouth too much, you could end up with an eight-to-twenty-five. I had told Warren not to say a word, even though Irv Waxman said it was okay to tell Palmieri any facts—he emphasized the facts part—that Warren knew, as long as he didn't say anything that could possibly be incriminating. The trouble is, how the hell do you know, at this stage, what's incriminating and what isn't?

What really pissed me off was that Palmieri wouldn't let Waxman in. He even tried to keep me out. Hah! Lots of luck, Sergeant. "Why can't Waxman come in too?" I asked. "You have to. It's the law."

"Only if I arrest Warren. That what you want me to do, Baer?" Palmieri was definitely not in a good mood. I didn't push it, but Palmieri wouldn't let it drop. "If Mr. Warren Baer feels he needs an attorney at this time, all he has to do is ask for one. In which case I just might decide to have an assistant D.A. present and record the questioning. Okay,

Mr. Baer?" I hate when they go all formal on you, so I just nodded. "In fact, Baer, I don't even have to let you in here. The only reason I'm doing it is because you helped out on the Kassel case and because all I really want is information from Warren as a witness. As long as you keep your mouth shut, right?" I nodded again. How many nods did he want?

"I don't want a lawyer, Sergeant," Warren said. "I'm happy to cooperate." He hesitated a second, then said, "So it was a murder? I was right?"

Palmieri hesitated too. "It'll be public in a couple of hours, so . . . But you have to keep your mouth shut until then." He looked around carefully, even though we were all alone in the bare room; old habits die hard, I guess. "Mr. Brodsky didn't die of a heart attack. He was asphyxiated."

Warren was quiet, thinking. "Wait a minute." I broke the silence. "If Brodsky was strangled, Palmieri, how come you didn't notice the marks when you first saw him?"

"The M.E. said asphyxiated, Baer; not strangled."

"So it could have been an accident? Like he accidentally choked on something?"

"In the steam room?" Palmieri looked at me, disgusted. "Come on, Baer, you know better."

"So it was a murder." Warren looked pleased, like an idiot. "Logically, it had to be."

"We don't know that," Palmieri said. "We don't even know if a crime's been committed. All I want is information."

"It was a murder," Warren insisted, like a good little philosopher who had to be right even if it killed him. "Look at the facts." Another thing they don't teach you in philosophy is when to keep your mouth shut. "He didn't strangle himself or choke on a fishbone, otherwise you wouldn't be talking to me here."

"The M.E. didn't say it was murder. Not yet, at least."

"It *was* murder," Warren insisted. "A carefully planned, perfectly executed murder."

"Premeditated?" Palmieri perked up. A first-degree

murder to a cop is like hitting the homer that wins the World Series. "How do you figure that?"

"From the time Mr. Brodsky went into the steam room to the time I yelled in, at which time he was already dead, was no more than about eight minutes. Subtract another minute for his pushing up the thermostat and settling down in his normal place. It had to take the killer a minute to go in without being seen and another minute to come out—he had to make sure no one was watching the steam room door both times. I didn't see anyone coming out of the steam room when I approached and asphyxiation takes two or three minutes, so . . ."

"Probably less," Palmieri said, "at Brodsky's age and condition, with the heat and all that steam in the room."

"Accepted. Also, the murderer didn't come in exactly one second after Mr. Brodsky; he had to have waited until the place was so steamed up Mr. Brodsky wouldn't see him coming."

"You're sure of that?" Palmieri asked.

"Reasonably. You don't kill someone you love in that way; only someone you hate. And Brodsky knew who hated him."

"Which was everybody who knew him," I said, to take some of the heat off Warren.

"More important," Warren continued, "no one would use the steam room when Mr. Brodsky was there. It was like his own private place. If he saw someone come in, he'd be suspicious; he wouldn't just lie there quietly."

"Maybe he got up, and the perpetrator killed him, and laid him down again."

"There would have been marks, signs of a struggle, the towel crumpled. When I saw Mr. Brodsky there, it looked like he was sleeping. He was flat on his back, with his hands by his sides, and the towel was smooth and straight."

"Okay, that ties it down to a five-minute period when the asphyxiation happened." Palmieri was writing in his notebook and figuring. "Leaving two minutes leeway for the killer. Less, because we're figuring perfect conditions. That's crazy. Nobody in his right mind would time it that close. Either the perp is a moron or we're missing something."

"Or nobody killed Brodsky," I pointed out. "When the coroner finishes, maybe you'll find out that Brodsky died a natural death."

"It's possible," Palmieri conceded, "but I wouldn't bet my life on it. If Warren is right, it was a very slick murder, but not necessarily as risky as we're figuring. If Warren hadn't happened to run a couple of minutes over in the gym, nobody would've even tried to go into the steam room until after nine. With the heat and all, we wouldn't have been able to pinpoint the time of the murder so exact. The perpetrator could've been in his office in New York by the time we got on the job, and we would've had a hundred other suspects and never had a chance to close the case, and that's what the killer had to be counting on."

"So you owe Warren and me another one," I said, "but who's counting? Can we go now? I got a business to run."

"While it's still fresh, I want Warren to tell me who he saw near the steam room around the time of the murder."

Warren leaned back in his chair and closed his eyes. "When I went into the wet area, all I was thinking of was would I beat Mr. Brodsky into the steam room. Hurrying; not trying to observe who was where. I don't like the sauna, it's too dry and too hot, but I was considering going in there if Mr. Brodsky was already in the steam room. Or maybe to relax in the hotter whirlpool or in a hot shower. And I don't know the names of all the members."

"Yeah, fine, just tell me what you remember."

"As I entered the big shower room, there was a man shaving at the far bank of basins. On my right, the farthest one at the end of the room, next to the shelves we put our towels and shampoo on. He was tall, about my height, a

24

light tan except around his hips, heavyset, very muscular, blond hair cut long."

Palmieri consulted the computer printout on the desk, checked some notes, and turned to me. "Sidney Hoffman?"

"From the description," I said, "could be. He's Gold Coast Mercedes."

"I might talk to you later about the suspects, Baer. Get the background, the gossip, everything. After I get the M.E.'s report." Back to Warren. "Was Hoffman shaving? Or going to shave? Almost finished? What stage?"

Warren opened his eyes wide. "Yes, good point. He was fully lathered and just starting to shave."

"Do they have aerosol containers of shaving cream handy?"

My respect for Palmieri went up; a dummy he wasn't.

"Yes, and razors, plastic disposables. Not brushes; you have to bring your own. So if Mr. Hoffman had killed Mr. Brodsky and had come out of the steam room just before I saw him, he would've had time to lather up. It wouldn't take him more than ten seconds to get from the steam room to the first basin. You open the steam room door— it's on the right side of the passage leading into the pool— and walk into the big shower room, six or seven feet, and make a left turn past the towel shelves. About ten feet, and you're there."

"Okay, that's what I mean, Warren." Good sign that Palmieri was still calling Warren by his first name, sounding friendly. "Try to be very specific and look at it from my point of view; that I'm trying to see if any of the men you saw *could* have had the time to . . . While you're memory's fresh. In case a crime was committed."

"And to check if what they told your men jibes with what Warren says," I said. And if what Warren says jibes with what *they* say. I didn't say that out loud, but I wanted Palmieri to know I wasn't born yesterday.

"Weren't you supposed to keep your mouth shut,

Baer?" He glared at me. "Go on, Warren, who else did you see?"

"Carl Lerman, the big developer. I know him because he's the landlord of Nassau Venture Capital's office. On my far left. He was taking a shower at the other end of the big shower room. Directly opposite Mr. Hoffman."

"You saw his face?"

"For a moment. He had backed out of the shower enclosure to lather himself. It's only about six feet from where he was standing to the opening into the small shower room, and a few feet more from there to the steam room door on the right. He's short, fat, gray hair, getting bald, pink complexion."

Palmieri checked the computer printout and his notes, and made a few marks. "Who else?"

"George Rubin. We had once discussed investing in his company—Rubinetics; manufactures electronics—but he was able to get bank financing himself, so it never went ahead. He's sort of stocky, average height, black hair, deep tan. As I entered the wet area, he had just finished wringing out his swim trunks in the basin next to the sauna and was going over to the centrifugal swimsuit drier. That's just to the right of the entrance into the small shower room, under the towel shelves. If he killed Mr. Brodsky, it would've had to be a minute or two earlier. The sun room door is right next to the sauna door, between the two banks of basins and about twenty feet from the entrance to the small shower room. For him to come out of the sun room, rinse his trunks, and go over to the drier . . . At least one minute, maybe more."

"You don't know, though, if he had been in the sun room, do you? Or if he'd been inside, how long he was in there?"

"I only saw him finish rinsing his trunks. He seems the least likely to me because of the distance he had to cover."

"Another ten seconds would take care of that." Pal-

26

mieri grunted. "Doesn't mean a thing, since we don't know exactly to the second when Brodsky was killed. Who else?"

"A man in the passage going into the pool area. That passage is between the small shower area and the steam room. I only saw his back as he made the right turn to the pool door. A spa bath towel was wrapped around his waist."

"So he could've just come from the steam room?"

"It's only a couple of steps away."

"How do you know it was the spa's bath towel?"

"The gold color and bigger than the hand towels."

"What'd he look like?"

"Very tall, slim, brown hair turning gray, pink skin. About mid-forties."

"Who's that sound like to you, Baer?" Palmieri asked.

"I don't know everybody in the club, but it has to be Arnold Greenleaf. He's a lawyer. Office in Mineola."

Palmieri looked at his computer printout. "Yeah, that checks." Naturally. Hoffman, Lerman, Rubin, and Greenleaf. Warren had to finger four of the biggest wheels in the club, all of them already mad at me for running for the board and a couple of them we once had some not-too-good business dealings with. He couldn't have noticed some stranger, some sneaky-looking ex-con who'd just gotten out of jail and had sworn to kill Barney Brodsky for screwing up his case? Nah, nothing but the best for my-son-the-philosopher. "You didn't mention what the others were wearing."

"Mr. Lerman was naked; he was taking a shower."

"You don't have to wear trunks to go into the pool? And take a shower first?"

"Oh, yes, the lifeguard won't let you in unless you're showered."

"So it wasn't automatic that Mr. Lerman was naked, was it?" Warren turned red; it's not often he gets caught in a mistake in logic. "Don't jump to conclusions, Warren;

27

just report what you saw." Palmieri didn't rub it in. "What were the others wearing?"

"Mr. Rubin was naked, but he had washed out his brown bathing trunks," Warren said in a subdued voice. "Mr. Hoffman had a bath towel around his waist."

"You'll be ready to identify all these guys if it becomes necessary, Warren?"

"If I can. But is a naked identification parade legal?"

"We'll worry about that when we come to it. You see anyone going into or coming out of the steam room?"

"No one. It only took me a few seconds to get from the wet-area entrance to the steam room, and I was looking at the steam room door all that time. If anyone came out, I would have seen him."

"Who else did you see?"

"No one, Sergeant. That's all."

"You sure?" Palmieri checked his notes again. "Positive? *Nobody?*"

"Positive," Warren said firmly. Palmieri kept staring at him. Hard. Warren stared back, then blushed. "Oh, yes, of course. One of the fellows who cleans up. Ramon, I think he's called. Short, dark skinned, slim, small mustache. I saw him, but I didn't really notice . . . He was just wiping the mirrors over the basins. Next to Mr. Hoffman. I'm sorry." Thank God, at least we got one poor schnook. Now if only he had a record and Barney had given him a hard time in front of witnesses . . .

"It happens. People don't notice. Like in Chesterton's *The Invisible Man*. Certain people you take for granted." Palmieri caught the surprised look on my face. "Policemen read too, Baer. We're not all dummies."

"I never said—"

"Forget it, Baer." He turned back to Warren. "Anyone else there? Anything else you noticed that was out of place? Looked funny? Unusual?"

"No, everything normal." Then he blushed again. "Now that you mentioned it—Ramon, I mean—I also

28

saw another one like him. I mean an invisible man. I
didn't actually see him *in* the wet area; he was leaving the
toilet—that's right after the wet area—and going into the
quiet lounge. Bill Carey."

"You saw his face?"

"His back was toward me, but I know him well."

"How was he dressed?" Palmieri asked, very casually.
Too casually.

"Sweat suit and running shoes. He takes an early
workout every day."

"Clothes wet?" Palmieri leaned forward intently.

I could smell that Bill Carey was working his way up
to being suspect number one fast. Thank God, sort of.

"They looked sort of damp," Warren said. "All over,
not sweated in spots like from a workout. The wet area is
warm and very humid."

"You know for sure he had been in the wet area?"

"I deduced it. He had to be, to get wet. I would've seen
Bill if he had entered the corridor from the locker room to the
wet area when I was walking toward it, so he had to be already
in there somewhere. Then I saw Bill just going into the
lounge when I entered the passage. He didn't get wet in the
toilet, so he had to have just come out of the wet area."

The way I saw it, Bill had come out of the *steam* room
just before he went into the toilet, and that was the way
Palmieri would see it. Guaranteed, Carey was on his way to
the clink that second. Sure I wanted somebody else to be
the obvious killer, to take the heat off Warren, but not Bill
Carey. It never fails: Just when you think nothing worse
could happen, it does. And who makes it happen? Who
else?—my son, the philosopher. And who does it happen
to? To the one man I didn't want to be a suspect, a real nice
kid, just the kind of guy I'm knocking myself out to help. To
Bill Carey, who I had to complete the deal for by Friday or
else he'd be ruined. And so would Sharon Edel, Brodsky's
granddaughter. Who I loved like she was my own. Own
daughter, I mean, not granddaughter; mine and Thelma's,
may she rest in peace. I had to talk to Carey fast.

6

"I'm sorry, Mr. Baer," the Oakdale Spa receptionist said, "Mr. Carey is downstairs with the police. I expect him back shortly. If you'd care to wait?" From where she was sitting, she could check who went downstairs into the gym and who came up, which guests had been invited by which members, who had massage appointments when, who was on duty at which periods for what, and everything that Carey might want to know.

"Okay, we'll go down and find him."

"I'm sorry, Mr. Baer," she said, and she really sounded sorry, "but no men are allowed downstairs until further notice. Only women, and they can't go into the pool area."

"But I was talking with the police earlier today," I pointed out. "Right up here."

"Yes, Mr. Baer, but I can't let any men down. You can read a magazine; we got some new ones in today."

"Okay, we'll wait," I said. No reason to give her a hard time. Instead of picking up a magazine, I tried to think about the case, to figure out why Brodsky was killed in the steam room and why it had been done just now and if it had anything to do with the coming election of the board of

30

directors and how to make sure that Warren wasn't accused, and that he and Lee . . . Useless; too much I didn't know yet. I visualized a meadow with buttercups and tried to relax.

The Oakdale Country Club is a beautiful place, well designed and well built; I should know, I used to be in the building line myself. It's on the Sound, on Nassau County's North Shore—the Gold Coast of Long Island—in Oakdale, one of the richest suburbs of New York City. It was founded right after *the* War, when the returning soldiers moved to the Island so they could raise their kids where you could see green once in a while instead of only asphalt. As they prospered and had time to relax, they discovered that not only were some of the villages on the Island restricted, all country clubs were. Screw them, was the attitude; we'll make our own club. And they did. The Oakdale, one of the nicest country clubs within commuting distance of New York.

Oakdale's buildings and grounds are always perfectly maintained, and the links, the courts, the marina, and the dining room are as good as you'll find anywhere on the Island. Some of the employees have been here since the club opened, and they're tops at their jobs; the managers make sure to hire the best. Not only are they all well paid, but the tips and bonuses effectively double their salaries, so there's always a waiting list for every job. At the club, you get what you pay for—which is not all that common these days—but you pay for what you get, so Oakdale is not exactly for poor people.

The members own the club. If you're accepted, you have to buy a share of the club stock, which is not cheap. The annual dues aren't exactly low either, and that's just to belong. Fees for the special services—golf and tennis pros, bodyshaping, karate, yoga, swimming lessons, the spa, boating instruction—are all out of this world. It was only ten years ago that I could afford to *think* of joining, and even then the business had to pay for it. It was a smart investment. In addition to the pleasure—if you can call playing golf with Iris Guralnik a pleasure—the company

31

got some business contacts and I met some real nice people, plus a few who were not so nice. Once Warren joined the firm, I put him up for membership too—there's no such thing as a family membership at Oakdale—and he got in easily; everybody likes him, especially the women. We could afford the money and, if he was going to have a desk job at NVC, he had to get his exercise regularly. Not golf— one of us getting ulcers is enough—but pumping iron to put a little muscle on his bones.

There's a regular crowd of women—golfers and tennis players and exercisers—who come to the club right after the husbands leave for work. Not *right* after; it takes time to put on the makeup and to pick out the right clothes and the right leotards and the right jewelry so the other women in the club should all drop dead from envy. But by ten they're ready, and nothing—absolutely *nothing*—will keep them out. The club is the best place on the North Shore to meet your friends and it's also the most reliable source of the latest gossip. Next to shopping, the club is the center of everything that's important to half the women in the village.

Then there're the men who like to start the adrenaline flowing before heading for Wall Street or Madison Avenue, to warm up for the *real* battles for King of the Hill. Some of them are very big big shots, not just on the Island but in New York too, and not all of them are as polite as I am. When someone like that comes to the club, ready for a workout, a tennis game, or nine holes of golf, he doesn't want to hear he can't change his clothes just because somebody died. The way I figured it, Palmieri had decided to close off the whole spa to make life easy for himself and avoid destroying evidence. Knowing there was going to be loud screaming from the women and real heavy bitching from the men, he told Bill Carey to do it, so Bill would have to take the heat. But Bill is no fool, so he convinced Palmieri to let the women into the gym and their locker room, their lounge, and the massage cubicles. Why not the pool area, I couldn't understand.

Obviously it wasn't a woman who had killed Brodsky. Not that a woman couldn't have gotten into the men's steam room easily; the door from the pool leads directly into the men's wet area, with only a couple of right-angle turns for privacy. That door is never locked, and it's only a few steps from there to the steam room. Anyone could have come from the pool and been in the steam room in about three seconds. The problem was that a woman anywhere in that area, where the men go around completely naked—there's a small bank of showers directly opposite the steam room and a large bank just outside the passage—would have stood out like a man in the women's wet area. Besides, the lifeguard's station is right between the doors to each area. If a guest who isn't wearing his glasses or who doesn't look at signs starts to open the wrong door, the lifeguard has to remind him which door not to go in. So if Palmieri wanted to seal off the pool, all he had to do was station a cop outside the door to the men's side.

Better still, he could have had Bill Carey lock that door, period, and let the women have the pool area and saved Carey a lot of explaining. Unless Palmieri figured there might be some clues in the pool? Ridiculous. With all that water slopping around the tile—there's the big main pool, the two whirlpools: hot and hotter, and a big wooden Japanese hot tub—there was no way to get fingerprints or footprints or *anything* that he could use. Still, Palmieri's no dope, so he must have had some reason to close the whole pool area and put Carey on the hot seat. The outdoor pool was still being cleaned in preparation for the official opening of the season next week, so Bill couldn't even offer that as a substitute.

Under the best of conditions, I don't envy Bill Carey's position. How a kid that young can be manager of the spa and handle some of our prima donna members is a miracle. I don't mean that he's not up to it—he's pretty smart: has a master's in Hotel Management and was also a top wrestler in school—only that he's just twenty-eight. These days, it seems to me that absolute *kids* are running the country, and it looks like they're all on a road that goes straight to the top without any bumps. I wondered how they'd do if they hit any *real* problems, the kind they don't even *tell* you about in school.

Why Bill chose Oakdale is easy; I figured it out before he told me. The average guy who goes to business school today is preparing to get on the corporate ladder and to climb—or backstab—his way to CEO. He goes to work for a big company in a fast-track position, sales or marketing, where a bright, aggressive young guy can make a big splash and come to the attention of the top executives. In twenty years he could end up at the top of the ladder and then, if he can get the financing, there's no limit to where he can go. Financially, that is. In terms of happiness, doing good, or even just *feeling* good—well, some sacrifices have to be made if you want to succeed. *That* kind of success.

For a country club, Oakdale is big, but as a business it'll never make the Fortune five million. On the other hand, each of the five division managers—Dining Room, Grounds, Office, Marina, and Spa—is like captain of his own ship. The general manager doesn't tell them what to do or how to do it. Each manager runs his division the way he wants to and if he doesn't do a good job, keeping costs in line and services working perfectly, he's out. But if he does everything right, he's set for life in a nice area close to his house—no fighting traffic and no Long Island Railroad to drain your energy—with good pay and lots of benefits. Plus one more thing that would interest an ambitious young man. Harold Gordon, the general manager, is getting ready to retire, so there'll be an even better job open for one of the five division managers a year from now. Except that Lorenzo Blackwell will never give up the dining room. He's a frustrated cook and he prays for the days when Thomas, the chef, is sick so he can cook some of his hot Cajun specialties with his own hands. And Yoshi Fukuda, who is even older than Harold Gordon, says he would die if he had to work indoors; he even does his paperwork in the greenhouse office. Jerry Macdonald, who runs the marina, lives on his houseboat and gets seasick whenever he sets foot on dry land. So the battle is between Bill Carey and Grace Dauber, our office manager.

By me, it's no choice. I like Bill, and I'm willing to go all out for him, but he's twenty-eight—been out in the real world for only four years—and Grace is forty-eight. Grace never went to college, came to us right from business school, but she's intelligent and smart—the two are not the same thing—and efficient like you wouldn't believe. Also, she raised three children without a husband while she was working full time, and if you think that doesn't take doing, then you don't know business. She runs the place with a smile, never raises her voice, and can handle the worst troublemaker—even a sonofabitch like Barney Brodsky, may he rest in peace—so he's left with nothing to bitch about. Because I say what's on my mind, some people think I'm prejudiced against women. I'm not. I like most women. Even Iris Guralnik, sort of, except when we're playing golf, and that's only temporary: an hour or two for the game and a couple of hours thinking about what I'd like to do to her, then it's over.

So if it comes down to it, if I get elected to the board of directors, I'm going to surprise everybody and vote for Grace Dauber. Unfortunately, there are a few directors, some of them women, who would never vote for a woman to be general manager. Stupid. You vote for the best one for the job. If sex is a factor—like for locker room attendant—consider sex. But if it isn't, then get the best. Which means I'll have to do some heavy explaining to some people when the time comes to vote. And some arm-twisting too, if necessary. It'll be necessary, I'm sorry to say.

"You wanted to see me, Mr. Baer?" Bill Carey asked. "Come right into my office." He was dressed in his usual neatly pressed white shirt and black slacks. They weren't a bit wet. Or even damp.

1

It was a little over three months ago that Bill Carey had come to my office. One minute after he started talking, I knew we had another potential winner. "Stop," I told him. "I want Warren to hear this."

Doris brought in caffeine-free diet colas. I not only have to watch my weight, but I stopped using caffeine a month ago and, believe me, I'm even calmer now than I ever was. The four of us settled down around the table instead of across a desk. Doris was taking notes, of course, but mentally. This way it's a more friendly atmosphere; the less formal the presentation, the more you can learn about the deal.

"I want to open a gym," Bill said. "I know I'm taking a chance coming to Nassau Venture Capital; if word about this leaks out, Mr. Brodsky would have me fired immediately, contract or no contract."

"What you tell us stays in this office," I said, "but I hope you realize that since I'm running for the board chairmanship, this puts me in a very difficult position."

"I know, and I'm sorry about that, but I've tried every other possible source that might consider my proposition."

"There are other venture capital companies on the Island," I said.

"I don't know them; you're the only ones I trust."

"All the banks turned you down? Private investors?"

"I don't have enough assets for a bank loan and I don't want partners to tell me how to run my business."

"If we invest in you, we'll be your partners; that's how we work. Fifty-one percent, minimum, depending."

"But inactive."

"Unless you screw up," I said. "Then I become very active. In fact, I take over, but good." Another thought struck me. "Why don't you wait until you marry Sharon Edel? Her family has more money than God. You're waiting till she graduates? Okay, so can't your deal wait another few months?"

Bill turned red. "You know about me and Sharon?"

"Everybody knows; there are no secrets in the club. Why do you think her grandfather is giving you such a hard time?"

Bill swallowed hard, then decided to say what he really thought. "Because Mr. Brodsky's a bigot. He's against me because I'm a Catholic."

"Wrong," I said. "He's against Sharon not marrying a Jewish boy. There's a big difference. He isn't trying to get rid of Grace Dauber, who's also a Catholic, or Jerry Macdonald, or Yoshi or Lorenzo."

"Then why . . . ? I really love Sharon and she loves me. I was even willing to convert, which would have killed my mother, that's how I feel."

"If you're converting, I'm sure—"

"The rabbi wouldn't take me. He said you're not supposed to become a Jew just because you want to get married; you can only do it if you believe."

"That makes sense, doesn't it? But if you and Sharon

37

really want to get married, no one's stopping you. You're both over twenty-one; have a civil ceremony."

"That's what we've decided to do, even if it kills both sets of parents. In June, right after she graduates. But I'm not going to marry Sharon while she's rich and I'm just working for somebody else."

"You have a great job with the country club," Warren pointed out. "A high salary, big bonuses, set your own hours, and you have a good shot at becoming general manager when Mr. Gordon retires." To Warren, at twenty-five, age and experience aren't as important as they are to me. He'll learn. I just hope it won't take him as long as it took me. I'd have to work out a way to speed up the teaching process.

"I'd still be an employee," Carey said, "no matter what my title is. I never want anyone to throw up to me that I married Sharon for her money. I fell in love with her before I knew her family was rich."

"Wanting to prove you married a rich girl for love," I said, "isn't the best reason in the world to make me invest NVC's money in your proposal."

"It isn't that way at all," Bill protested. "If I wanted to work for someone else, the club would be the ideal place, but I've always wanted to be my own boss." That was what I was waiting to hear. True entrepreneurs hate working for *anybody*. "As a matter of fact, according to my projections, for the first two years I'll be taking home a lot less money than I am now. Sharon said she's willing to help, to work in the gym alongside me. It'll be a hell of a struggle at first, but it'll pay off in the end."

That's the next thing I was waiting to hear. If you know you can't take money out of a growing business to raise your standard of living, you have a good chance of succeeding. And if your wife is willing to sacrifice for the business, that's another big plus. I was almost ready to go ahead right then and there but, for the sake of my potential limited partners, I had to ask Carey a lot more questions.

"Aren't there already a dozen gyms in Nassau County, all competing for business? I don't see the need for one more; you're fighting for a share of a limited market."

"There are some franchises where you can get a good workout cheap but they have to pile in the customers with specials and deals, so they're often uncomfortably crowded. They're not luxurious in any sense of the word and they offer very few amenities. The lockers are half width and half height, and the ceilings are low. Some don't even offer massages. They don't have sun rooms or tanning booths because of the insurance costs, and they don't have snack bars or lounges or hot tubs. A minimum of everything."

"Isn't that the sensible way to run a gym?" I asked. "The margin of profit on such an operation isn't all that great, and rents for commercial space are going through the roof. Since they cater mostly to young people who have to work for a living, they're packed right after working hours, in the evening, and weekends. It's to be expected."

"If I wanted to have a gym like that," Bill said, "that's exactly how I'd run it."

"You want to duplicate the Oakdale Spa?"

"Of course not; one of these is all Nassau can support. It's for the rich; the only thing missing is a polo field."

"What's wrong with that? I like having attendant parking instead of cruising around to find a slot, and a golf course where I don't have to get up at three A.M. to play. I like a gym where there's enough equipment so I don't have to wait for somebody to finish a set, and enough room between so I don't feel crowded. It's quiet and clean, there are enough masseurs around so I can get a massage exactly when I want one even without an appointment, and I can take a nap afterward on a recliner in the quiet lounge. I can choose between two whirlpools, a Japanese hot tub, a sauna, or a steam room, and we have so many showers I never have to wait. A double-size locker—just for me; I never have to look for an empty—is exactly what I need to hang up my suit before I go to work so it doesn't get creased. And best of all, whenever I show my key number to the linen boy, in thirty seconds I get a wash cloth, a hand towel, a bath towel, a massage sheet—my own, which nobody else ever uses—washed, sterilized, and ironed, with my locker number on the corner of each one. It's like the old Roman baths; the way a spa should be. If I'm willing to pay for this, why shouldn't I have it?"

"I agree, Mr. Baer, but have you ever seen, for instance, the size of my linen rooms? I carry six of each item—three here and three in the laundry—for each member, male and female, and if anyone uses more than three items a week, I have to supply two more for that person permanently, with his number ironed on, and recorded for billing. I keep two hundred extra of each item in stock for that alone. And my payroll? I have one man and one woman on duty at all times just to handle the towels and sheets, to keep my linen rooms stocked and each item in numerical order so you can get what you want in a minute. We're open a hundred fourteen hours a week so, with the overlap, that's six people on the payroll full time for linens alone. In the summer, when the outdoor pool is open, I add another male and another female attendant during the day. You'd be surprised how many bath towels can be used on one hot day. If you've ever been here at noon on Fridays, when the truck comes from the laundry, you'd see everybody on the maintenance crews working a full hour just to get the clean linens in and the dirty linens out. I also have extra ventilation in the linen rooms to prevent mildew. On top of that, have you noticed how much room those big lockers take up? There's one for each male and one for each female member. My locker rooms alone are bigger than some gyms. All this luxury costs a lot more than ninety-nine percent of the people in Nassau can afford."

"That's something to be ashamed of? I worked hard all my life—I didn't steal—and I was lucky enough to have made money. I shouldn't enjoy the fruits of my labor?"

"Of course you should, Mr. Baer. All I'm saying is that there's a hole in the market. Where does the moderately successful middle-class family go? Or people retired on a fixed income? Or single men and women on their way up? Maybe they'll be rich someday, but meanwhile they can't afford Oakdale and they don't want to go to the cheaper gyms. They want some luxuries, but not an outdoor pool, or two whirlpools plus a hot tub. They can manage without individual oversized lockers, personal linens, or squash courts. What they want is the basics, properly done. Also, and this is usually forgotten but it's very important for marketing, where do these young people meet others like themselves? Possible spouses? For the most part, our potential clients don't hang out in bars. What they need is a nice place, slightly luxurious, a place where, when you meet someone, you can see what you get. Where the men and women you meet are likely to be health-conscious and attractive and intelligent, and at your own economic level. That's what I'm proposing."

"What do you think, Warren?" I asked.

"I'd join a gym like that myself when it opens," Warren said.

"That's what I figured. You think Lee would like it?" Might as well give a little push; keep his mind on her.

"She'd love it, Dad, but she's away at school now."

"Ask her next week when she comes home for the spring break." I turned back to Bill Carey. "Where would you put it, assuming we agreed to help fund you? All the good commercial space I know of is tied up."

"There's going to be a new mall, a very nice one,

right near the intersection of Jericho Turnpike and Oyster Bay Road. It's a two-minute drive from where Wantagh State intersects Northern State and the expressway. Right in the heart of Nassau County and only minutes from five major highways."

"Forget it," I said. "I know all about the Lerman Mall. My own landlord is putting it up, Carl Lerman; took him five years to assemble the site. That mall's too fancy; the rent per square foot will kill you."

"No, it won't. All I'll have on the ground floor is the reception desk and the stair leading down to the main lounge; everything else'll be in the cellar. I'll be paying a small fraction of the first-floor or mezzanine rent, and I'll have the clientele of the mall to draw from too."

"Will Lerman allot enough parking for you?"

"He agreed to put in another hundred parking spaces, which the town planning board wanted him to do anyway. Don't forget, the mall will bring me more clients, but my clients will also shop in the mall."

"I'm sure old Carl figured that out already," I said dryly. "Is the cellar deep enough for a pool?" I asked. These business types, with their MBAs, sometimes forget about practical matters.

"It will be now. Since it was still in the design stage when I was negotiating the deal, all I had to do was pay Mr. Lerman for the architectural and engineering costs and for the extra structural work at the pool area. Plus the extra plumbing and heating and air-conditioning."

"You paid him already? You've *committed* yourself?"

"I'm the first minor tenant, so I got a good deal, and my being in the cellar won't hurt the developer's rental plans."

This was crazy. "You *signed* a lease?"

"I got a ten-year lease, with two five-year extensions at reasonable increases."

"Carl Lerman gave you a lease without any downpayment?" I couldn't believe this. "No rent in advance? No security?"

"I only paid for the cost of the structural and mechanical changes and three months rent as security."

"Which is still a lot of money to lay out, especially at this stage. Are you sure that's all? Will this hold you until you take over the place and start the alterations?" I knew Lerman too well to wonder what the answer would be.

"I just have to pay the first six months rent in advance and half the cost of the additional parking. In four months from now; the lease is in escrow until then."

"And if you don't make the payment you lose everything?"

"That was the only way Mr. Lerman would make the changes in construction, and I didn't have any time left. Another few weeks and the plans would have been finalized for the planning board meeting. If he missed that date, the project would have been delayed three months."

"You paid for the architectural and engineering revisions, and the structural and mechanical changes already? I didn't know you were that rich," I said sarcastically.

He didn't hear the sarcasm. Or maybe he didn't want to hear it. "I'm not rich. I took all my savings, and I borrowed all I could. Then my parents . . ."

"Sharon too?"

"Oh, no." He looked shocked. "I wouldn't touch her money. Not even after we're married."

I liked that, but he had still done a stupid thing. He had not only stripped himself, he had stripped his parents, his friends, whoever he had borrowed from, and was left with no money for the construction of the gym itself or for running the business at a loss for the first year—which was absolutely certain—and no place to get more money from. With no assets left, no bank would touch him. The major cause of business failure is undercapitalization and Carey was not only *under*capitalized, he was *minus*capitalized.

"I'm sorry, Bill," I told him. "I like you, and I like your idea. But I don't want to be associated in business with a gambler and I won't recommend to my limited partners that we invest in this deal."

He looked shocked. "I'm not a gambler, Mr. Baer. I've figured out everything very conservatively. This is a sound business proposition with a great potential. I wasn't gambling; I was betting on myself. There's a difference."

Maybe there is, but it's not such a terrific difference. If it was all my own money, maybe I'd consider it; I've bet on riskier things in my life. But half of everything NVC lays out—whether it's invested cash or loans or guaranteeing bank loans—comes from the limited partners, so I have to think very conservatively. "I'm sorry," I said, "but—"

"Do you have a full proposal?" Warren broke in.

"A complete pro forma, including demographics, a short market survey, cost of construction and equipment, fee schedule, a five-year projection, the works. Everything conservatively figured."

"What formula did you use for your demographics?" I asked. As long as Warren had brought it up, I'd have to act like I was really considering Carey's proposal.

"I really believe this kind of gym will draw from a bigger area, but to be conservative, I applied the standard formula. Within a five-mile radius, one percent of the potential gym population in terms of age and income will become members, and I set the fees accordingly. The numbers come out very close to what I believe the average member will pay for what we'll give him."

Well, at least he knew the business end of his business.

"Let's at least see the proposal, Dad," Warren said.

Even if Warren didn't own half the business, I still wouldn't overrule him in front of a client. I'm trying to build up his confidence, not break it down. "Yes. Good idea. Leave the papers with us, Bill; we'll give you an answer inside of a week." Bill gave Warren the proposal and left.

I'd go over the papers, really go over them, but it was the wrong thing to do. Warren may have thought he was helping Bill, but sometimes when you think you're helping, you're hurting. As long as Carey felt he had a chance with us, he wouldn't try any other venture capital groups, which could cost him a week he couldn't afford. If he missed the deadline, Carl Lerman would hold him to the letter of the agreement, and properly so; Lerman had timing problems and financial obligations too. So Bill and his family would be dead broke and he'd be paying off his debts for the next ten years. Knowing him, that meant he'd never marry Sharon.

Two broken hearts, on top of everything else. On the other hand, he said he didn't have any other sources left. So maybe he should have stopped being so goddamn proud and taken money from his intended. Or her family. On the third hand, if he proposed that, Barney Brodsky would have told Sharon's parents that Bill was only after her money and they'd never get married. And on the fourth hand, if Bill took Sharon's money before they were even engaged, I'd lose all respect for him; a man has to take care of his wife, not depend on her to support him. No matter what I did, with the best will in the world, I was going to hurt Bill, whom I liked. And Sharon, whom I loved. And Warren, my and Thelma's only child. Which was something I'd never do. I'd die first.

While I was thinking over the deal, and except for the tight deadlines it looked pretty good, Warren had grabbed the proposal papers and made three sets of copies. He gave one to Doris. "Set up a spreadsheet," he told her, "and check the arithmetic, so Dad and I can juggle the parameters and analyze the intangibles in the deal." Doris took the sheets to her own office, where the big-screen computer was.

It was good that Warren was starting to act like an

executive, but he was picking the wrong deal to do it on. "Are you thinking," I asked him, "of dropping all our other business to analyze Carey's proposal right now?"

"Every minute counts; you know that, Dad."

"Which is exactly why this is not our type of deal."

"If the numbers are accurate, and they probably are, it's a very good deal."

"The stupid bastard has stripped himself of every asset."

"He still has the one that counts: himself."

"Which I can't deposit in a bank. Are you letting friendship affect your business decisions?"

"I'm taking into consideration what I know of Bill Carey. He's exactly the kind of guy you set up NVC to help."

"Not at the expense of our investors; they're our first responsibility. And two of them are Lee's parents, remember?"

"You're right, Dad," he admitted. "But I still want you to go over the deal. If your analysis shows it's good, but you feel the time pressure makes it too risky for our investors, I'll take the deal myself."

"Yourself? Without me?" This was crazy. I mean, it was great that Warren had developed so much nerve, so much confidence in his decision, to put all—and that's what it would take—all of his liquid capital into this deal, but it wasn't exactly the safest way to live. Maybe he'd make a bundle, but he could also end up very broke very quickly. Still, it gave me the chance to get the two of us back to where we were a couple of months ago. "No," I said firmly. "We don't work that way. You own fifty percent of the NVC stock. Whatever we do, we do together. And I'll tell you what else. I'll make a careful analysis, and you do the same. Doris should have the spreadsheet ready by three today. Four at the latest. We'll play several scenarios on that. Then *you'll* make the decision. There's no point in making Bill sweat blood any longer than is necessary. Whatever your decision is, I'm with you."

And that's how I got into this stupid, no-win situation. Every time I try—with the best of intentions—to do good, I end up ass-deep in alligators. Warren is now number-two suspect only because Bill took over the number-one slot. I'm going to have a lot of explaining to do—and I can't even imagine where to start—to our investors. Among which are Iris and Marvin Guralnik. Whose daughter, Lee, was supposed to give me six beautiful blond grandchildren, four girls and two boys. And if Lee finds out that Warren was the one who stupidly got me into . . . Of course, I could always take the full blame on myself. If I was allowed to make the choice, that is. Which I won't be. You think anybody's going to blame Warren? Skinny, undernourished, handsome young Warren? Forget it. It'll be my neck, guaranteed. Automatically. So what else is new?

Warren and I settled ourselves on the hard wooden chairs opposite Carey's desk. "I always take a light workout before I start my day," Bill said, sorting the memos on his desk into three piles. "Every day, even Sundays. Otherwise I'd never have time to exercise." His office was spare, simple, and businesslike; no photos of himself with famous people, no medals or awards, just a few nature prints to soften the look. "I exercise right after I make a quick check of the spa to see if everything is clean and in good order."

"The women's areas too?" I asked.

"I do those areas just before the spa officially opens. Locker room, linen storage, wet area, steam room and sauna, sun room, massage cubicles, and the makeup area."

"How long does that take?"

"Less than ten minutes. When the spa is empty it's easy to see if those areas are in good shape. Mark goes with me, the chief instructor. I tell him what I see that needs

48

taking care of and he gives the orders to the appropriate people."

"Then you take your workout?"

"Low resistance, high reps. I'm not interested in building bulk and strength anymore, but I have to maintain good muscle tone. How would it look if the manager of the Oakdale Spa had a pot belly? Besides, I have to work off steam to stay sane; there are big pressures in this job."

"There are big pressures in every worthwhile job," I said. He knew what I was driving at. "You check the men's area after your workout?"

"I can go through the men's areas while they're in use, so there's no point in paying Mark overtime to come in earlier than he has to. I notice things in each gym room while I'm exercising; it makes a pattern in my mind. After my workout, I check the pools and the men's wet area, the toilet and the quiet lounge, another few minutes. Mark finishes his rounds about the same time I do. He tells me his immediate problems, I tell him what I want done, and I'm up here a little after eight to start on my paperwork."

"You go through the men's wet areas by yourself?" It would help if he had a witness.

"I only take Mark with me for the women's areas."

"Can't he do all of this himself?"

"I'm responsible, so I walk the factory floor every morning. And at odd times during the day. There's a lot you can't tell about an operation sitting on your ass in an office. When I'm in the gym, anyone has a complaint, he doesn't need an appointment to see me."

"You work out in your official uniform?" I indicated his shirt and slacks. I already knew the answer from what Warren had told Palmieri, but I wanted to hear how he said it.

"In a sweat suit. I change up here and take a quick shower in my private bathroom. It sounds like a perk, but it's really more efficient for me to be in the office first thing. It also cuts down the griping there would be if I happened to be using somebody's favorite shower at the time he wants to use it."

"Favorite shower? You got to be kidding."

"I am not. Some of the members resent seeing employees using any part of the spa. To them, we're servants. There aren't many of them, but they're the ones who have the biggest mouths." He suddenly remembered he was talking to a director who could possibly be chairman of the board next year. "I hope you understand, Mr. Baer, I'm not talking about anybody in particular. Most of our members are nice people."

"Yeah, sure, don't worry. The same guys you got trouble with, I got trouble with." And Warren too, though Bill didn't know that. "What did the police want with you?"

"Sergeant Palmieri? He asked me a lot of questions about who was where, during the time Mr. Brodsky was in the steam room, and exactly when I saw them."

"Who did you see?" I asked. "Around the steam room at that time, I mean."

"Why? What difference does that make?"

"He asked Warren the same question. If your answers jibe, it may be useful."

He looked at me suspiciously, but I was, after all, a potential chairman of the board and I held his future in my hands in other ways too; we hadn't yet fully closed on the various loans and notes the bank required for NVC to invest in his new business. "Mr. Hoffman was at the basins, shaving. Ramon was polishing the mirror next to Mr. Hoffman." So he was a better observer than Warren, but then, of course, he was interested in what his employees were doing and would be more likely to remember them. "Mr. Lerman was taking a shower in the corner of the big shower room. Mr. Rubin was in the sauna. Mr. Brodsky was in the steam room."

"You saw him? When?" This could be critical.

"I didn't exactly see him: I just went into the steam room for a few seconds. It was so hot and steamed up, I knew he had to be in there; no one else could stand it."

"You didn't talk to him?"

"What for? I wasn't concerned with who was doing what, you understand, just what needed to be done. There was no way I could see anything and, since Mr. Brodsky hadn't called me on the intercom to complain, I assumed everything was okay."

So far, everything fitted. "Who else did you see?"

"When I first entered the wet area," Carey continued, "Mr. Greenleaf was standing near the far bench in the large shower area." That tied Arnold Greenleaf down as the guy whose back Warren saw later, going into the pool complex. Hoffman, Lerman, Rubin, and Greenleaf; the four Warren told Palmieri he had seen. Plus Ramon, the wet-area attendant, who didn't really count. I don't mean he couldn't have done it, just that he wasn't a power in the club. "And when I went into the pool area," Carey concluded, "in the near whirlpool, the hotter one, there was Mr. Kaner." Kaner? That was all I needed. Another suspect—it was only a few feet from the steam room to the first whirlpool—which was good, but why did it have to be Joel Kaner, who was as powerful as the other four big-wheel suspects? Even worse, I was running against Kaner for chairman of the board of directors. Anything I did to show that he had something to do with Brodsky's death, everybody would think it was because I wanted to knock him out of the race.

"Why are you asking me these questions, Mr. Baer? The way you're . . . It's just like Sergeant Palmieri. He kept asking too. Over and over. The way he was acting, you'd think there was something . . ." Bill looked at me curiously. "He was killed, wasn't he? Mr. Brodsky, I mean."

"If he wasn't—" If Palmieri found out I told Carey something five minutes before it was in the headlines, I'd never get any cooperation out of him again. "—the police are spending a lot of time and money for nothing."

"And Palmieri thinks I know something about it?"

I didn't want to upset him yet. "He questioned Warren too; everybody who was in the spa at the time Brodsky died. If it turned out that Brodsky was killed and Palmieri didn't do a thorough job, the town could be hit with a big lawsuit and Palmieri could get transferred to the South Shore."

"He didn't question everybody in the gym," Bill said stubbornly, "just those who were around the steam room at eight o'clock. He thinks one of us did it, doesn't he?"

As long as Carey was taking for granted it was a murder, I might as well do what I had to do. "One of you did do it; who else could it have been?" God, I was talking like a—a—a Palmieri already. Well, why not?

"You think I could have done it?"

Warren, who had been sitting without saying a word all this time—which has to be torture for a philosopher—spoke up. "You have to face the facts, Bill. Lots of people hated Mr. Brodsky. Most of us did, but none of us had the motives you did. It's clear that Sergeant Palmieri is going to concentrate on you and you'd better be prepared for it."

Carey got good and red. "I thought you were my friend, Warren. Now you think I did it too?"

"I'm just saying that from the viewpoint of the police, you had the best motive."

"You leave Sharon out of this; she had nothing to do with it."

"You can't leave Brodsky's own granddaughter out of it," I pointed out, "or how much Brodsky hated you. Everybody knew he was trying to get you fired and that's going to come out, sooner or later. You also can't leave out about you and Nassau Venture Capital, what we were planning. I'm not going to volunteer anything, but if Palmieri asks me, I've got to tell him the truth."

"But—but—Mr. Baer—" Carey was trying to suppress his anger. "If you tell him about that, he'll think . . ."

"He already thinks." It was time to hit Bill with the facts, and I was watching his face as I spoke. "Why else would he have interrogated you so long? You had the opportunity: You were in the steam room—your sweat suit was damp all over—at the time Brodsky, may he rest in peace, was killed. You had the means: However Barney was asphyxiated, it didn't require any weapons other than your own hands, palm over his mouth, thumb and fingers closing his nostrils. You're an ex-wrestler and in real good shape, while Barney was old and weak. You had the motive: Barney hated you more than he hated anybody else in the club. He was trying to get you fired because you stood up to him and didn't let him have any special privileges, and he wasn't using only fair means. Then he was trying to stop you from seeing Sharon. And, if he found out about our deal, he'd be in a good position to ruin that; he's got a lot of influence around here with the banks and the zoning boards. Motive, means, and opportunity: It looks to me like you're not only a prime suspect, you're the most likely suspect in Palmieri's eyes."

"I don't care what it looks like," Bill shouted, "I didn't do it. Do you really think I did it, Mr. Baer?"

His reaction was what I would have expected from an innocent young man, but that didn't guarantee he was innocent either. "No, I don't," I said, "but my opinion doesn't carry a hell of a lot of weight with Palmieri."

"To hell with Palmieri," Bill said. "I'm not worried about him. I know I didn't kill Mr. Brodsky, so there's nothing the police can do to me. I'm more worried about you, Mr. Baer. My option is up on Friday, and if we don't close by then, I lose everything, every penny I've got. And maybe Sharon too. You told me the papers were almost ready; I want to sign them today."

"The papers are ready, but under these conditions . . ." I didn't want to say it, but I had to. "As long as you're under suspicion of murder, I'm going to tell my group to put the deal on hold until this matter is settled."

"Why? If it was good yesterday, it's good today."

"Wrong. The whole business depends on you: your ability, your personality, and your character. If I've misjudged any of these, the business will go to hell and my investors will lose their money. Or if you're in the clink, or even out on bail, with your whole mind on how to get yourself a verdict of not guilty, then who's going to watch the store?"

"I keep telling you I didn't do it."

"That doesn't mean you won't be arrested, does it?"

Warren stuck his nose in again. "I'm sure you're innocent, Bill," he said firmly. "We'll prove that before Friday. Won't we, Dad?"

I keep telling him and telling him: In business, follow my lead. If you disagree with me about anything—*anything*; I'm easy to talk to—discuss it with me in private, never in front of the guy you're negotiating with. And never, never, *never* contradict, in public, the guy who's carrying the ball for the company. But too late, it was out on the table now, and I couldn't contradict *Warren*, not after all I'd told him, so what else could I say? So I said it, trying to sound sincere and confident. "Yeah, sure. We'll do it. Before Friday." Before *Friday*? In my spare time? Hell, we'd be lucky if we could get to first base by then. If that far. And that's only if I *wanted* to prove Bill didn't do it.

I couldn't let my feelings show in front of Carey; what goes for a business goes double for a family. And I couldn't tell Warren how stupid . . . No, I wasn't allowed to say that; not after the hard time we had with each other after Thelma, may she rest in peace, passed away, and not after how long it took for me and Warren to get to understand each other a little. It wasn't much, but better than nothing. What I meant was that later, when we were both relaxed, I would point out to Warren that it isn't smart to

54

make promises that you aren't absolutely sure of being able to . . . To hell with that. It *was* stupid of Warren to promise. Just plain *stupid*. And I'd explain to him how he might be digging his own grave if he . . . And mine too; goes without saying. That on Palmieri's list, right after Bill Carey—and not too far behind—was Warren Baer, prime murder suspect number two, so if we cleared Bill Carey, guess who Palmieri'd zero in on next? Not to mention the six beautiful blond grandchildren I'd never have if Warren—my guaranteed-innocent Warren—went up the river and didn't marry Lee Guralnik real soon.

I had to talk it over with somebody. But who? The only one I knew with experience solving the problems children cause their parents was Iris Guralnik. *Iris Guralnik?* Now? Right after I'd lost another game to her because of her lousy needling? Over my dead body I'd ask her *anything*. But who else? Whom did I know who was smart enough, wise enough, and a working psychologist? Who could keep her mouth shut? And was as interested as I was in getting Lee and Warren married fast? And who had already helped me on my last case? Well, if it had to be, it had to be.

9

"I'll just have a diet cherry," Iris told the waiter.

"I take you for lunch to the best deli on Long Island," I said, "and you order *nothing*? You sick or something?"

"Maybe I'll nosh a couple of your french fries."

"My french fries you don't touch. Bring another side order," I told the waiter. "Also we'll split a fried onion rings. And a pastrami on one of those miniature rolls for the lady." I turned back to Iris. "Let's see you resist that."

The waiter nodded, satisfied, and left. "I really shouldn't," she said. "I've been trying to lose weight." Iris has been trying to lose weight all her life and not doing too good at it. Not that she's all that fat; it's more like she's built solid. Her pectoral muscles are so big it's a wonder she can see the ball, but she can get a drive off better than most men. The trouble is that, for a psychologist, she has no willpower when it comes to food. I wouldn't say that out loud, though, especially now that we're going to be in-laws. If Warren ever gets moving, that is. "Besides, I already had lunch," she explained. "With Marvin."

56

"Even though you knew you were going to eat with me?"

"I bring Marvin a good lunch to the office and eat with him every day; helps him relax. That way I can control what he eats and make sure he gets lots of vegetables. I've been worried about his health lately. Being a dentist isn't as easy as you think."

"It's a lot easier than being the guy he's torturing."

"Like hell. Not only do you get scoliosis and phlebitis and ulcers, plus intention tremor while you're working in a tiny field where a thousandth of an inch is critical, but your patients are afraid of you. Most of them even hate you subconsciously; you think that doesn't take a toll? The suicide rate among dentists is the highest of any profession."

"Yeah, my heart bleeds for all the poor suffering dentists. Like it does for the IRS." She gave me a *look*. "All right, Iris; I was just kidding. But if he hates it that much, why doesn't he just retire?"

"He can't; we need the money. I want to give Lee the kind of wedding she deserves; the kind I didn't have myself when Marvin and I got married."

"What for? From what I know of Lee and Warren, they'll want a quiet little wedding; just close family."

"A wedding is for the mother; the bride has nothing to say about it. It'll be the biggest, fanciest wedding in the history of Oakdale. Lee deserves it. My only child; my only opportunity. *I* deserve it."

"Yeah, if they ever get around to it, which was one of the things I wanted to talk to you about."

The waiter brought our orders. "Later," Iris said, and started in on the onion rings. I started too; there was no point talking until we were finished. I can't think straight with a hot pastrami-on-rye in front of me uneaten. And french fries. And fried onion rings.

When I was done, I leaned back in my chair. Iris was already done. "See," I said. "If you hadn't stuffed yourself

57

on salad, you could've had a full-size sandwich. Just once you couldn't tell Marvin you're having lunch with me?"

"You think that would help him relax? Hah!"

"What's with the 'Hah!'? It's okay to take my money on the golf course but not okay for me to buy you a lunch in exchange for advice? To bounce some ideas off you, I mean?"

Iris hesitated for a moment, then said, "Anybody but you, Ed. He's jealous."

"Jealous? Of me? What the hell for?" Suddenly it struck me. "You? He thinks that I . . . ? With you?"

"You're single now."

"So what? Did I ever even hint at . . . ? Not just you, but anyone you know? From the day I met Thelma, there was only one girl for me. And there still is, even though . . . If he doesn't know that, maybe you better tell him."

"Never; better he should be a little jealous. But it's not just that, Ed; it's the whole general thing. That you're so—so strong-minded, so sure of yourself, so decisive. Different from him."

"So? Everybody's different from everybody. If he tried to be like me, he'd be just as miserable as I'd be if I tried to be like him. You gotta be yourself."

"Exactly, Ed. So you just answered your question."

"What question?" Iris can drive you crazy, at times. "I didn't hear myself asking any questions."

"You didn't have to say it out loud. Warren and Lee. Let them be themselves. At their own speed. Without you putting on the pressure. Or did you want advice on how to play golf"—she smiled nastily—"instead of donating a hundred bucks to the wedding fund every Monday, Wednesday, and Friday because you'd rather kill the ball than break a hundred?"

"I'll make that two hundred a game if you'll keep your mouth shut when I'm ready to swing."

"This you say to a psychologist? Dream on, sucker; to

me it's worth the money ten times over just to see your reactions. I may even do a paper on you."

"You'd write me up in a case history? Your only daughter's father-in-law? To be? If they ever make their minds up, that is?"

"I'll change the names to protect the guilty. And don't worry about Warren and Lee; they've made up their minds."

"They have?" I couldn't believe this. "And he didn't tell me? I'll kill him. When?"

"The moment they met. What they're doing now is exploring, checking, making sure."

"What do you mean *exploring*? They're fooling around? Without even being engaged?"

She sighed. "Ed, you're a century behind the times. I was a virgin when I got married, and probably Thelma was too. We were both lucky—and you and Marvin were too—that we married good men. In every way. But today? The divorce rate? The young people don't really want to get divorced, but they look at the statistics and they want to change the odds a little more in their favor. They want to see if they can *stand* each other. Living together is not the same as being married, but it's as close as you can get."

"But they're not living together—she doesn't graduate till June—and what the hell's wrong with announcing the engagement now? I'd feel a lot better if they said it out loud. At a formal engagement party."

"They'll be living together as soon as Lee graduates."

"Warren's going to move out on me? You know this for sure? She *told* you?"

"Of course she didn't tell me, but I know it for sure. I'm her mother and I'm also a damn good psychologist."

"And you'd let her? You didn't say a word?"

"Come on, Ed. Warren's twenty-five and Lee's twenty-two. You think either of them are innocent virgins?"

"I never even thought of it. I just . . ." Iris was right.

I'd been so used to thinking of Warren as a boy that I didn't . . . "I want them to get married right away."

"You *want?*" Iris smiled at me crookedly. "Good idea. Let's go out and buy a big whip. Two big whips."

"I didn't mean *force*, Iris, and you know it. What I meant was talk, that's all. Soft and sweet. You talk to Lee and I'll talk to Warren."

Her face grew hard. "You try that, and I'll break a driver over your big fat head. Your idea of soft and sweet is like using a ten-ton steamroller instead of a twenty-ton. Pushing Warren and Lee is the best way to ruin everything. Let nature take its course; the wedding will be this fall."

She had been right about some things before, like in the Kassel case, that ended up bringing Warren and me a little closer, so I figured I'd play along with her for the while. But if anything looked like it'd interfere with having my first beautiful, blond granddaughter next year, then I'd step in, do things my own way. "Look," I said, "I'm in favor of a big wedding too. So if there's any problem with the cost . . ."

"Thanks, Ed." She smiled nicely as she said that; back to friends again. "But it's not just the cost of the wedding; it's the investment in your new gym deal." Marvin Guralnik was as big a pain as an investor as he was on the golf course, but when NVC was starting out I offered everyone who came in on its initial venture first refusal for the same percentage of the deal on all future NVC ventures. It's very flattering that all my investors stuck with me on every project, but it's not so good to have a superconservative nervous twitcher like Marvin as a limited partner. "That's the biggest deal you've brought us so far," Iris said. "The partnership's responsible for two and a half million? That's not peanuts. Especially when the guy running the company has no assets at all."

"I know, but I've checked it out good; it fills a real hole in the market. Maybe it won't pay off as fast as some of our others at first, but it'll give a good steady yield for at least twenty years and build up lots of equity too. When the nut is paid off, our profit will triple."

"I didn't say we wouldn't take our usual share of the deal, Ed; just that it's a lot of money."

"Look, Iris, if it's a strain on you, why don't you take a smaller percentage? I can easily get other investors to take up the slack and I've always advised you to diversify. Some tax-exempt bonds, some CDs, some solid stocks, things like that. Putting all your eggs in my basket worries me. One of these days I could make a real bad call."

"If we're going to gamble, Ed, I'd rather trust you than some of those geniuses on Wall Street. You're a stubborn schmuck on the golf course—one of these days maybe you'll listen to me and stop trying to destroy the ball—but you're pretty good in business. It isn't that we're starving because we took our full share, but when we gave you the money it left us with nothing liquid for emergencies. And it took a big bite out of the wedding fund."

"Don't take this wrong, Iris, but since we'll soon be *mishpocheh*, I could—"

"Marvin would die first, but thanks anyway."

It was time to get to the reason why I had brought her here in the first place. "Cheer up, Iris; maybe we won't close the deal on Friday. Or ever."

"Barney Brodsky?" Well, I never said she was stupid. "Bill Carey's involved?"

"The prime suspect. He was in the right place at the right time, and he has the best motive of anybody."

"Because Barney hated him doesn't mean he hated Barney."

"Thank you, Dr. Guralnik, but maybe you should try to convince Sergeant Palmieri of that. It's not just that Barney was working to get Bill fired from the club, but he was also trying to keep him from marrying Sharon Edel."

"Never. They love each other; I can tell. If her parents don't approve, Bill and Sharon will elope when she comes home from school."

"Your word in God's ear, Iris. But there's worse. One of my friends in our bank told me that three days ago Barney started pushing them not to approve the NVC loan because Bill's name was on it too."

"You think Barney knew about the gym?"

"He had to. Not officially, of course, but I'll bet somebody at the bank let something slip."

"So why didn't Barney get Bill fired from the club?"

"Guaranteed he'd have tried to push it through this Friday at the board meeting. If he'd already told Bill about it—you know what a mean bastard Barney was—and Palmieri finds out about it, Bill will be in the clink five minutes later."

"Does Warren know this?"

"Positively not. He'd kill . . . I mean, after the trouble he had with Barney last year, he would've had it out with the old bastard in public, and I couldn't have stopped him. You know how Warren is about doing right."

"Did you ask Carey if Barney . . . ?"

"To tell you the truth, Iris, I was afraid to."

"Because if Carey told you Barney had threatened him, you'd have to tell Palmieri yourself?"

I nodded; couldn't speak.

"And because you felt guilty about putting Bill down as a signatory to the loan?"

"Guilty? He was borrowing the money along with us."

"It was stupid of you to put him down on the loan, Ed, and you know it. We didn't need Carey for that; he's broke."

"I need him; that's NVC policy. If our necks are on the line, our partner's neck gotta be too."

"He's already put in over twenty percent of the gross startup cost; isn't that enough?"

"If you tell me how to do business, Iris, you'll have

all the responsibility of the general partner and none of the benefits. So shut up for your own good."

Her face got red. "Are you trying to tell me you're not going to close on Friday?"

"If Carey's under arrest at that time, definitely not. If he's still under suspicion, probably not."

"He'll lose everything," she protested. "The poor kid'll be in hock for the rest of his life."

"The poor kid could also end up with an eight-to-twenty-five, if he killed Barney Brodsky."

"He didn't. My professional reputation on that."

"Yeah, that's what Warren said. But Palmieri doesn't believe in ESP."

"What exactly did Warren say?"

"That we'd prove Bill didn't do it." I could barely get the words out. "Before Friday."

"In front of Carey?" I nodded. "Did you contradict Warren?" She stared at me intently.

"No. Like an idiot, I said I'd help him do it." There, it was all out. In front of Iris, yet. I felt like the biggest schmuck in the world.

She let out a breath of relief. "Good. So do it."

"Do it? Do what? Prove Carey didn't kill Brodsky? Are you crazy? How the hell do you prove somebody's not guilty? And you know what else? If I prove Carey's not the killer, you know who's second on the list? Warren. My Warren. Your future son-in-law. I hope."

"The problem's simple," Iris said smugly. "Don't try to prove anybody is innocent. Find out who the real killer is."

"Just like that? By Friday? Brilliant! Today's Monday, and it's half over already. Actually, it has to be *before* Friday. Four days *maximum*. You're crazy, Iris."

"You did it once before, didn't you? You and Warren? The Kassel case?"

"Not with this time limit, we didn't. Not with the kind of suspects we got here—all powerful people, all club members. And Warren's a philosopher, Iris, remember? How the hell's he going to . . . ? A *philosopher*, just what I needed."

She ignored that completely; by her, philosopher's not a dirty word. "Just remember, let Warren take the lead. Back him in everything. Give him credit for everything. If he succeeds, he and Lee will get married sooner."

"What does that have to do with—"

"Living with a domineering father like you takes a lot of—of energy." I could tell she was going to say something else. "You keep building up Warren's confidence, and he'll . . . Trust me on this, Ed."

Even if I didn't trust her, I had to. What else could I do? Four days to find who did it? With my six grandchildren at stake? No problem, right? A real terrific team we had to find a murderer in four days: a philosopher and a schmuck. With a psychologist for the cheerleader. How could we lose?

10

When I had phoned earlier to invite her for lunch, Iris told me she would drive down to the deli herself. This I couldn't understand. When I invite a lady out, I figure I'm supposed to pick her up and see her home safe. Iris explained that God forbid Marvin should hear from some big-mouth yenta that I had picked up his wife at home while he was tied up in his office, had taken her to a real hot spot like the Oakdale deli, and had gotten her drunk on diet cherry soda. It's only six months since Thelma, may she rest in peace, passed away and I'm going to start fooling around with a married woman?

Anybody who knows me . . . Crazy. Phlebitis isn't the only thing some dentists suffer from. How a terrific girl like Lee could be his daughter . . . And as far as fooling around with *anybody* is concerned, Iris would positively not be my first choice for female company, even off the links—close to the last, in fact—especially when she's acting like a psychologist and ordering me around.

So as soon as Iris left the deli, I called my office to see if there were any messages. Doris told me that Palmieri

had called a half hour ago and wanted to see me and Warren right away. At the station house. Now. *Immediately.*
And that he had sounded very mad. Warren was already
on his way so the faster I got down there, the less time
Palmieri would have to give Warren a hard time without
me to protect him. It's always Warren, with the women.
How come they never worry about me being given a hard
time?

"I called an hour ago" was the way Palmieri greeted
me when I got there. "What the hell took you so long?"
Warren was sitting opposite the desk. I remained standing.

"I was having lunch and my secretary didn't know
where I was. As soon as I talked to her I came over. Why
are you giving me a hard time, Palmieri?"

"You held out on me, Baer. Practically lied to me."

"Me? Lie?" I tried not to yell, but nobody calls me a
liar. *Nobody.* "To you? About what?"

"Not exactly lie"—Palmieri inched back—"but close.
You withheld vital information from the police. Why
didn't you tell me you had a run-in with Mr. Brodsky last
spring?"

"You didn't ask me. I—Warren and I—answered
every question you asked."

His face got red. "I don't have to ask you, Baer; I
want you to tell me. Volunteer. Remember how I cooper-
ated with you on the Kassel case?"

"Damn right I do, Sergeant. I also remember how
that let us solve the case and give you all the credit."

He clenched his jaws visibly, then took a deep breath
and relaxed. "Okay, so long as we understand each other.
Now tell me all about your fight with the victim."

"What fight? We had a little disagreement."

"Little?" Palmieri smiled nastily. "Wasn't that when
you decided to run for the club's board of directors? When
you called him a miserable old bastard in public and said you
were tired of his running the club like he owned it?"

66

"He *was* a miserable old bastard and he was ruining the club. Can I help it if my voice carries a little?"

"Carries a little? They said you could be heard on the twelfth hole."

"So what? If you think I'd kill Barney for a little disagreement a year ago, you're crazy. I was out on the links when he was killed and I can prove it. Jerry Fein, Iris and Marvin Guralnik, and maybe fifty others. Who told you?"

"Never mind who told me. And I didn't say you killed him, Baer; all I said was that you didn't give me important information. I talked to you twice this morning, *twice*, and you didn't say a word once."

"It wasn't important; didn't have any bearing."

"I decide what has bearing, not you. Talk."

I pulled over a chair and sat down. "In the club, you can be chairman of the board two years in a row, no more. After that you can run for the board and be voted in again as chairman a year later, as long as you're out of office at least one year. But Brodsky, may he rest in peace, liked to be boss of whatever he touched. So he got a bunch of people he controls to run for the board regularly so there's always a majority to vote him in as chairman."

"But he's still out as chairman for a year, right? Like he was going to be right after the coming election."

"Means nothing. He always made sure one of his stooges would be elected chairman, so he was still in control."

"Joel Kaner? The one you're running against?"

"That's why I'm running against him. Joel's a good guy and I don't really want to be chairman—I got a business to run and enough headaches as it is—but Brodsky's been running the club for fourteen years, and enough is enough."

"You objected to Mr. Brodsky's policies?"

"Not all of them; he was pretty efficient. But this term is important. Harold Gordon, the general manager, told us he was going to retire next year. I believe in promoting from within whenever possible—Grace Dauber was the logical choice—but Brodsky would never let a woman be in charge."

Palmieri glanced at the notes on his desk. "The way I heard it, you were expected to favor Bill Carey."

"Bill's good, but he's too young for the job."

"Your son is two years younger than Carey and he's vice-president of Nassau Venture Capital."

"Warren owns half the company, so he's entitled. Besides, neither one of us makes a binding decision alone."

"Like should you finance Bill Carey in his new gym?" He glared at me. "You forget to tell me about that too?"

"That was supposed to be private." Did the whole world know my business? "Who told you? Somebody at the bank got a big mouth?" Probably the same guy who tipped off Barney.

"Never mind who; just answer the question."

"We both agreed on that; it was a good investment."

"Did you support Grace Dauber so Carey would have to quit the club and take your deal?"

"You calling me a crook, Palmieri?" Cop or no cop, I stood up ready to slug him, but Warren dived from his chair and grabbed me from behind. He was stronger than I thought; the workouts must've been doing him some good.

"Sit down, Baer," Palmieri said calmly. "Hitting a cop in his own house is looking for big trouble." I hadn't noticed him taking the sap out, but it was already in his right hand. "All I'm doing is repeating what some people said about you not getting along too good with Mr. Brodsky."

"People? What people?"

"People I've been talking to about the murder."

"They know all about the gym deal too?"

"Only about the fight you had with Brodsky last year."

Thank God for little favors. "Then let me tell you

something, Palmieri, that you don't know. You got this information from the suspects; that's who you've been talking to this morning. And you know who they are?"

"Sure. Arnold Greenleaf, Sidney Hoffman, Carl Lerman, George Rubin, Joel Kaner, William Carey, and Ramon Velez. All the people who were near to the victim when he was killed, who were physically able to commit the murder."

"Yeah, but do you know *who* they are? They're Brodsky's gang, all five, the directors he controlled. Except for Bill and Ramon, I mean."

He jumped at this. "You sure?"

"They're the ones I'm fighting. That's why one of them told you about my business with Brodsky. Now that I've given you something important, who told you about me and Brodsky?"

"All of them, Baer; what'd you expect?"

I should've known. These guys—I thought they were my friends, or at least not my enemies—but when it comes down to his skin or mine, each one would've pulled the switch on me without hesitation. And did. "Who told you about Kaner? He was in the whirlpool, so Warren didn't see him. Warren only told you about Greenleaf, Hoffman, Lerman, and Rubin."

"Bill Carey told me. And the lifeguard confirmed it. So now we have eight suspects."

"Six," I said automatically. "Ramon didn't do it."

"Probably not, but I'm not dropping him from the list officially."

"With Ramon, I still only count seven," I said. "Where do you get eight?" Then it struck me. "Warren? You think *Warren* could've . . . ? He's officially a suspect? You're crazy, Palmieri. You know Warren. He could never—"

"You never know who could. I gotta suspect anybody who had the opportunity, the means, and the motive."

"Warren just happened to be there accidentally at the

time. Everybody in the club had the means. Choking a weak old man? Two hands is all you need."

"Brodsky wasn't choked; he was asphyxiated. Suffocated."

"Same thing. Anybody could've done it."

"Including Warren?"

"Warren didn't have any motive."

"No?" Palmieri looked real mean now. "That's another thing you forgot to mention to me, isn't it? What about that big fight Warren had with Brodsky only a few months ago? How come you never told me about that?"

"It wasn't a big fight and it had nothing to do with . . . Look, Brodsky was a bastard, ask anybody. He was on the board of our bank, the one we use to finance our deals. We never had any trouble with them before, always fast service and reasonable rates. Why not? I got a clean record and I stand behind our loans personally. Which I'd do even if NVC wasn't the general partner in all our deals. All of a sudden—"

"Let me tell it, Dad," Warren broke in. Remembering what Iris had told me, I shut up right away. "I was the one involved, Sergeant," Warren said. "I do all the work with the bank now, while my father does the analysis and evaluation. I had the routine down pat, the paperwork computerized, a good relationship with the vice-president who handled our loans, and we were closing even faster than before. Suddenly everything's at a standstill. Even small loans had to be referred to committee. Large ones had to go back two and three times, taking weeks where before we could close in days. My friendly vice-president was making trouble over typos and trivial matters. I was spending all my time on petty details and neglecting other work. NVC boasts that we can give an applicant an answer in a week; now we were lucky if we could do it in a month. Finally I asked the VP what was wrong. He wasn't supposed to tell me, but he did."

"Brodsky?" Palmieri asked.

"He was on the board and passed the word down."

"Why? What did he have against you?"

"Only that I was Bill Carey's friend and we all thought my father was going to support Bill for general manager. Mr. Brodsky wanted Carey fired so he'd leave the area."

"And not marry Brodsky's granddaughter?"

"Partly that and partly that Bill refused to kowtow to him. Bill ran the spa the way he thought best, and wouldn't jump every time Mr. Brodsky whistled."

"That's when you had the fight?"

"It wasn't a fight," Warren said wearily. "I went to his office—though he's retired, he maintains an office in his son's law firm, Brodsky, Burns, and Brodsky, where he's 'of counsel'—and spoke to him. Quietly. I pointed out that applying pressure to NVC would not affect my father's actions in the club—might even make him more stubborn—and that tactics like this were unworthy of a man of his years and standing. He got all excited and started screaming, accused me of threatening him, and called in his son, Gene, and his secretary to witness my threats and call the police to . . . It was totally ridiculous. I'm sure his secretary had been through scenes like this before. She escorted me out and apologized. When the story went around the gossip circuit, it took on the usual exaggerations. That's all there was to it, and you can check with Mr. Brodsky's secretary and his son."

"I will," Palmieri said, "but even if everything you said is true, don't you still have a motive for killing Mr. Brodsky? In your own words?"

Time for me to get back in the game. "You think I'd let that condition continue?" I said. "Let a bastard like Brodsky kill my business and hurt my investors? I was in the building business for a long time, and I've faced tougher guys than Barney Brodsky. As soon as I found out what was going on, I went to each of the bank directors and talked to them man to man. None of them knew what

71

Barney had been doing; the bank officers couldn't go be-hind one director's back and snitch to another. The direc-tors were decent guys and good businessmen, so I hit them with the ethics, mentioned the State Banking Commission in passing, and showed them figures, how much we'd bor-rowed in the past. Not just NVC, but my construction company and the companies we'd invested in. I added up how much new business we had brought to the bank, how solid we were, how we paid on time, how much profit they had made on us, things like that. I told them that in spite of our good relationship in the past, and much as I hated to do it, if this stupidity went on, I'd be forced to take my business to another bank, their most hated rival, so what did they think I should do? One week later we were back to normal again. They must've raked Brodsky over the coals, but good. So maybe Brodsky had a reason to hate me, but since Warren didn't have a reason to hate Brodsky, take him off the suspects' list."

"Sorry, Baer," Palmieri said, "but after what I just heard, he's on it stronger than before."

"Didn't you hear what I said?" I could feel my neck swelling. "Warren didn't—"

"It's okay," Warren interrupted me for the second time, not that I'm counting. "Leave me on the list if you have to."

"That's how I have to work; it's not like the games private eyes play in books."

"But leave me a way to get my name off that list," Warren said. "To clear my name."

"Stop sweating," Palmieri said quietly. "You're not at the top of the list."

"Bill Carey?" Palmieri didn't change the expression on his face. "He didn't do it," Warren went on. "I know him. He couldn't. I want to clear him too."

"You clear him," Palmieri said, "and you move one name closer to the head of the list."

"What if we find the killer?"

"Forget it; this is police work."

"Like the Kassel case," Warren urged. "We'll stay out of your way, no interference, and you'll get the credit."

Palmieri thought for a while, then said, "You tell me everything you do, everything you find out, clear everything with me *before* you do it?"

"My word," Warren said.

Palmieri looked at me. "Me too," I promised.

"But you have to give us some information to work with," Warren pressed.

"Whatever I can," Palmieri said.

I knew what that meant: zilch. It was going to be a one-way street; we tell Palmieri everything we find out, he tells us nothing we don't already know.

Warren stood up, smiling. What the hell for, I couldn't figure out. Well, what can you expect from a philosopher? God, was I ever that young and stupid?

11

Even though Barney Brodsky's murder had already cost me over half a day's work, I couldn't keep my mind on business. The numbers kept swimming before my eyes, and when I found myself going over the same page for the third time, I closed the folder and went into Warren's office. Warren's desk was empty and he was staring off into space like a philosopher, which he wasn't supposed to be during business hours. We're into small businesses that haven't been around long enough to stash away the capital they need to weather the rough times that come when you least expect them, so we have to be thinking business all the time. Remembering what Iris Guralnik had warned me, I kept my voice soft and calm, and was careful not to criticize Warren. "You beginning to see now how stupid it was," I said, "to promise Bill Carey that we'd close the case before Friday?"

"It has to be before Friday, Dad," Warren said. "Otherwise we won't be able to close the deal and pay Mr. Lerman the rest of the lease money."

"The world will end if we're not in the gym business?"

"Bill Carey's world will. He relied on us."

"Normally, the deal would have closed on time. But go figure on a murder. That's my responsibility?"

"I thought you liked Bill." Warren's eyes looked at me just like Thelma's used to when I let her down.

"I do, I do. I want Bill to be successful, I want him and Sharon to be happy, I want our limited partners to make money, I want peace on earth, I want . . . I want . . . There's no limit to what I want, but when it comes to what I can do—me alone, Ed Baer—then there are limits. Boy, are there limits."

"It's not you alone, Dad. I'm with you."

I deserved that. "Yeah, I'm sorry. I didn't mean it the way it sounded. But even with the two of us . . . Even if we decided to let the business go to hell for a week . . . Just because we were lucky once doesn't mean we can do it again."

"You never gave up before in your life, Dad. Why now?"

"In the Kassel case, I knew the business. I had some leverage over the suspects, so they had to talk to me. Here? Some of those guys can buy me and sell me before breakfast. If I try to question them . . . They don't even have to say hello to me. And they've all got it in for me since I started running against Joel Kaner for chairman; they're all Brodsky's boys. A couple of them are tough bastards too."

"If the logical conclusion is that we won't get any cooperation from them, it's logical for us to use non-Aristotelian logic to get them to cooperate."

He's always doing that to me. As soon as I have something figured out clearly, he comes in out of left field with one of his crazy philosophy ideas that make me dizzy. "I don't even want to know what that means, Warren; I got enough trouble just being logical."

"Look at it this way, Dad. We were going to go to each suspect and question him to find who the murderer is, right?"

"There's something wrong with that?"

"If we had a cooperative group of people who were willing to help us, no. Or people we had some element of control over, that we could force to help us. Since we don't, we have to approach them with reverse logic. We're going to help them."

"We are? Those bastards? Help them what? Ruin my business? Cheat me out of the chairmanship?"

"Help them by giving them the one thing they need that they can't get anywhere themselves: We're going to help each one clear himself of the suspicion of murder. Remember what Palmieri said? That they're all suspects?"

"Even the murderer? We're going to help clear him? Is this some more of your backward logic?"

"*Especially* the murderer. We're going to try to clear all of them. The only way we can do it is to talk to each one and have him tell us everything he knows."

"You think he's going to tell you anything that might incriminate him? Or even throw suspicion on him?"

"He's only going to tell us things that throw suspicion on the others. By putting together what they tell us, we'll know everything about all of them. Then we'll try to clear each one, and the one that we can't clear—he's the murderer."

Brilliant. Typical. Brilliant *and* typical. Of Warren. In his enthusiasm at finding a way to get the bastards to talk to us, and to tell us the truth about the others, he forgot one little detail. What happens if we clear *all* of them? Who's left? Bill Carey, that's who. And if we clear him too, there's only one other suspect. Warren Baer, my son the philosopher, who will search for *the* truth, and find it, even if it kills him.

12

Warren wanted to start with Greenleaf, Hoffman, Lerman, and Rubin, the suspects who had offices in Long Island, but clearly, we had to start with Joel Kaner, the only one who worked in Manhattan. "Palmieri interrogated you three times," I told Warren, "and it's still only midafternoon, so he's got to be talking to the others the same way."

"I thought that was because I discovered the body."

"Partly, but also because the police have to get the information while it's hot. If a case gets cold the odds against solving it go up very fast."

"But three times in one morning?"

You never know what a cop'll do in a big murder case, but I wasn't going to let Warren worry that he was a real suspect. "That's how Palmieri works. First he gets the stories from each witness. Then he questions them again, checking what each one said against what the others said, as well as against the background information he's gotten in the meantime. He looks for discrepancies and talks to them all again about what doesn't fit. At least three times for each witness; it's not just you, believe me. So he won't let Kaner go to New York today, but he can't keep Kaner away from his office two days in a row. Which means we have to see Kaner first."

So even though I don't drink, we were sitting at a table in the club bar, waiting for Joel Kaner to meet us. To make it clear that he was doing us a favor even if we were going to clear him, he was a good fifteen minutes late.

Kaner was a casting director's perfect choice for the owner of a midsize New York accounting firm: short, richly plump, thinning dyed-brown hair gray at the temples, styled sideways, and smooth, smooth all over. His suit alone had to have cost more than most people make in a month, and his watch, ring, and gold chains could've fed a family for a year. Kaner ordered a tequila, with lime and salt, and licked it down like a real tourist. His father, who had probably come over in steerage with ten kopeks in his pocket, should have seen his son now. He'd have disowned him on the spot.

After his hand had been cleaned of salt, Kaner started with his usual graciousness. "What the hell do you mean you're going to clear me, Baer? I don't need clearing, especially from you."

"Yeah? How many times did Sergeant Palmieri call you down to interrogate you today? Two? Three?" His face gave him away. "Four? You think he did that so he could have the pleasure of seeing how an expensive tailor with a phony accent could hide your pot belly?"

"You're not going to get a hell of a lot of votes by insulting people, Ed. In fact, you got a hell of a nerve running against me in the first place. I earned the job, climbed up through the ranks for ten years. This is the first time anyone's opposed the nominating committee choice."

Honey's better than vinegar, so I said, "I'm not trying to get votes, Joel. As a matter of fact, I don't really want the job and I think you'd make a hell of a good chairman

78

now that Barney, may he rest in peace, is gone. So why don't you relax and talk like a human being, okay?"

He looked at me suspiciously. "Are you saying you're going to withdraw? If I make you head of a committee?"

Everything with him had to be a deal. Left side of the ledger and right side; balancing debits and credits. "Not head of anything. When this case is over—assuming you're not the killer, which I'll do my best to prove—I'll withdraw my nomination. You want to make me chairman of the building committee, I'll consider it. You want somebody else to handle it, that's okay with me too. Now are you happy?"

He was still guarded. "And why the hell should you want to help me? Not that I need it."

"You need it, Joel, believe me. Everybody who was near the steam room when Barney was killed is under suspicion. And it's not just you I'm trying to help; it's all the club members. I don't want Palmieri to charge any of us with murder; it's that simple. That a member of Oakdale should turn out to be a murderer . . . ? It would shame us all."

"That include Warren?" His fat little eyes were wary. "You're doing this to clear Warren, aren't you?"

"Sure." Why lie? Especially to someone as smart as Joel Kaner. "But I'm also trying to clear everyone in the club."

"Everybody? Or just members?"

Kaner didn't inherit a big accounting firm, he earned it, so there was no reason to assume he wasn't smart enough to understand the facts of life. And the same went for the others I had to talk to. I had a rough three days ahead of me. "Not just members. I don't believe Bill Carey had anything to do with the murder either."

Kaner just stared at me. For a full minute. "How could an outsider get into the club," he asked, "much less the locker room and the wet area, without being seen?"

"I don't know," I confessed. "But that's my theory."

"Impossible. Unless you're thinking of one of the Puerto Rican kids? No way; Barney was killed by a member."

I passed the ball back to him. "Why do you say that?"

He took a deep breath and let it out slowly. "I'm going to trust you, Ed; tell you everything I know. You're not the sweetest guy in the world, and I don't agree with you on a lot of things, but I've never heard about you lying or screwing anybody. And I know what kind of a job you did on the Hamilcar Hi-Fi case. Since I didn't kill Barney, I'll help you find who did. And in case you think this has anything to do with the chairmanship, I don't care if you don't withdraw; I'll beat the pants off you anyway."

Beat the pants off me? That'll be the day. "Maybe I won't withdraw," I said, "just to prove you're wrong. And after I win, I'll resign and recommend you."

"Cut the bullshit," Kaner said, "I got to get back on the phone to my office. What do you want to know?"

"Everything you know about this morning."

"I got up early and played a fast nine holes. Took a quick hot shower and went into the extra-hot whirlpool to relax before I took the train in."

"When was that?"

"Around eight o'clock, maybe a little before; I didn't check the time exactly. Who knew there was going to be trouble?" He shrugged his shoulders. "A few minutes later, Arnie Greenleaf came in. Big hurry, like always; a towel around his waist. Threw the towel on a chair and zipped right into the pool with me. After a while I got out and Arnie got out right behind me. I took a shower to get the chlorine smell off and cool down. Dried off, shaved, blow-dried my hair, and went into the locker room to get dressed. Just as I was ready to leave all hell broke loose. Medics, cops, noise and confusion. That's it."

"You used the small shower room?"

"Just for a minute. Rinsed my trunks too."

"Arnold with you?"

80

"In the next stall."

"Did you use the swimsuit drier?"

"I don't put wet trunks in my locker." He didn't try to hide his annoyance.

"Did Arnold say anything?"

"When he came into the whirlpool? He said 'Hi,' and I said 'Hi.' He closed his eyes, put his head back against the tile, and relaxed. I did the same, let the jet work on my back. I have a bad back—comes from leaning over a desk all day—and the hot-water massage takes away the tension."

"You didn't see anything else? Anyone?"

"No, just me and Arnie. Unless you mean the lifeguard."

"He'll verify what time you went into the whirlpool?"

"Out, yes. In, no."

"He wasn't there when you went in?"

"He's supposed to be there at eight and no one's supposed to go in any pool unless he's there, but I'm not that fussy."

"Exactly when did he come in?"

"I don't wear a watch in the water, I'm not facing the clock, and I close my eyes when I relax. All I know is he was there when Arnold came in. You suspect him?"

"Not at this time. Just trying to get background."

"So why are you concentrating on me, Ed? I was in the pool when Barney was killed, you can ask the lifeguard. Arnold came in after me; concentrate on him."

"I'm not concentrating on you, Joel; you're just the one I'm talking to right now. I'll talk to the lifeguard, and everyone else too. I'm sure what you say will stand up but if I'm going to have a chance to solve this case, I have to ask everybody everything. Now tell me again: You didn't see anybody but Greenleaf and the lifeguard?" Palmieri's method.

It worked too. "Nobody," Kaner said. "Unless you mean . . . No members came in, but Bill Carey walked around the pool a few minutes after I got in. That what you mean?"

"Exactly. How about when you first went into the wet area? Who'd you see?"

"Sid Hoffman taking a shower. That's all. And the kid who cleans up, washing the showers at the other end of the room, away from Sid. That's *positively* all."

"Okay, but later, when you've got a clear head, what I'd like you to do is think a little more, see if there's anything you can add to what you've told me."

"Sure." Kaner got up to go. Then I remembered what Iris Guralnik had told me and said, "Warren has some questions. Would you mind sitting down for a couple minutes more?"

He sat down reluctantly. Warren hesitated for a moment, then asked, "Who hated Mr. Brodsky?"

"Hated?" The question sort of stopped Kaner. "I don't think anyone actually *hated* Barney. Not real hate."

"Somebody did kill him, Mr. Kaner."

"I guess . . . Nobody really liked Barney, you understand, but hate? I don't know. I can't think of anyone who hated him enough to . . . Unless, maybe, your father . . . ? Actually, even your father didn't hate him; just sort of disliked him."

"Weren't you part of Mr. Brodsky's group? Saw him socially? Associated with him in business?"

"Oh, sure. Not socially; he was a different generation and we had very little in common. Also, he could be a real pain with his needling; went a little too far at times. Not a real fun guy. If we were talking business, sometimes we'd have a drink or two, but that's about it."

"What kind of business?"

"I was his personal accountant as well as for the law firm: Brodsky, Burns, and Brodsky. They used to recommend me to their clients and I used to recommend them to mine. Barney wasn't really active at his age, just 'of counsel,' but I'm sure that when he told Gene to do some-

82

thing, Gene did it. Barney could be very—very forceful with his children."

"His daughter too?"

"He gave Ellen a hard time about some things."

"Like Sharon going with Bill Carey?"

Kaner blushed. "I wasn't going to mention it, but there was no way Barney was going to let Sharon marry Bill. Ellen did her best to keep it peaceful, didn't even tell Maurice about it at first, but Barney managed to find out. Barney always found out about everything. His greatest pleasure was getting the dirt on somebody and then bugging him about it in public." He turned to me. "If you ask me, Ed, the one who had the best motive to kill Barney was Bill Carey."

Just what I needed to hear. To get off the subject, I asked, "As Barney's accountant, you had to know all about his business affairs. Did Barney screw anyone in business so badly that the guy wanted to kill him?"

"Absolutely not. Barney was sharp, very sharp; he'd drive hard bargains, cut corners very close, but nothing illegal. Insisted on obeying the letter of the law, very rigid. I know; I invested along with him in some deals myself and, as an accountant, I'd never take the chance of doing something that could cost me my business. Or my freedom."

Then it struck me. "Invested in some deals like the Lerman Mall?"

Pay dirt. "That was one of them, the best, in my professional opinion. Within one year after it opens it'll be the most profitable mall on the Island."

"Was that Barney's deal?"

"Carl Lerman's. Barney, Gene, and Maurice were limited partners like the rest of us."

"The rest of you?" It was suddenly clear. "Greenleaf, Hoffman, and Rubin too?"

"There are thirty of us who always went with Lerman. He didn't tell you? Barney either?" Kaner laughed nervously. "You used to give Barney a hard time at the board meetings and I guess he asked Lerman not to approach you."

"Even if he had," I said, "I wouldn't put that much into a single deal; it's better to diversify. From the size of the project, with thirty limited partners, each share has to cost over five hundred thousand." I always did numbers in my head, faster than a computer. Comes from being brought up on a slide rule, where you have to know the rough answer before you compute. A big advantage in business; while the other guy's still punching buttons, you already know the score.

"Yeah, I forgot you were in construction once. Actually, it was six hundred each."

"Even if it was a lot less, I wouldn't invest in another guy's deal; I got plenty of my own on the fire. By me, money's got to work full time; I keep the minimum liquid."

"So do I, but when Carl's ready to sell limited partnerships you have to move. He waits till it's all set: zoning, permits, mortgage, construction loan, everything, then he takes the money. I like that; there's no maybes. But one week; that's it. Actually it's not that sudden. He always lets us know when he's sure it's a go; two weeks ahead. His regular guys get preference, but if you don't take a share on time, there's a dozen guys anxious to take your place."

"His deals are that good?"

"The best. He's honest and efficient and conservative; never goes over budget and finishes on schedule."

"You had six hundred liquid?"

"Come on, Ed; nobody keeps that much in cash."

"So you had to liquidate some assets to raise the money for your share?"

"It really hurt; some of my investments I should've held onto longer to maximize . . . Yeah, it cost, but in one year I'll be even and after that, with the tax benefits, I'll be way ahead of the game."

84

"Still, putting six hundred grand in cash together in one week, that takes a little doing."

"Carl's had his own money tied up in the deal for five years, so if that's the way he wants to do it, who's to argue?" He looked at me shrewdly. "Now that we're talking about it, Ed, what do you think of the mall? Your professional opinion as an ex-contractor?"

"I wish I owned it. It'll be the best mall on the Island. But why ask me now? You already put your money in, didn't you? And went over the paperwork? You know numbers."

"Never hurts to get a second opinion." He looked at Warren. "If you're done . . . ? I still have a business to run."

"Thank you for your cooperation, Mr. Kaner," Warren said. "We still have to talk to the others, and we may have some more things to ask you about later." Warren stood up and shook Kaner's hand, so I did the same. Kaner took off fast.

What Joel had told us was an interesting complication, but right now, with less than four days to go, complications were what I didn't want. As for interesting—like in the Chinese curse, 'May you live in interesting times'—the less interesting, the better. What I needed was *plain*, not fancy. Dull, boring, routine. Fat chance.

13

As soon as Joel Kaner was gone, I got up to go to the phone, but Warren stopped me. "Were you going to call one of the others? To see if we could talk to him now?"

"The working day is almost over," I said, "and there's no way I'm going to talk about the murder to anyone in his own home. You want me to give his wife a heart attack? So maybe I can catch one more guy in his office."

"Shouldn't we analyze what we've learned before we talk to the next one? So we'll know what approach to take?"

Analyze. Always with the analysis. Philosophers. But I spoke nicely. "Under normal conditions, Warren, yes. But this is not a normal condition. We've got to tie this up by Thursday night. If you want to help Bill Carey, that is. For my part, if we don't get the killer, ever, it's not the end of the world. Barney Brodsky, may he rest in peace, was not a nice guy, and whoever killed him . . ."

"But Justice . . ." He pronounced it with a capital letter.

"Of course we'll do what's right. But the facts are that it's almost five o'clock and a Jewish funeral's got to be in one day. Tomorrow. Between the funeral service and going to Gene Brodsky's house to pay our respects and the family's sitting *shivah* after that, tomorrow's shot. You can't interrogate people when they're in mourning or visiting the family to show sympathy. So I have to talk to as many suspects as possible now. At least one more today."

Warren sighed. Hated to give up a two-hour analysis of all the different theoretical possibilities, no matter how improbable. "Who're you going to call?"

"I figured Carl Lerman. With a big project underway, he's most likely to be in his office now. And we know him best. Sid Hoffman we can always catch at the automobile agency, and Arnold Greenleaf . . . ? A lawyer should be able to fit us in for fifteen minutes between clients." I started off, then turned back; I didn't want to get yelled at by Iris for putting down Warren. "Maybe we can do some analysis in the car on the way to Lerman's office."

His secretary told me Carl was on the job site of the new mall, a fifteen-minute drive, which gave me and Warren some time to talk. "So what's on your mind?" I encouraged him.

"Let's start with your questions on the mechanics of the murder," Warren said. "Did you learn anything useful?"

"Not a thing. Just because Kaner was in the whirlpool ahead of Greenleaf doesn't mean he's innocent. Nobody does anything to the exact second, and this killing . . . A minute one way or the other, and it could've been any of them."

"Does that mean you don't care who was where, or when?"

"I didn't say that. We have to keep checking if each

one of them was seen by somebody every minute between, say, ten to eight and ten after, or if one of them was *not* seen at all for a couple of minutes during that period, or if there are any other holes in the stories."

"So they all had the opportunity. As far as means is concerned, they're all strong enough to asphyxiate a skinny little old man. Motive? Isn't it significant that all the suspects are limited partners in the Lerman Mall?"

"You asked a good set of questions, Warren." My first chance to compliment him. "And it might be important, but you have to remember that it's perfectly normal for them to do business with each other. Aren't all of our own limited partners members of the club? I'll bet that at any one time you'll find two or three of our group in the club at the same time."

"Yes, but for five of them—six, counting Mr. Brodsky—to be near the steam room at the time of the murder . . . ? That's stretching the odds too much."

"Maybe yes, maybe no. This morning I was playing nine holes with Iris and Marvin Guralnik and Jerry Fein. All of us, four out of four, were part of every one of Nassau Venture's deals."

"Nobody was murdered then."

He should know how close I'd been to wrapping a club around Iris Guralnik's neck. "There's another difference. We're a small group; they have thirty limited partners. More likely it's twenty-nine, to keep them a small closely held partnership instead of a public offering. Six out of twenty-nine in the wet area at one time is not so unusual."

Warren shook his head stubbornly. "Over twenty percent of the limited partners in the mall deal there at the time one of them was murdered? There must be a connection."

"Actually, only five were limited partners; Carl's corporation has to be the general partner."

"I still want to ask Mr. Lerman about possible

motives. I have the feeling that Mr. Brodsky's murder was closely tied to the ownership of the mall."

"So ask; you're running this investigation, aren't you?"

"I am?" Though he tried to hide it, he sounded a little bitter. Angry even. "With you asking all the questions, deciding whom we're going to talk to, when we're going to talk to him, and what we're going to look into?"

I hadn't realized it, but he was right. How could I know it would bother him? Everybody's used to my taking the lead, and Warren never complained before. If Iris heard about this I was in real trouble. "You're right, Warren. Sorry about that. I got carried away, wanting to help Bill Carey and all that. And Sharon Edel. She'll be flying in to be with the family for the funeral and to sit *shivah*; might even be home already. We'll go over to Gene Brodsky's house tomorrow, right after the funeral. I'll tell Sharon I'm—*we're*—going to find out who . . . *You'll* tell her. By Friday. And that everything'll be okay for her and Bill."

But that's only if Bill didn't do it. Kaner was right; if it was motives Warren was looking for, Carey had the best. And what I had just done—but what else could I do?— was to put Warren on the spot. If we didn't solve the case by Thursday night, Warren would now take the full rap. In his own mind, at least, which was the only place it counted. It might even affect, God forbid, when he and Lee Guralnik got married. Or engaged. Or *something*. And how could I tell Warren that what I was doing was not to put him down, but to get him off Palmieri's list as the prime suspect? Just like a doctor doesn't operate on his own family, and a lawyer doesn't handle his own litigation, a detective—even if it's just as a sideline—shouldn't try to solve his own case. But if I didn't, who would? And if not now, when?

14

Carl Lerman, bald head wet with sweat, was on the phone when we entered the construction trailer at the mall site, so he waved me and Warren to sit down and be patient. Standing next to him was a worried-looking young man dressed in chinos, evidently Carl's construction superintendent. "Like hell I will," Carl yelled into the phone. "I screw up, I pay for it. You screw up, make me open the mall late, lose a month's rent and pay penalties to the tenants, *you* pay for it. Believe me, it'll be a lot cheaper for you to okay the few hours' overtime." He listened for a few seconds, then broke in. "Okay? Okay, so we understand each other." Again he listened, nodded, grunted, and hung up.

"Tell Tony," Lerman told his construction super, "the overtime is okay." The young man looked relieved and ran out.

It was a pleasure to watch a pro at work, and it was a double pleasure to know I'd never have to live like that again. Once in a lifetime is enough to be in the stinkingconstructionbusiness. That's one word to me, which is why I'm in the venture capital business now. Thank God.

Lerman turned to us and said, "So what brings you here, Ed? You want to get back in the business, we could talk." His normally pink face was red from the anger he had to be feeling about the job almost getting behind schedule, and that's just one of the things I used to hate about the business. "I'm getting too old for this kind of crap, and I wouldn't mind giving out my next job on a construction management basis. Even to you, if the price is right."

"Don't talk dirty," I said. "I took a big licking when I left the business, and it was worth every penny. Added ten years to my life. Not that I don't have problems now, but at least I got some control of the situation. As long as you brought it up, why don't you get out while you're still sane? Money you got plenty of; you and your wife should enjoy life while you can." Like I had planned for me and Thelma, only it didn't work out that way.

"I can't. What would I do? Developing and building is all I know. You can't play golf all day."

"Charity, temple, hospital, orphans. Lots of things."

"Leave my investors hanging? How do I walk away?"

"Easy. Just stop. You started this job; you got to finish it. Okay. But sell off your other projects, in whatever state of progress they're in now."

He looked at me suspiciously. "You aren't looking to buy one of my projects, are you, Ed? At a bargain price?"

"Not if you gave it to me for nothing. I'm still waiting for my first grandchild." I couldn't help glancing toward Warren. Big mistake.

"Then what are you here for?"

"Barney Brodsky's murder." I thought that would shake him up. It didn't. "You're one of the prime suspects, Carl, and I'm going to help clear you."

"I'm a suspect? What gave you that idea? And why do you want to clear me?"

"Not just you, all the members. That one of us is a murderer is a scandal. And you *are* a prime suspect; everyone who was in the vicinity of the steam room during the time Barney was killed is a prime suspect."

"Not me. I talked to the police and they were satisfied with what I told them I did. I don't know the exact times, but maybe fifty people saw me."

"Not every second, otherwise why would Sergeant Palmieri call you in so many times?"

Carl got a little redder. "He called in everybody a few times. The ones who were near the steam room."

"Greenleaf, Hoffman, Kaner, and Rubin. All were limited partners in your mall. Barney was too. You think there's no connection?"

"Absolutely not. There are lots of partners. Barney's son, Gene, is also an investor. And his son-in-law, Maurice. And Ellen Edel too. In fact, Ellen's family took three shares, one for her, one for Maurice, and one is for Sharon."

"But only if she marries the right guy."

"Why not? You wouldn't do the same thing?"

"Positively not. In fact, I—and Thelma, *olav hasholom*—didn't. Warren owns half the company and he can marry whoever he wants." As long as it's Lee Guralnik, please God.

"I was trying to show that in spite of the coincidence, there's no reason to think there's a connection between the mall and . . . Bad publicity I don't need."

"Exactly. But the only way to convince the police one of your limited partners didn't do it is to find the real murderer. I—Warren and I—did that once, and we're going to do it again. With your cooperation."

"I already told the police everything."

"Tell me."

Lerman sighed. "I took a light workout, just to get the day started. Then I went in the sauna for five minutes to relax. Maybe ten; not more. Then I took a hot shower—I don't go to cold right after the sauna; it's a shock to the system—and gradually turned it down to cool, dried off, and checked with Tommy, my masseur. I have a standing appointment for eight-thirty, but if he's early, he takes me when I'm ready. I was maybe half finished when a cop came into the cubicle and told me to see Sergeant Palmieri, and that killed the day. Palmieri kept me hanging around for hours, otherwise I would've been able to straighten out that overtime business by noon, instead of this last-minute headache."

"Did you see anything? Hear anything?"

"Not a thing."

I kept on questioning, but everything he told us didn't help at all to put anyone on the spot. Or take anyone off it. Finally I said, "Five of the suspects—all but Warren and Bill—are investors in the mall. Plus the victim. That's coincidence?"

Lerman's voice grew hard. "Don't make trouble for my project, Ed; I got enough problems as it is."

Warren suddenly spoke up. "Did Mr. Brodsky's firm do the legal work for the mall?"

Lerman laughed. "You think I'm crazy? A limited partner give legal opinions to the company? Or Kaner be our accountant? No way. I use my regular lawyer, accountant, architect, engineers, the ones I always use. Anybody who has to give me advice, I wouldn't let him into the partnership for anything. I want completely impartial advice. I don't even buy my Mercedeses from Sid Hoffman, that's how careful I am."

"Weren't you, and the others we mentioned, part of Mr. Brodsky's group on the club's board of directors?"

"Group? It's not a group like I think you mean, but sure. Barney wanted to control the board and he did a good job running the club. When he got out of line—you know Barney, always picking, picking, making trouble—we had a little talk with him and he'd back down." Carl turned to me. "You should withdraw your nomination, Ed. This battling doesn't do the club any good. Joel'll make a good chairman."

"I probably will, now that Barney's gone. Assuming Joel's not the murderer."

"Joel? Forget it; he's not the type. None of us are."

"Somebody did it, Carl. It had to be an insider."

"Sure, but why should Joel, or any of us, kill Barney? Think. Who had the most to gain from Barney's death?"

"Bill Carey didn't do it," Warren said.

"Because you're friendly with him?" Lerman said. "Well, for the same reason, I'm sure none of my friends did it."

"Were you friends, Mr. Lerman, with Mr. Brodsky?"

Carl sucked his breath in on that one, and I wondered where Warren got the nerve to stick the knife in so deep. He was learning the wrong things from me, and too fast. "Not friends," Carl said. "Not socially. We ran the club, and he was in some business ventures with me, but that was all. I don't pick my friends for business reasons; business is business and pleasure is pleasure. You don't mix them."

"I understand," Warren continued, "that Mr. Brodsky got pleasure from finding out about someone's foibles and needling him about it in public."

"I already told you we weren't friends; that was one of the reasons. I like friends you could turn your back on."

"Do you have something to hide, Mr. Lerman?"

"Don't you, Warren? And you, Ed, after thirty years in the building business? Doesn't everybody?"

"Nothing dishonorable, Carl," I said. "Ask anybody."

"Same with me, Ed."

Just then, Lerman's construction super came in. "Footings and foundations'll be ready on time," he announced.

"Good," Lerman said. "Now call the steel erector and tell him to start erecting the first tier steel eight sharp, Thursday morning. As per the original schedule."

Shrewd, Carl. Just the way I would've played it. Push the job as fast as possible, but don't take unnecessary risks. It showed the same kind of mind and nerves that were needed to kill Barney Brodsky, may he rest in peace, and get away with it.

15

Doris, my secretary, must've called Violet and told her everything that was going on and what a hard time Palmieri had given Warren. In the early days, when Warren was a baby and I couldn't afford a secretary and Thelma had to be one, Violet spent more time with him than Thelma did and today Violet still looks on him like he's her baby as much as her own kids. Not just the way all the women who know Warren want to feed the poor skinny kid, but I think Violet would kill for him. For me, no; but for him? No question.

What she did tonight was to make his favorite dishes: broiled lamb chops with mustard and rosemary, home fries, and a thick chocolate malted, and she made sure he ate every bit. And brownies. For him; not for me.

Violet's not so young any more, and I keep telling her that I can afford a nice-size pension, so she should find me a good young housekeeper, train her for six months, and then retire. She won't. Keeps telling me there are no good young housekeepers left—the ones with ambition are all big-shot executives on Wall Street and the trash she won't

let into the house. I offered her extra help, even two help-
ers—part time, full time, whatever she wants—for the
heavy work, and she turned that down too. She's taking
care of us, running the house, nobody else, and that's
that. Her daughters? Never. When they were little, she
trained them to take care of a house. For when they got
married. Not that they should ever do day work, God forbid, but so when they were rich enough to hire help—as
they were now—they should know what had to be done
and the right way to do it. The best boss is the guy who
used to do it himself for a living.

I don't mind when Violet yells at me for not being nice
enough to Warren, but no way am I going to let her outsmart
me. I retained a cleaning service to come in once a week—
for now; next year it'll be twice—to do all the heavy cleaning, but Violet, instead of resting, stands over them every
second. Not to see that they don't steal the furniture—
they're bonded—but to catch them leaving one tiny streak
on an upstairs window so she can tell me I have to get rid of
the lazy worthless slobs. I also arranged for a pick-up laundry
and cleaners and Violet can't do anything about that either,
though she still hides Warren's shirts, washes them by hand,
and irons them the way they *should* be ironed for her baby.

We have plenty of room in the house, but she won't
live in; wants to be near her friends and neighbors and
church when she's done working. That's reasonable, but
it's an hour trip each way by bus, railroad, and another
bus, so I bought her a car. She wouldn't even try sitting in
it, much less take driving lessons.

"What am I going to do with Violet?" I asked Warren,
over our malteds and brownies. I knew I shouldn't, but they
tasted so good . . . When I finally realized Violet was working ten or eleven hours a day, I changed her from daily pay to
hourly pay. Knowing her, I figured she'd be ashamed to take
the overtime money. She thanked me and said she'd use the
extra money for the day-care center in her neighborhood,
and kept working the same hours. "Violet misses a train at

night and it could be another hour till the next one comes. And who knows how safe the station is at that time?"

"I hadn't thought about it," Warren said, "but the solution is obvious."

"Obvious? More of your reverse thinking?"

"You're looking at the problem from the wrong angle, Dad. Don't try to change Violet; nobody can do that. Change the circumstances so that, given her personality, she'll adjust in the way you want. I remember seeing, in a museum, an old poster put out by the Technocrats. You know who they were?"

"Of course. In the Thirties. They thought you could use technology to change the world. Never got anywhere."

"The world *is* changed by the technology available, so they did get somewhere. The poster showed a streetcar, with a sign that said 'Please don't ride on the platform; it's dangerous.' That didn't work. So the streetcar company put up another sign that said 'Riding on the platform is illegal; you will be fined.' That didn't work either. Finally they built a streetcar without a platform. Problem solved."

"Great. How does this apply to a stubborn old woman who won't let me help her? I even offered to pay for a taxi door to door, but she won't take more than her friends get. Worse, if I raise the cost of household help around here, a number of the day workers who come to Nassau will lose their jobs; some of the women who use them are on very tight budgets. The people who hire day workers—men as well as women—who need someone to take care of their houses and children while they work will have to give up their jobs or take less demanding jobs at lower pay. Not everyone who lives on Long Island is rich. Most aren't, in fact."

This didn't stop Warren. "Ask Violet if she knows a reliable, ambitious man in her neighborhood, any age, who is willing to risk everything he's got to go into business. There must be dozens. This man has to put together half the money for a used nine-seater minivan in perfect condition. A recent model. Nassau Venture Capital puts up the rest and all other costs. He'll offer a door-to-door service in this area for the same price that the women are already paying for the buses and the railroad, which is considerable. But all the women must come at the same time and go at the same time, so Violet can't work more than eight hours."

"I already thought of that. Won't work. The owner of the car service can only make one trip a day here and back. When you have little kids, the housekeeper must be there before you leave for work, and when you work at a job, you must be there when the place opens. That's why you see those beat-up old unsafe vans on the parkway every morning and night. There isn't enough income from one round trip a day to support a business, so the passengers chip in, buy a wreck—that's all they can afford—and one of them drives it to their factory. The vans are usually heavily overloaded; these are not high-paid workers. Remember that accident a few months ago? Eight people dead? Haitians? All good people, working to make a living, but the van was in such bad shape that sooner or later it had to happen. I'm sure they all knew it, but with a family to support . . . I won't let Violet take the risk and I won't be associated with anything like that."

Warren went on as if I hadn't said a word. "Now we come to point two. Since there isn't enough income for the owner of the car service to live on, we're going to hire him as the NVC chauffeur during the day. It's a business expense, so our net cost'll be about half what we pay him. Also, since we spend a lot of time in the office, the chauffeur will be able to do minor maintainance on our company cars and keep them clean. We can also use him for delivering and picking up papers. Putting it all together, the cost won't be much more than we're paying now for those services. But the main thing is that it'll make NVC more efficient. In two ways. First of all, we'll never have to worry about finding parking again, even in New York, so we don't have to start out a half hour early to get to a meeting on time. Second . . . What do you do while you drive, Dad?"

"Same as I do during any routine operation. Think."

"Which makes your thinking less efficient and your driving more dangerous. With a chauffeur, you can even go over papers while you're traveling." I nodded. The whole idea made sense. And Violet would have to go along. No way out for her. "We could do this ourselves," Warren went on, "but Violet would suspect. Besides, we must share all our ventures with our investors. With the right man—or woman—the business should grow to where it could show a nice profit, both for us and for the owner of the service. There must be fifty people we know in the club for whom a chauffeur would be the cheapest way to make their businesses more efficient. And there have to be hundreds of men and women around here who need good reliable help that would come on time so they could get to their own jobs on time. And that's just in Oakdale. There's the rest of Nassau County, Suffolk, Westchester, no limit." He was getting excited, his face glowing.

"I take it all back," I said. "What I said about your backward thinking. It's a great concept and it's going to make money for us as well as for the people involved. It's all your baby, Warren; arrange it with Violet."

"Thanks, Dad, I will. Right after we take care of Bill Carey. Just one more thing. Since Violet will be taking home less money—no overtime—why don't we donate part of our profits from the car service company to the day-care center that Violet was giving her extra money to?"

"I'm all for charity—you know how much we give a year—but that idea goes against the NVC concept. We help start businesses that will grow; charity we give personally, not from the business. You know the saying: 'Give a man a fish today, you'll have to give him another fish tomorrow. Teach him how to fish, and he'll catch his own from then on.' Also we have no right to give away our investors' money or the business owner's money; only our own. You want us to donate personally to the center, no problem. But I have a better idea. Have Violet also find us someone in her neighborhood who's qualified to run a day-care center and has ideas on how to run one profitably. Without government subsidies, if possible; it takes a lot of time and money to process the paper and to follow bureaucratic directives, so I'm sure it can be done profitably without all that. We'll invest with her. Or him. With a place to take care of their children, we'll free more women to take jobs or go to school or whatever they want. And to use our new van service. Or to drive the vans and be chauffeurs; no reason why they couldn't. The combined businesses should feed on each other; the more one succeeds, the greater will be the need for the other. I have a feeling that in six months, our chauffeur will own ten vans and will be too busy running the business to do any driving himself. And something else, to keep the vans running weekends: a catering operation, also from Violet's neighborhood. We'll combine it with our first business venture, Ruthanne's Gourmet Cakes. As long as the van's in Nassau County, the car service could become their delivery service too. In fact, we could offer a small package and delivery service anywhere on the Island cheaper and faster than the big companies, and after that, a safe transportation service for factory workers, and then—"

"Slow down, Dad," Warren said, laughing. "You're going too far into the future to predict accurately."

"But this venture has real good possibilities. There's a hole in the market here for local delivery services."

"Let's see how I do with the first step," Warren said, "then we'll look into the day-care center, which has to be a much bigger problem. Thanks for the compliment about my backward way of thinking, Dad, but it really isn't backward, just different from the way most people think. Your straight-ahead way of thinking isn't so bad either, Dad, at least the way you do it. If it can be done, I have a feeling that Violet will be running the center two years from now."

"If it works, there'll be ten centers by then. And I know the people Violet's going to go to for ideas: her daughters. Probably for the initial investment too. For the car service company as well. From what I know of her daughters, they'll probably set up a national franchise operation. And since what we're offering is a strictly business proposition, Violet can't object."

Warren smiled. "Now that we've solved the problem of how to make Violet retire and put two new businesses into our pipeline at the same time, can we analyze the Brodsky murder?"

"We don't have enough information yet; we've only talked with Kaner and Lerman so far. And Bill Carey. The problem is the timing. Everything took place over such a short period that any one of them could have done it. We don't know enough to point the finger at someone specific."

"We know that if Mr. Kaner did it, Mr. Greenleaf can't be the killer, but we don't know if Mr. Kaner did it. And if the murder took place after Mr. Greenleaf entered the whirlpool, neither he nor Mr. Kaner is the killer. But we know the murder occurred before Mr. Greenleaf went into the pool area. I saw his back as he went in and I was watching the steam room entrance from the moment I went into the wet area. So we can't clear either him or Mr. Kaner yet."

"So we're back where we started. Either Kaner or Greenleaf could have killed Brodsky before you came into the picture. So could Lerman, Rubin, or Hoffman. Or Carey. Even Ramon. Two seconds when nobody's looking and any one of them could've slipped into the steam room. A minute or two for the actual murder, crack open the steam room door to peek out, and, if nobody's looking, another two seconds to get to where you're supposed to be. So where does that leave us?"

"I have a feeling that we'll never solve this case by working on the opportunity. Let's look at the motives."

"There are no motives, Warren. So far they've all said—even Bill Carey—that they disliked Barney but didn't hate him. We'll probably get the same story from the others."

"There has to be a motive; no one kills just to kill. Maybe it wasn't hate. What about sex, money, fear, revenge?"

"Sex? *Barney?* Never. Money, maybe, but how could anyone make money killing Barney? Fear? Barney was a big pain, but nobody feared him. As for revenge, maybe something from the past, when he was an active attorney, but nothing that I know of since I joined the club."

"Still, he was killed, and it wasn't for a trivial reason. If these motives don't fit, perhaps some others will, or a combination of motives."

"What we need is more information. After all, it's only twelve hours. I think we did a lot for one day."

"Agreed. So what do we do tomorrow?"

"The funeral's probably going to be after three; certainly after two. Sid Hoffman's usually in his showroom; we can drop by anytime without calling. If he's busy, we come back later. George Rubin, guaranteed, is going to be at the Rubinetics plant, which is not too far from Gold Coast Mercedes. Greenleaf we have to call first; he could be in court or something. So what I'd suggest is we call Greenleaf first thing in the morning and play everything else by ear."

"Shouldn't we talk to Ramon too?"

"Positively. I'm sure he didn't do it, but people talk in front of the help like they don't exist. We should grab him after we leave Gene Brodsky's house. Check with Bill Carey if we can talk with Ramon and what time he goes home."

"I already did. Ramon's done at four. We'll talk to him in Carey's office, not in front of the other help. Anytime we want to, even first thing in the morning."

"Not in front of Bill either, right?"

"He didn't even ask, Dad." Warren hesitated, then

said, "Did you notice, when we were talking with Mr. Kaner, about the lifeguard?"

"That he wasn't there just before eight? Yeah, but I'm not even considering the lifeguard. There's no doubt in my mind that one of those five did it and that it's connected to the Lerman Mall in some way."

"I didn't mean it that way. What I have in mind is that we may have more than five suspects, if the lifeguard wasn't in his place until after eight. There's a door in the gym that leads into the pool area. What if somebody came into the pool that way a couple of minutes before eight, went through the pool area and sneaked into the wet area, into the steam room, just before Mr. Brodsky got there? There was no one in the pool area to see him go in, and it would be almost impossible for anyone in the big shower area to see him. He turned up the steam and, when Mr. Brodsky came in a minute later, killed him. Anybody in the gym could have done it."

"But how about coming out?"

"That depends on exactly when the lifeguard was there and when Mr. Kaner went into the whirlpool."

I turned it over in my mind for a full minute. "Possible, but I don't like it. If the killer left through the big shower room, the odds are one of the guys there would've seen him. If he left the way he came in, through the pool area, he'd be cutting things so close that only a desperate *meshuggener* would consider it. How could he know exactly when the lifeguard would come on duty? How could he know when anyone, like Kaner, would come in?"

Warren sagged, suddenly looked tired. "There's only one man who could've known if the lifeguard habitually came in a few minutes late. Who wouldn't have been noticed if he left through the pool area—part of his normal daily checkup—or even through the big shower room. None of the men in either area would know—if they noticed him at all—whether he was starting or completing his daily morning tour."

"Bill didn't do it," I said firmly. "This murder is connected with the Lerman Mall. I feel it in my bones."

"But isn't Bill's new gym part of the Lerman Mall? What if Mr. Brodsky decided to kill the gym deal?"

"He couldn't; after last year, he wouldn't dare. You and I—we're the only ones who can kill it."

"Maybe not kill the deal directly, Dad, but are you sure Mr. Brodsky couldn't *delay* the closing past Friday?"

This hit me like a load of bricks, just when I was going to compliment Warren on how he was getting really smarter—not just book smart—every day. That business with how to retire Violet was pretty damn good. My influence, naturally. And Thelma's genes. I loved it, though it would make Warren harder to handle about the important things. Such as setting the date for the wedding with Lee. Still, look how far he'd come in only a few months. Iris would be proud of me.

Would have been, but not now; not after Warren brought up . . . The worst part was, it was Warren who caught it. Not Palmieri, not me, but Warren. And being Warren, he'd have to tell Palmieri. Which would make Warren the guy who hanged his friend. And that would be the end. Not just of Bill, not just of Sharon, but of Warren too. And if Warren, then me too, because Warren was all that I had left. And Lee, and my six grandchildren? Gone, all gone.

Warren was right, I was sorry to say. All Brodsky had to do was ask the bank's closing attorney to clarify a couple of minor points on the loan application, and there'd be an automatic delay. And no one could blame Brodsky for Bill's losing his option—that's all it really was—and going broke and being unable to marry Sharon Edel. If ever there was a time for Bill to go crazy—become a desperate *meshuggener* was the way I had put it before—and kill Barney Brodsky, this was it.

104

16

"I don't know nothing, Mr. Baer, like I tell police man," Ramon said, standing stiffly in front of Bill Carey's desk. I had invited him to sit down but, having been sent in by Mr. Carey and with me sitting in Carey's chair behind Carey's desk, he must've assumed he had to treat me like a boss. "I just clean, that's all. Clean good," he added for emphasis.

"I'm perfectly satisfied with the way the wet area is maintained, Ramon," I said. I hadn't slept too well Monday night and had gotten up very early this morning. So had Warren, although he had probably stayed up late doing his philosophical thinking. After breakfast, Warren had suggested that we visit the wet area before talking to Hoffman, Rubin, and Greenleaf, in case we noticed something there we'd want to ask them about; another of Warren's good ideas. Amazing how many good ideas he'd been having lately; came from watching me in the Hamilcar case. And as long as we were here—the wet area we could always see—I decided to talk to Ramon. "I just want to ask you a few questions about what you saw the morning Mr. Brodsky was killed."

"I don't see nothing, Mr. Baer."

I ignored that; typical answer from someone who'd learned, even in his short lifetime, that when he was asked a question, he was in trouble to begin with, trouble that could only get worse no matter what he answered. "You're in charge of keeping the men's wet area clean?"

"Yes, sir. And toilet room, pool room, sun room, dark room, and massage room. Lotsa work. I so busy all the time, I don't see nothing, just work. Also toilet paper, paper towel, fill up soap, everything."

"Dark room? Oh, the quiet lounge."

"Yes, sir. Too many lounge. Please, I study, but my English not so good. Not *too* many; I can do."

"But you start work in the wet area, don't you?"

"Yes, sir. Nobody come for lounge first. Come first in shower, so first I clean shower. Floor and wall and—and—*dividir*?"

"Dividers? Partitions?"

"Yes. With hose. Cold water. Don't like cold water on feet when take hot shower, so I do shower first."

He went on to confirm everything we already knew about who had been where and doing what at the time of the murder. Too bad, but I really didn't expect anything different. "One last question, Ramon. Did you ever hear any of the people you mentioned fighting with each other? Arguing? Disputing?"

Ramon looked shocked. "Oh, no, sir. All nice gentleman. Talk nice, not fight. I don't hear nothing; too busy clean."

Warren looked at me. I indicated I was done, so he said, "Thank you, Ramon. We're done."

Ramon turned and walked to the door. I could see the weight go off his shoulders; he had come through the ordeal unarrested and unfired, not even yelled at. A tremendous relief. At the door he turned and said, "I sorry I don't see nothing, don't hear nothing, don't know nothing. Please." He shut the door quietly behind him.

"No way was he going to admit he heard anything that had to do with the murder," Warren said. "Although I doubt that any of them would be so foolish as to quarrel in public."

"He tuned out deliberately," I said. "And his measure of time, based on what jobs he completes, is not exact enough to tell us who was where at the time of the murder. Also, he couldn't know what went on on the other side of the wall separating the large shower room from the small one and the steam room. Still, now we know that what we were told was accurate. And what you saw."

"Why, you didn't believe me?"

"That came out wrong. Of course I believed you; I was thinking of Palmieri. Now we can concentrate on who did it."

"We'll know who did it when we find out who had a motive to kill Mr. Brodsky."

"You do it your way, I'll do it my way." I could've bitten my tongue. There I went again, challenging him. Anything you can do, I can do better. When I really wanted to lose. No, not to lose; to have him win. Not quite the same. I think. I hope.

11

Arnold Greenleaf said if we got to his office fast, he could give us fifteen minutes. I grabbed the opportunity; with the funeral that afternoon, it would be very hard to see anyone after twelve, and I had too little time to coordinate with Hoffman or Rubin, each of whom had a business to run.

Which reminded me that I had a business to run too. Fourteen businesses, to be exact. Well, not run, exactly, but keep an eye on. With four new ones in the pipeline. And two more that had just been thought of by us. Plus Bill Carey's spa. The papers for which had to be signed on Friday. Assuming we cleared Bill by Thursday afternoon, before three. Because if we didn't, that was when Warren had to tell the bank the deal was off. Otherwise, Friday morning they'd have all their legal and financial talent sitting around a table, waiting for us with the meters ticking, and I didn't want them to question our competence. Or to charge us for the wasted time and talent in addition to the forfeited origination fees. Which would make our limited partners question our ability. Which could put us out of business. For a moment I thought of going back into the stinkingconstructionbusiness. Scary.

I had never been in Greenleaf's office before. It was near the courthouse in one of the old buildings on Old Country Road, and a lot smaller than any lawyers' offices I had ever been in. Just two rooms, the reception area and his office. Inexpensively furnished too. And no help other than the receptionist who, I was sure, doubled as the secretary.

I also noticed that Arnold wasn't wearing gold chains or a ten-thousand-dollar watch or a thousand-dollar suit. He noticed me noticing. "I don't dress here like I do at the club," he explained. "I work with individuals and families, not corporations. Estate planning, wills, trusts, intestates, guardianships, escrows, individual home sales, transfer of assets, things like that. The decor tells my clients I'm not one of those overpriced attorneys who'll charge them more than the case is worth to pay for the fancy office and the British receptionist. When I took over my father's practice I didn't change a thing. The old-style wooden furniture, the pictures, the law books, everything's the same. It gives the client a feeling of confidence, of warmth and stability, that we've been established a long time. Which is true." He settled his tall, skinny body in the creaking wood and leather chair behind the desk.

"Don't knock it, Arnold," I assured him. "There's a great need for lawyers like you. Most of the guys around here won't touch anything that doesn't involve a big corporation. You fill a need; that's why you make a good living."

"It's the volume; there're a lot more of people like my clients than there are big and small corporations combined, and some of my regular clients are quite well off, old money. The work is mostly routine, and a lot of it's steady, goes on for years. Once I set it up, administering an estate just involves making prudent, conservative investments. If you treat the clients right, not only do they come back again but they recommend you to their friends and relatives."

"And you keep all the fees, don't have to share them with a partner. Sounds like a good deal."

"It lets me work a reasonable number of hours too; I don't have to account to anybody, so I have time for my family, for tennis, for fun." He leaned back in his chair and swept his hand across his thinning brown hair, starting to go gray. "I have to be at the county clerk's office soon, so I won't offer you coffee. Let's get down to business."

"Good idea," I said. "It's about Barney's murder, may he rest in peace. The police think it was done by a member of the club. We'd like to show that it wasn't. With your help."

Arnold leaned forward and put his forearms flat on the desk. "I've been thinking about it too, and I've come to the conclusion that it wasn't a member—there's no motive—but it still doesn't take away . . . Is it any better for our image if they charge Bill Carey? After all, we hired him."

"It would be best if it was an outsider, but I don't see how an outsider could get into the spa."

"That's no problem; you can come in through the supply entrance. It'd be easy to fix the panic bar and the alarm so you could come in, but once in, what do you do? We all know each other by sight, especially the ones who come in early. A stranger in the shower room would be noticed immediately."

"What if a stranger came in real early," I asked, "and hid?" I knew the answer, had been over it in my head for hours last night, but I wanted to get his ideas.

"Where? In the sun room? The sauna? One of us goes into those rooms and sees a stranger, he'd tell somebody. If not right away, then later. The steam room? Barney'd notice and raise a stink; he wasn't shy, you know. And getting out without being seen by one of us? It had to

110

be someone you'd expect to see there, and if it was, my money's on Bill Carey. He had the best motive."

"How about Ramon? The kid who cleans up."

"Why would he? Even if he had a reason, he wouldn't do it in a place where he'd be suspected. Actually, the best thing for the club would be if the killer isn't caught."

"Do you want to live with the knowledge that one of us, a member, a friend, our spa manager, is a murderer?"

"Not really, but given the alternative, yes."

"Maybe you're right, Arnold, but good or bad, I'd like to know. What did you do and see around the time of the murder?"

"Why? You think that I . . . ?"

"Not you; not anybody. I'm trying to put the facts in line and clear everybody, then give those facts to Palmieri. If he knows we're clear, he can work on other angles."

Arnold nodded wearily. "I've already given all this to the police, but if it makes you happy . . ."

As I expected, he went over the same information we already had. I turned to Warren. "Anything else?"

"Motive," Warren said. "I understand Mr. Brodsky used to dig into people's private lives and discuss them in public."

Arnold sighed. "Not just discuss, Warren, needle, and he didn't know when to stop."

"Could this have been a motive for his murder?"

"Doubtful. A lot of what he harped on was gossip, not necessarily true. Then it was usually minor crap. But even so, it could get irritating."

"Did he needle you?"

"Of course; he didn't miss anybody."

"And yet you were a limited partner with him on the Lerman Mall."

"That was business, not a social occasion."

"Isn't it odd that everyone in the wet area at the time

111

of Mr. Brodsky's murder was a limited partner in the mall?"

"That's not quite accurate; Lerman was the general partner. Ramon and Carey aren't partners, and neither are you. There were several mall partners there, but this may have been because we all go to the spa at the same time, which is how we became partners with Lerman in the first place, over five years ago. In the gym or the sauna, there's a tendency to talk to each other, and sometimes we talk business."

"And aren't you all directors of the club?"

"We became directors the same way. Barney was the one interested in running the club, and one by one, he recruited us from the fellows who came there at the same time."

"Did you hate Mr. Brodsky too?"

He caught that. "*Too?* No one liked Barney, but no one *hated* him that I know of."

"Did you have any other business relationship with Mr. Brodsky?"

"With the firm, yes; not with Barney directly, though he sometimes referred old friends to me, ones who had become inactive in business. With my low overhead I can charge less than the big firms and still do well. Gene sometimes referred a client to me if a case was too small for him, or if it posed a possible conflict of interest. Even some larger cases; dealing with the bureaucracy can be very time-consuming, unless you know your way around. I also referred people to them if the case was wrong for me. We both benefited from that. Gene's a highly competent lawyer; anyone I sent him was in good hands."

"Did Mr. Brodsky ever have a case where the client wanted to kill him?"

"I suppose so. Every lawyer has cases that the client blames him for losing or messing up, myself included, and some clients get very upset. But I think you're going at this wrong. It's highly improbable that an outsider killed

112

Barney in the steam room; there's a hundred better places. It had to be someone who was there." He glanced at his watch. "I have to be at the County Office Building by ten."

We all got up; I had nothing more to ask, and Warren didn't say anything. "You going to the services?" I asked.

"Of course. And to Ellen's house, where they'll be sitting *shivah*."

"Not Gene's house?"

"I guess they decided the older child has the privilege. You going to the cemetery?"

I looked to Warren. He nodded. "I guess so." I'd watch the reactions of the suspects there. Which, if it was as much help as our interviews so far, would be no help at all.

18

I phoned first, just to make sure. George Rubin was busy, but he could see us in an hour. Sid Hoffman was free to see us, and he had a batch of cars in he was sure we'd love. I have nothing against foreign cars, but to me a car is a way of getting from one place to another, not to establish how much richer I am than you. If it's safe and reliable and comfortable—and there are plenty of medium-size American cars that fill the bill— why should I spend a fortune on a new car every year? Whom do I have to impress? I don't wear jewelry either, except for my wedding ring. That I'll never take off.

Sid was as big and muscular as his cars. And as handsome, in spite of the thick glasses, with a full head of wavy brown hair, not a bit of gray, though he must've been almost my age. He insisted on showing us some of the latest models in his showroom. One of his perfectly dressed, handsome young salesmen demonstrated all the sexy features while one of his perfectly dressed, beautiful young saleswomen gave us brochures and explained the technical advantages; a nice twist on what I'd been expect-

114

ing. I said ooh and aah—you don't criticize someone's wife or children—and we finally went into Hoffman's chrome-and-glass office. He sat down behind his desk and Warren and I sat on the big leather couch.

"I hear you're trying to find who killed Barney," Sid said.

"I'm trying to clear us all," I said, "the members as well as Bill Carey. If we don't find who did it there'll be a cloud over our heads that'll affect everything we do. Would you invest with Carl Lerman if you thought he was a murderer? Or have a drink with Joel Kaner if he was the one?"

"If I knew for sure, I don't think so. But don't forget, I sell Mercedeses. I can't prove it, but I *know* in my gut that some of the guys working for the company had to have been Nazis. Or if not them, the steel suppliers, the paint manufacturers, *somebody*. What do I do? Make a full check of everybody I do business with? Take fingerprints? Tell me something, Ed. When you were in the building line, everybody you did business with—he was a hundred percent pure? No record? Never stole? Never killed anybody? Nothing?"

He had me there. "Maybe some were connected. I didn't know who, and I didn't ask. I worked straight and so did everyone I did business with. That was all I asked."

"Then let the police do it, Ed; why get involved?"

"The police can't handle a case like this."

"It's more than that." Warren stood up, face flushed, sounding like a prophet from the Bible. "Because murder is wrong, Mr. Hoffman; it's that simple. There has to be a guide to human relations that we all follow, otherwise there's no way to predict anything. If you have to go through life worried about whether or not the next person you meet on the street will cut your throat, then civilization will die and the human race will die with it. If you aren't certain that the coming car will stop at the red light, then there's no way to drive a car anywhere, at any time. If

115

we can't trust each other to obey the basic moral laws, the only recourse is to kill the other guy first. We've had a great set of rules given to us, the Ten Commandments, rules that most of us follow most of the time, for our mutual benefit. Whoever breaks these rules has to be prevented from interfering with the lives of the rest of us. Whoever commits the worst crime of all, the taking of human life, must be eliminated from society, so we can all be safe. And just as important, so we can all *feel* safe."

Sid sat quietly for a few seconds, letting it sink in. I had never thought Warren was particularly religious, so what he said surprised me too, but it was a good answer, sensible and practical, and had its effect. "Okay, Warren," Sid said, "that makes sense. What do you want me to do?"

"Just answer a few questions about what you saw and heard at the time of the murder."

"There's not much I can tell." And there wasn't—or anyhow, nothing we didn't already know.

"You didn't see Kaner or Greenleaf, Lerman or Rubin either? Carey?"

"If I moved back three feet, without my glasses I wouldn't have seen myself."

"Did you have any reason to kill Mr. Brodsky?" Just like that. I don't know what's come over Warren lately.

"You know, Warren," Sid said heavily, turning red, "that's a pretty insulting question. And not too smart either. If I did, why should I tell you?" His voice softened. "Look, I know you're one of the guys Palmieri's working on, but this is not the right way to go about clearing yourself." He thought for a moment, took a deep breath, then said, "No, I didn't have any reason to kill him. Nobody had. He was a *noodge,* and nasty sometimes, irritated a lot of people, but you need a better reason than that to kill."

"Do you know who did have a reason to kill him?"

"What goes for me goes for everybody I know, and that includes Bill Carey. Bill was the guy Barney was giving the most trouble to, but as a reason to kill Barney. . . ?"

116

Forget it. Even if Bill was sure of getting away with it, how would killing Barney help him get the family's okay to marry Sharon? How would being *suspected* of killing Barney help him become the next general manager of the club?"

"Somebody did kill Mr. Brodsky, Mr. Hoffman. Are you saying it was done without any motive?"

"Yes. No. That is, not any motive that . . . I'll put it another way. I wasn't always a car dealer; I started in the selling business right out of high school. Magazines. Door to door. You want to learn about human nature, try that someday. I found that people do the craziest things for the craziest reasons, reasons that you wouldn't consider reasons. For example, a guy kills his wife and kids; you read it in the papers every week. For what? She made him meat loaf twice in a row? Or she *didn't* make it twice in a row? Who knows?"

"You think Mr. Brodsky was killed in a fit of passion? Mr. *Brodsky? Passion?*"

"Not passion like he's fooling around with somebody's wife. But there's passion and passion. I'll give you an example." He came out from behind the desk and sat next to Warren. "First, I want you to know that this is just an experiment, to prove something. I like you and I'm not trying to give you a hard time; just want to prove a point. Now what I'm going to do is poke you in the chest with my finger. Gently, wouldn't hurt a baby." He began poking Warren with his first finger. Poke, poke, poke. "I'm going to keep doing it while we're talking, every second, without a stop. All the time." Poke, poke, poke. "We'll talk about the weather, business, politics, we'll tell jokes and stories, but I'm going to keep on poking all the time. It doesn't hurt, it won't leave a mark, but it's all the time." Poke, poke, poke.

"All right, Mr. Hoffman," Warren said, "you've made your point. You can stop now."

Poke, poke, poke. "Talking won't help, Warren. In

this experiment, I'm immune to talking. You have to get mad enough to take a swing at me." Poke, poke, poke. "How much longer will that take?"

"I don't want to swing at you, Mr. Hoffman," Warren said, "but if you don't stop, I'll go away. Now."

"Good, you're getting mad. But it won't help to go away. I'll follow you. How much longer?"

"I'll take a poke at you, Sid," I offered, "if you don't stop."

He stoppped. "That's great, Ed. Proves my point. And I wasn't even touching you." He turned to Warren. "Tell me, could you have stood it for another five minutes?"

"I don't think so, Mr. Hoffman. It's a form of the Chinese water torture, isn't it?"

"Similar. But faster, because the water isn't personal; it doesn't hate you, doesn't want to hurt you, doesn't *enjoy* what it's doing."

"Are you saying," I asked, "that somebody, one of the guys in the wet area, finally decided he had enough and took the opportunity to kill Barney?"

"A crime of passion, without the passion. Look at it this way: I'm the killer. I walk into the room and I see a few guys, all busy, backs turned. It's the time when Barney's usually in the steam room all alone. Nobody's looking. I put down my razor and go into the steam room. Nobody sees me. In fact, once I'm past the towel shelves, even if they're looking they can't see me or see the door to the steam room. I go in, kill Barney, come out, start shaving again. A couple of minutes, that's all. You ask anybody where I was. They'll swear I was shaving all the time. And believe it."

"You'd risk your life on a gamble like that?"

"Me? No. But if I'd had enough, couldn't take any more . . . ? A crime of passion doesn't have to be somebody going crazy in a minute; it can build up over weeks, months, years."

118

"You really think that's what happened?"

"Something like that, Ed. At needling Barney was the champ. You know what his trouble was? No sense of humor. When I was a kid, some of the other kids used to call me Four-Eyes. But after a while it wasn't funny any more, and they stopped and we became friends and then I was Sid. But Barney didn't do it for fun, needle people; he did it to hurt them. For that, there's no stopping. Like when I poked Warren."

"That openly?"

"Hell no, Barney was too smart for that. And he was a lawyer, knew how to use words. He'd say things that sounded perfectly normal, but only one of us would understand them. Plenty of times I saw one of the guys turn white, his jaw muscles get hard, stand out, from something Barney said. You knew Barney had struck again; you just didn't know what."

"He did this often?"

"Not enough for somebody to slug him in the club. But this time it must've been once too often."

"You really think it was a spur-of-the-moment killing?"

"We're all pretty smart guys, the ones who were in the wet area. Even Carey is sharp for his age. The situation was ripe, so the killer took advantage of it."

"So who was Barney torturing?"

"All of us. Not real torture; little pokes. No one thing you could take offense at, but all the time."

"Four-Eyes?"

"Nothing that crude. Different things. There were times even I felt like beating his brains in. But how the hell does a guy my size, my age, lay a hand on a skinny, little old man? So I'd shut up, smile, and go on to other things."

"Why associate with him at all, then?" Warren asked.

"I didn't associate with him. We were on the board of

119

directors of the club and limited partners in Carl Lerman's developments, that's all."

"You don't have to go into every one of Lerman's deals," I pointed out. "Or stay on the board."

"Yes, I do. I deal in a check business; nobody buys a Merc for cash. At least, around here they don't. I need the real estate tax losses so I can save a few bucks from the IRS. And Lerman's deals are the best; I wouldn't miss one for anything. As for the board, the club is important to me, so I want to make sure that it works right. It's up to us guys who work on the Island to do the job; the poor bastards who work in New York don't have the time or strength."

"Kaner works in New York."

"He thinks it's an honor to be on the board and that chairman is an even bigger honor. But he does a good job."

"Don't you think it unusual," Warren asked, "that everyone in the wet area at the time Mr. Brodsky was killed was also a board member and part of the mall ownership?"

"Not really; that group happens to be there at that time." He thought for a moment. "But in another sense, maybe you're right. The only ones who were needled by Barney are the ones he came into contact with. He had no friends, so that had to be through the board or through business. If my idea is right, the killer is definitely somebody who couldn't take him any more. One of us, or Bill Carey."

"You're exonerating me?" Warren asked.

"Just being polite," Sid said, with a friendly smile.

I knew what he meant. It could've been the way he said, that somebody's string snapped. But it could also have been someone who had a real beef with Barney Brodsky. Like Bill Carey. Or Warren Baer. Not that Warren had a real beef, but from Palmieri's point of view . . . ?

120

19

The Rubinetics plant was 50 percent bigger than I remembered it from last year when George Rubin was talking about funding an expansion, so the company must've been doing well. In a sense. More production, more sales, it all sounds good, but it's not the greatest thing if you can't handle them. George himself was looking a bit frazzled, his black hair mussed up and his tie open. Comes from running a one-man business, which he shouldn't have been doing, but I could see why. Between the payments to the bank and the need to pump out product fast to meet the payroll, he had to be having difficulties paying his material suppliers and subassembly contractors on time. So they, in turn, were stalling on deliveries, which was the start of a vicious cycle that could easily turn into a tailspin. George's deep tan didn't fool me; it came from the sun room in the club. I knew he hadn't had a vacation, not even a day off, since he went on his own.

All new businesses go through this, especially the ones that are undercapitalized, like George's still had to be. It sounds good to grow 50 percent in one year, but it takes a lot of money to do it. Some banks tend to lend you a little less than the minimum you need rather than a little more. That little more could mean life or death of a business. If Murphy's Law strikes, and it guaranteed will, and you don't have any extra cash handy, you sink without a trace. Some banks don't understand that; they think they're being prudent by lending too little. They're not. What they're doing is guaranteeing that the loan won't be paid off. So they'll foreclose, sell the assets, lose money, and congratulate themselves that they kept the losses down because they were smart enough not to lend the borrower all he asked for.

The smartest thing for George to do at this time would be to sell some equity in the business, get partners to help with the work and to take the pressure off the cash flow. The right kind of associates, that is; the wrong kind could drive him into the ground faster. But I knew George; he wouldn't sell even 1 percent of his company. These engineer types—and I'm one myself, sort of—are very proud of their work. The designs are like their own children and the product is made with love. We'd still like to work with him, but I can't bring it up; he'd think I was trying to talk him into giving NVC a piece of his business now that it was about to be a great success. In his mind, he had to be seeing Rubinetics as a business ready to take off—that *had to* take off—go public next year, and make him a zillionaire overnight. It could happen, but I wasn't going to hold my breath until it did.

George was drinking a glass of milk at his desk, even though it wasn't lunchtime yet. Bad sign. Another six months of this and he'd have an ulcer. He offered us coffee and danish, but I wanted to eat lunch with Warren at the club and talk, and I've got to watch my weight, so I politely turned him down.

"I hate to bother you in the middle of a workday," I said, "but I have to ask you about the murder."

"You *have* to?" he asked. "Why do you have to?"

"I'm trying to clear us all, you included, and you're the only one I haven't talked to yet."

"I already talked to the police, Ed."

"So talk to me too. Just a couple of minutes. Tell me what you were doing at the time Barney was killed."

"I don't know exactly when . . ."

But he went through it. Again, nothing new. I tried another tack.

"Barney never bothered you? Stuck in a few needles?"

"Barney was always bugging me, but I tuned out."

"Can't that get to be too much sometimes? On top of all your other problems?"

"You can be a big pain too, Ed, like right now, and I'm not killing you."

"Yeah, but I'm not trying . . . All I want is a little information. Did you go into the steam room at any time?"

He was still glaring at me. "No, and I didn't see anyone go in either. I was in the shower, not the least bit interested in the steam room."

Warren broke in at just the right time. I could tell George was under pressure, and maybe I was pushing too hard. "Can you think of a motive for anyone to kill Mr. Brodsky?"

"You don't kill somebody for talking too much."

"If you disliked him, why talk to him at all?"

"If you're on the board together, how can you avoid it? Or if you're limited partners together."

I took hold of that fast. "The Lerman Mall?"

"All of Carl's projects since I went into business."

"If you're that tight for money . . ." He started to object, but I waved that aside. "Look, I have all your papers from last year, when we were negotiating about going in with you. I treat them confidentially, but I got a good memory. Also I can see how the business is booming, which means you got to be short of liquid cash. So where do you get six hundred thousand to invest with Carl on a week's notice?"

123

Now he was really angry. "That's none of your business, Baer. Get the hell out."

"Relax, George, I'm not here to make trouble. Unless you're the killer, that is. You throw me out, not satisfied you have a good answer, I have to tell Palmieri what I know. So let me talk and then you decide what to do with me."

"Talk," he said through gritted teeth.

"You took all your savings and all your vested pension money to start your own business. You did well on a small scale, manufacturing your own electronic designs, and made some good money. Last year you felt you should expand. That's when you came to us. Unfortunately for us, and I mean that sincerely, you got funding from a bank, so you didn't have to give up any equity. Right, so far?"

"You're talking like I'm starving. First of all, I was one of the highest paid engineers in the business. I not only had a vested pension, I had stock options. Rubinetics wasn't started on a shoestring; it was properly funded. I expanded to make my new transducer. It moves the read-write head of a computer disk to the exact track required thirty percent faster than the present voice-coil drive, without feedback, and so accurately that the tracks can be closer to each other by twenty-five percent. *Twenty-five percent!* You know what that means? A 1.44-megabyte disk can now hold 1.8-megabytes and a 40-megabyte fixed disk can now hold 50 megabytes. And I'm doing it for six dollars less a unit."

"Which is why I was interested in doing business with you, George; I know how good you are. So why did you go in with Carl Lerman? Why not use the money for additional production facilities? Or for managerial help?"

"Because I'm conservative, that's why. I know how easy it is for a business to fail, for reasons that have nothing to do with how good the product is or how smart the management is. With the mall, and with what I bought before, no matter what happens to me, my wife and children are taken care of."

Then I understood. "You're absolutely right, George,

124

two years from now, when the mall begins really paying off. But now you're killing yourself to stay alive. What you did . . . You mortgaged your house, hocked all your wife's jewelry except the wedding ring, and borrowed on your insurance and from every other source you could. You're juggling a lot of balls, hoping that none of them fall. Because if one falls, they all fall. Not a good situation."

"Wrong, Ed; they don't all fall. The business is in my name only; the limited partnerships are in my wife's name only. The family is safe."

I felt sick. What I was hearing, even though he wasn't saying it out loud, was that if Rubinetics fell, he'd kill himself. Accidentally, of course, for the double indemnity, so his family would live. Crazy. I know; I was once in that exact same position myself. Thank God I came out of it. I hoped George would too. But I didn't know how to help him. Unless he took NVC in with him. Which he'd never do. He'd die before he did. Really die. "How would killing Barney Brodsky help you?" I asked.

"You tell me," he growled. "Because if you can figure that out, you're smarter than I am. Or killing anybody."

So, like a good engineer, George had already computed every possible combination and permutation of people and events to see how he could best solve his problems. Including the murder of Barney Brodsky, which he had just admitted he had considered. Not that I could see how anyone could make a penny out of that murder, but then I didn't have Rubin's problems to stimulate my thinking.

I didn't want Warren to ask any more questions about motive; George was too tense already. I got up. "We have to leave now, George," I said, and turned to go. Then I turned back. "If your next projection shows that, uh, that an irreversible, uh, trend is foreseeable, don't take any, uh, action without talking to me first. There may be a way to solve your problems without your losing control of your business and your inventions."

I grabbed Warren's arm and pulled him out of there fast.

20

"Not today, I don't," said Clarence, my regular waiter. "Your face looks all puffed up and you're starting to gain weight again. I'm gonna bring you some nice crunchy vegetable sticks with a low-fat yogurt dip. Curry flavor. Delicious."

"I have problems, Clarence; got to keep my strength up."

"Okay, I'll bring you three sesame breadsticks too, but that's it. No butter. And black coffee." He turned to Warren. "And for you, Mr. Warren, how about a nice sliced skirt steak? A sandwich, so your daddy can't steal any off of your plate? On a seeded roll."

Warren nodded and Clarence took off, satisfied. Between him and Violet, I'd be skin and bones in no time. "So what do you think, Warren?" I asked. "We did a lot today—Ramon, Greenleaf, Hoffman, and Rubin—but I was so busy talking, I didn't have a chance to analyze a thing."

"There's nothing to analyze, Dad; we already knew that anyone of them could have done it."

126

"We also found out they all disliked Barney but that none of them had a motive to kill him."

"Only according to what they told us. Do you really think that if one of them had a good motive to kill Mr. Brodsky, he would have told us about it?"

"Of course not, Warren, but can you think of a way any of them could benefit from Barney's death?"

"All that means is that we don't know something; not that a real motive doesn't exist."

One does, I thought sadly. For Bill Carey. Clarence served lunch, if you can call vegetables lunch. I forced myself to eat the stuff; maybe later I'd have a chance to grab some real food before we went to the funeral chapel.

I persuaded Clarence to bring me a little milk for my coffee; he brought skim milk, must be related to Violet. "We've got an hour before we go to the funeral," I told Warren. "I'd like to try something, but I need your help."

He looked at me suspiciously. "What? Reenact the crime?" When he was little, he thought everything I did was wonderful. They grow up too fast.

"Not really. Just check the timing of what each one told us." I didn't want to tell him what I really had in mind.

"How will that help?"

"If I know how long it takes to do each thing, I can form a picture in my mind of who had to be where at what time. What else do I have to do tonight?"

"We have to find the motive, Dad. If you're looking for something to do after the funeral, we could go back to the office and catch up on work."

"Humor your poor stupid old father," I said. "I'll catch up on my work this weekend."

He sighed.

We stopped in front of the wet area. On the right was the in door; on the left, the out. "You saw Bill Carey coming out of the toilet," I reminded Warren, "as you entered the corridor to the wet area and, since you didn't see him go into the corridor ahead of you, he had to have been coming from the wet area, right? Okay, you're Bill Carey. Do an inspection the way he would've done it. Go." I pushed the button on my watch—even cheap watches today have functions I hardly ever use—and Warren opened the door.

He walked slowly, looking around the big shower room. There were people all over the place—lots of members come in at lunchtime—who looked at us like we were nuts; nobody goes into the wet area in a suit and tie. I ignored them; let them wonder. Halfway through the large shower room, Warren turned right, went over to the space between the two banks of mirrored sinks, and opened the right-hand door, the one to the sun room. Shading his eyes, he peeked in for a second, closed the door, moved left a step, pulled open the wooden sauna door, and peeked in. He went back to the middle of the shower room and walked toward the entrance to the small shower room. Just before he went in, he stopped at the stainless steel towel shelves, took a quick look at each one, opened the cover to the swimsuit drier, glanced in, and moved on. I don't think Warren ever saw Carey make his inspection, but this had to be how Bill would do it.

Two more steps and the steam room door was on Warren's right. He pulled open the door and went inside. I followed. It wasn't too badly steamed up and you could see for several feet. I waited near the door as Warren walked around the U of tiled steps, looking at each level. It only took about twenty seconds, but by the time we left the room, my clothes were all damp and wrinkled. Warren

128

went straight out of the steam room and continued across the narrow passage into the space between the two banks of showers in the small shower area, two showers on each side. He pushed the plunger on one of the liquid soap machines and it squirted soap on the shower floor. Ramon had done his job well.

When Warren came out, he turned left into the Z-shaped passage that led to the pool. A quick right and left, and we were at the door into the pool. On the door was a sign that said YOU MUST SHOWER COMPLETELY BEFORE ENTERING THE POOL AREA. As soon as the door closed, the young lifeguard looked up from his homework. "I'm sorry, sir," he said, "you can't enter the pool area with your shoes on. The soles could have a fungus on them. Or germs. Or dirt."

"Sorry," I said. Warren and I took our shoes and socks off. They were soaked from the steam room anyway.

Warren walked straight ahead to the hotter whirlpool and looked inside. Then he went to the next one, the cooler one—which was still plenty hot as far as I was concerned—looked in, and moved to the hot tub—a real Japanese wooden hot tub—looked in, came back to where I was, then started walking around the pool. I didn't want to reset my stop watch, so I counted mentally; it took fifteen seconds to go from the gym door to the wet area door. On the way back, Warren dipped his hand into the hot tub, the cooler whirlpool, and the hotter whirlpool. I opened the door to leave—the atmosphere was too humid for a suit—but Warren stopped to talk to the lifeguard. "What's the temperature of the hot tub?"

The lifeguard looked embarrassed. "I'm sorry, sir," he said, "you'll have to ask Mr. Carey about that."

"It's all right," I said. "I'm Ed Baer, on the board of directors, and this is my son, Warren. You can call Mr. Carey on the intercom if you want to."

The lifeguard thought for a moment, then said, "It's a

state law that no public pool can be hotter than a hundred five degrees."

"I thought it was the same as the hot whirlpool," Warren said, "but everyone thinks the hot tub is much hotter."

"Yes, sir. Some people even brag how much heat they can stand, so we don't advertise that there's no difference. I check the temperature every half hour, and the pH, the chlorine content too. If it's too hot, somebody with heart trouble could have an attack, or if you're on certain drugs, you could faint and maybe drown."

"You keep a careful eye on everyone?" I asked, looking hard at his homework.

"I have the pattern in my mind of who's where, and I look up every few seconds. If I see anything different, I check it out immediately. No one's ever complained."

"I'm not complaining," I said. "Just wanted to see how you work. Were you on duty when Mr. Brodsky was killed?"

"It wasn't my responsibility, sir." He looked embarrassed. "It happened in the steam room."

"You saw Mr. Kaner in the hot tub?" I asked. "This one?" I pointed to the near one.

"A few minutes before Mr. Carey made his inspection. I didn't know his name at the time. Then the other member came in. I didn't know his name either."

"Mr. Greenleaf."

"Yes, sir. I know both of them now."

"They left together?"

"About five minutes after Mr. Greenleaf came in. I don't time each person, but I have a feel for someone who's been in too long and I warn them that it could be dangerous. If he objects I keep an eye on him and, five minutes more, I tell him he must leave the whirlpool."

"And if he doesn't want to?"

"I call the desk and they get the chief instructor or

130

Mr. Carey or whoever's in charge at the time. I'm not allowed to pull anyone out except to save his life."

"And Mr. Carey comes down for this?"

The young man looked embarrassed again. "What usually happens . . . Mr. Carey asks if the man looks faint to me. I always say yes, because he could die if I misjudge it. Then Mr. Carey says I'd better pull him out fast to save his life. And I do. Not too gently. Sometimes he swallows water and I have to pump him out." The boy smiled. "They always listen to me the second time. It's for their own good."

Bill Carey was smarter than I thought. Wiser. Maybe I'd reconsider voting for him next year. If he was around next year. For my own education—I never went into the hot whirlpool; torture I don't do voluntarily—I asked, "What's the temperature of the second whirlpool?"

"A hundred two."

"Only three degrees cooler? It feels much colder."

"The body's a lot more sensitive to temperature than most people realize," the lifeguard said. "Even one degree feels like a lot."

"And you keep it at the prescribed temperature?"

"Within half a degree, yes, sir."

"And the temperature of the swimming pool?"

"It's quite warm, sir; eighty-four degrees, but don't tell anyone. Some people complain it's too cold and some say it's too warm. We tell them it's seventy-eight, but we don't dare keep it that low. I've seen elderly men, men your age, sir, come right out of the hot tub and jump into the pool instead of going in gradually, getting used to the change. It's dangerous, a shock. Could bring on a heart attack, the sudden chill. So we keep it as warm as we can get away with."

Elderly? Men my age? Enough was enough. I motioned to Warren that we should leave, but he had another question. "Did you see anyone else besides Mr. Kaner,

Mr. Greenleaf, and Mr. Carey? Did anyone come in from the gym entrance and go through the pool area into the wet area?" So Warren had noticed it too. So had Palmieri, which was why he had closed off the pool. And I thought I was the only one.

"No, sir. Nobody came in at all, other than the two people I told you about."

"Nobody? Mr. Carey didn't come in?"

"Of course Mr. Carey . . . After he inspects the wet area, he comes in here. Every morning, but I thought you meant . . ."

"When did he come into the pool?"

"A little after Mr. Kaner. He checked the whole place, my inspection log, and went back into the wet area."

"What do you do if you have to leave your post?" Warren asked. "To go to the toilet, or for any other reason?"

"I call the desk and one of the instructors who has a life-saving license takes my place. You can't leave a pool untended. One minute's inattention and somebody could drown."

"Did you leave your post," Warren asked, "the morning Mr. Brodsky was killed?"

"Once I got here, I didn't leave that whole morning."

The way he worded it was a dead giveaway. "What time did you get here?" I asked.

"I'm on duty from eight to four, weekdays."

Now I was sure. "You wear your bathing suit in the car?"

He blushed. "I leave it in the locker." He knew what I was driving at. "My time starts when I enter the spa."

A clockwatcher; I could see he'd go far, especially if his major was economics. "So you were here," I said, "in your place as a lifeguard, a few minutes after eight?"

"It only takes me a couple of minutes to change clothes and get in here."

132

"Then you didn't see Mr. Kaner come in?"

"No one's supposed to use the pool if I'm not on duty."

"But you did see Mr. Carey and Mr. Greenleaf come in."

"Yes, sir."

So there was a period of two or three minutes, maybe four, when somebody—anybody—could have come from the gym, through the pool area, and gone into the steam room. And the most likely one was Bill Carey. Who would have no trouble coming back from the steam room to inspect the pool as if he had entered the wet area from the corridor; how would the lifeguard know? I looked at Warren, could see by the sick look on his face that he was ahead of me. And Palmieri? If he hadn't already figured this out, he would any minute.

I had to get Warren's mind off the idea that Bill Carey was the killer. "Come on, Warren," I said. "We still have five other sets of actions to time." I opened the door back into the wet area.

"I don't want to, Dad," he said, as he followed. "It's pointless. What good does it do to know if it took me five minutes to follow Bill's circuit or six minutes?"

"People's ideas of time are very inaccurate. Even yours. Actually, it took you three and a half minutes by my watch, not counting the talking with the lifeguard. But if you don't want to, that's okay. I proved that Bill could easily have killed Brodsky. We might as well go home and change our clothes. It's late as it is, and we'll barely make it to the service." What I also learned was that we couldn't rely on studying the pattern of who was where when. Which would save me a lot of work tonight, but would also make solving the case that much more difficult. I might even have to look into motives, the way Warren wanted. Only there were no motives that I knew of. Except Bill Carey's.

21

Warren and I got to the funeral home just as everyone was filing into the chapel for the service, so we put on yarmulkes and sat in the back. While the rabbi and the cantor went through the short service, I looked at the front row, which had been reserved for family. Barney's daughter, Ellen, sat between her husband, Maurice, and their daughter, Sharon. Ellen's brother, Gene, and his family were to their right. Filling the rest of the front row were men and women of Barney's age, relatives and friends of his I had never met. Scattered around the chapel were the people I wanted to observe, Rubin, Greenleaf, Hoffman, Lerman, and Kaner, looking solemn and sad, like you're supposed to look at a funeral, but not exactly rending their garments and beating their breasts.

I should have been paying attention to the service, but I hadn't liked Barney Brodsky in life and his death hadn't changed my opinion of him in any way. My major concern was to help Sharon Edel—her parents and her Uncle Gene too, who were nice people—and Bill Carey. And to build up Warren's confidence by letting him solve the case, so he would make the right decision about marrying Lee Guralnik fast.

At the end of the formal prayers, the rabbi called up some of the old people from the front row to speak of Barney's good heart, his kindness, his charities—there were a lot more of them than I had suspected; who knows what goodness lurks in the hearts of men?—and particularly Barney's strong support of HIAS, the Hebrew Immigrant Aid Society that had originally been set up, long before I was born, to help poor Jewish immigrants and was now helping poor Asian and East European refugees too. I hadn't even known about that side of Barney; just sent HIAS my annual check, as big as I could make it, in memory of my father and mother, both of whom had been given a hand by HIAS when they first came over.

I noticed that Bill Carey wasn't there. I was sure he wanted to see Sharon, to hold her and comfort her, but this was not the time or place to make problems for her parents. The rabbi announced that the family would be sitting *shivah* at the Edel house for the next seven days, and that anyone who wished to express his sympathy to Gene Brodsky and Ellen Edel, and to pay his respects, should go to the Edels' after the interment or at any time during the mourning period. The family had also requested there be no flowers, but if anyone wished, he could make a donation in Mr. Brodsky's honor to one of his favorite charities.

The funeral director announced that all who intended to go to the cemetery should follow the family limousines, and all others should wait in the parking lot until the funeral procession had left. I decided to go to the cemetery out of respect for the family, out of my duty as a fellow director of the club, and to watch my five suspects, to see if I could find anything in their faces that would indicate . . . I probably wouldn't, but what else could I do at this time?

The cemetery was in Suffolk, a half-hour's ride away. I made sure to stand on the opposite side of the grave from my suspects, so I had a clear view. After the prayers and the cantor's singing, the plain pine coffin was lowered into the grave and we all lined up to throw a shovelful of earth on the coffin. Judaism is a life-oriented religion—what kind of human being you are, what you do while you're alive, is all that counts—and the throwing of earth on the coffin is the ritual way of closing the cover of the Book of Life, so that new life may go on. One by one Greenleaf, Hoffman, Rubin, Lerman, and Kaner passed in front of me, threw their shovelfuls of earth. I could't read a thing in their faces.

The Edel home was one of the most luxurious in Oakdale. Very little had to be done to turn it into a house of mourning, but the atmosphere after the funeral was clearly that of loss and sadness. In accordance with Jewish ritual, all the mirrors were covered and there were only low, backless stools for the family to sit on. Each family member had a torn strip of black cloth pinned to his clothes, to symbolize rent garments, and none of them wore shoes in the house. It was clear that Ellen and Gene had loved their father and that Sharon had loved her grandfather, which I liked to see. That Barney acted differently with his own family than with me was only natural. That his business associates didn't like him, or even that one of them hated Barney enough to kill him, didn't change the fact that the man had love in his family.

I kissed Ellen, shook hands with Maurice and Gene, said a few words, and went into the dining room. The central table held a big catered spread for the guests. I was hungry, and piled a plate full. Later, and through the week of mourning, friends and neighbors would bring food. Not that the Edels lacked anything; it was symbolic of the requirement that the family do no labor during the period, to leave free their hearts and souls for prayer and remembrance.

When I finished eating, I went to find Sharon. She was surrounded by friends her own age—though not Lee Guralnik, who must've still had tests or something—and I waited patiently until I could cut her out politely. The makeup couldn't hide the paleness of her face or that her eyes were red from crying. I put my arms around her and held her closely. Sharon knew how much Thelma, may she rest in peace, and I loved her, and I could feel her relax and lean on me. After a minute, I led her into a corner so we could talk.

"Bill called you?" I asked. "Brought you up to date?"

Her soft brown eyes filled with tears. "Please, Uncle Ed," she said—we're not related, but ever since she was a baby, that's who I was to her, "you've got to help Bill. He didn't—didn't—do anything like the police think. He's so sweet, so nice, that . . . I *know*."

"I'm doing everything I can, Sharon," I said. "I don't control the police." I felt sick; later Warren and I would have to tell Palmieri about the lifeguard.

"You and Warren solved the loudspeaker case; you can solve this one."

I held her close again and smoothed her long brown hair. "We're spending all our time on nothing but this." And the more we looked, the more we found to show that Bill Carey was the most likely suspect.

"I know I shouldn't bring up business at a time like this, but is everything ready for the closing on the gym?"

"The paperwork has been completed and the closing is set for Friday morning." Everything I told her had been accurate, but none of what I said was true. Even though it was for her own good, I felt like the lowest kind of hypo-

137

crite, and looked around for a way to escape. Warren caught my eye; I motioned with my head for him to come over. "Here comes Warren," I told Sharon. "I know he wants to talk to you." I took off, not looking back.

Mingling with the crowd, I tried to keep an eye on my suspects. Maybe if one of them had a couple of drinks, something would show. But none of them was a heavy drinker, and there was nothing I could see in their faces.

Finally Warren came over to me. "Anything?" I asked.

"She'll be all right," he said. "Asked me if Lee was coming home this weekend for the spring break; she'd like to see her. I told her that Lee was scheduled to fly in Saturday morning but that I'd phone to ask her to try to come Friday afternoon and drop in. That made Sharon feel better."

"Nothing about Bill?"

"She wants me to bring Bill here. I told her it was sensible of Bill not to come, so that her mother wouldn't have an additional problem, but she insisted I tell him."

"Will you?" How Warren handled this was important to me.

"I'll give him the message, but if he asks me, I'll advise him to wait until they're no longer sitting *shivah*."

That was what I wanted to hear. Showed respect for tradition and for family. Wisdom too. Not just intelligence, but wisdom. And sensitivity to the feelings of others. At that moment I felt really proud of my son. Damn few kids of his generation had any *menschlichkeit* at all. It sort of means humanity in Yiddish, but that's not the full meaning. "Have you decided to tell Palmieri about the lifeguard?"

Warren's eyes looked tortured. "We have to, Dad."

"It may convince Palmieri to arrest Bill."

"That the lifeguard wasn't there for a few minutes doesn't mean that Bill killed Mr. Brodsky."

138

"With Bill's motive, it makes him the obvious killer. Palmieri has a lot of pressure on him to produce."

"I'll do my best to persuade him not to arrest Bill."

Lots of luck, Warren, even with my help. "When?"

"Right after we leave here."

"You know, if Bill finds out, he'll never forgive you. And Sharon will hate you." And who knows what Lee, Sharon's best friend, will think? Why does Warren have to be so goddamn honest? And would I want it any other way? I didn't know; I swear I didn't know. Between good and evil, there's no problem. But between good and good? God only knows.

"I'm calling a meeting of the limited partners for tonight," I told Warren. "To bring them up to date."

"Can't it wait two more days, Dad?"

"What's going to happen different in three days? Two and a half days, actually; it's already late Tuesday."

"We'll find the murderer. We have to, especially now."

"We're obligated to keep our investors informed; their money shouldn't lie idle. You know something I don't know?"

"Their money isn't idle; it's drawing interest. And we haven't explored the motives yet. If we must have a meeting, why don't you just report to them what we know so far?"

"Fair enough. But if on the basis of what I tell them, anyone wants to take his money out, I'm going to let him."

"It's not part of our agreement, but I don't mind; we can get another to take his place quickly, or lay out the money ourselves temporarily."

"You want to make the presentation?"

"Not really; I know you'll give them a fair picture."

"Don't worry. And don't worry either if I don't come home for supper. I had so much to eat here," I said, "that

I can't even think of eating any more." I was glad that Warren wasn't coming to the meeting. I never said he was wrong about the motive business—of course there had to be a motive—just that I didn't see how we could find a motive for any of the suspects in the time we had left. With Warren not there, it would be a lot easier for me to talk to Iris; about motives she was the expert. "I may be home a little late," I said.

As for Warren turning in Bill, telling Palmieri about the lifeguard, the only solution was for me to do it myself, to save Warren from torturing himself. My father would've done it for me. And his father for him.

22

"Got anything new for us?" I asked Palmieri.

"Oh, sure," he said. "It's a full day since the murder, so why shouldn't I have the case closed already?"

"A day and a half," I corrected, "but who's counting? I got something for you, if you got anything to trade."

His collar got tight. "No trades. You got anything, you tell me."

If he knew anything I didn't, I'd have to get it out of him later; no way to do it in his present mood. "The lifeguard. You interrogated him yourself?" First I had to know if I could talk straight or had to pussyfoot around.

"This is the police *department*. I interrogated the main suspects; one of my men talked to the witnesses."

"Pull out your notes on the lifeguard."

"If you think he did it, you're crazy." He took a folder off his desk and opened it. "He's a college kid; no connection with Brodsky." Palmieri read from the folder. "On duty at eight sharp. Nobody went past him to the steam room."

141

"*Where* was he on duty?"

"Where he was supposed to—" Palmieri read the report again and turned blue. "I'll kill the sonofabitch. I keep telling them and telling them, but do they listen? He's going to the South Shore for a year. Or until he smartens up, whichever comes last." He threw the folder down on his desk. "Okay, Baer, exactly where was the lifeguard at eight sharp?"

"By his locker, putting on his swim trunks. One of these clockwatchers who wants to make sure the boss doesn't beat him out of a couple minutes. He didn't get to the lifeguard's chair until three or four minutes after eight."

Palmieri hit three buttons on his phone. "Jerry? The Brodsky case. Pull in that bastard lifeguard you interviewed. Yes, *now*, I don't give a shit where he is. Ask him where he was—that's right, *was*—at eight sharp the morning of the murder. Give him a hard time, but good, for withholding information from the police, and get a signed statement where he was every *second*, from ten to eight to ten after. Then get your ass in here and explain to me why you shouldn't turn in your badge." He turned to me. "You know what this means?"

"Theoretically, Carey could've gotten into the steam room from the gym without going through the shower room."

"Theoretically, my ass. He's got the best motive and he had the best opportunity. I'm pulling him in myself."

"You're arresting him?" Warren must've been half expecting it, but he still sounded shocked.

"Arresting? Not yet. But I'm going to have a good long talk with him. And you know what else you've done? Now I've got to check everybody who was in that part of the gym just before eight, where each one was, what he saw, and exactly when he saw it. Two days later. At least twenty people to talk to. With all the other things I got to do."

"You want us to go out," I asked politely, "and make believe I never told you anything?"

He glared at me harder. "The last thing I need right now, Baer, is a smart-ass civilian."

"I'm not saying you should worship the ground I walk on, Ben; a simple 'thank you' would be nice."

He had the courtesy to look embarrassed. "Yeah, sorry. Thanks. Now get out; I got work to do."

"Bill Carey didn't do it," Warren said stubbornly.

"I didn't charge anybody yet, did I?"

"What Warren means," I said, "is that if you'd give us a little information, harmless stuff, maybe we could come up with something more. For which you'd get all the credit."

"Like what? I don't have a thing; I told you that."

"Warren—we—believe that the suspects, the guys in the wet area, at least one of them had a motive to kill Brodsky. There's no way we can get that out of them, but you must've gone into their backgrounds pretty completely."

"All I got's some gossip. Nothing solid."

"Every little bit helps, Ben. We'll be discreet with it."

He sighed. "Okay, but remember that none of this has been checked. I doubt that it can be checked." He opened his folder. "Barney Brodsky himself. Used to needle everybody he knew. Anybody who overheard him wouldn't know what Brodsky was talking about; only the victim would know. The suspects all swore it was bullshit that they tuned out on; none of them would tell me what it was all about."

"But you found out."

"Not for sure, but if different people in the club tell similar stories about this guy or that guy, it's gotta have some basis. Like Mr. Hoffman. The big good-looking car dealer? He's supposed to be screwing one of his salesgirls."

That could be a good wedge. "They say which girl?"

"Each source named a different one, so I ain't too

sure how accurate it is. Then Mr. Greenleaf, the lawyer? He's supposed to have a surrogate in his pocket, paid off, to assign him juicy probates. Again, nothing solid."

Just what I was looking for. "And the others?"

"Rubin, the electronics guy, copied his big invention from somebody else. Kaner, the accountant, faked an audit for a company going public. And Lerman, the developer, he's been paying off building inspectors."

"Did you follow through on these, Ben?"

"Too vague. Take the whole department ten years to check out. I brought up the dirt to each one, but none of them looked the least bit scared."

"Maybe if I . . . ?"

"Couldn't hurt, if you're careful. But remember, these guys, they're all solid citizens, taxpayers. And some of them got more clout than you do."

"With *you*? After all I did?"

"With the commissioner. So don't make waves. If anyone asks, you heard this on your own; didn't get a thing from me. And call me about anything you find out. Night or day."

What Palmieri had told me sounded like the kind of stories that float around every successful man: possible but without foundation, and no way to prove a thing. And since Barney had been doing his hinting privately rather than coming right out with names, dates, and figures, he probably had nothing firm either. Blackmail? Impossible. Barney had as much money as any of the suspects and besides, if he was really blackmailing them, the last thing he'd do is needle his victims in public. What I had to do was figure out how to use what Palmieri had told me to pry the *real* motive out of the killer.

144

23

It didn't take long to tell the investors in the gym deal all I knew about the murder situation. Not because I'm a fast talker, but because I didn't know a hell of a lot. Like I promised Warren, I tried not to influence them, but maybe I tried too hard; the message didn't get across. "Why are you telling us all this?" Jerry Fein asked.

"This deal is different from the others we've done," I said. "Usually we have four sources of money available to the new business: the owner's own investment, a bank loan to the business based on the forced-sale value of the assets, a bank loan to the owner personally that's cosigned by us, and our own money, which goes in half loan and half investment. In this deal there's no way for Bill to borrow any more from a bank. On top of that, the bank loan to the business is relatively small; in case of a default, there's a limited market for the gym's physical assets, some of which aren't transferable: the pool, the sun room, the whirlpools, the steam room, the sauna, and so forth."

"But you took all that into account," Bob Pasternak said, "when you decided to go ahead with the deal."

"That's the point. This is a business where the owner's ability is of primary importance. With Bill Carey running the gym, it's a good deal. Without him, who knows?"

"Do you think he killed Barney Brodsky?" Dan Tumin asked.

"No, but how do I prove it? And as long as Bill is under suspicion, I'm seriously considering not going ahead with the closing on Friday."

"Won't that cost us?" Bernie Weber asked. "The bank is ready to go, made a firm commitment, allocated the money, did the paperwork, everything."

"You never read the fine print on the papers I gave you?" Bernie shook his head. "That's very flattering, Bernie, but it's stupid. Anyway, in my deals, I don't touch your money until the closing; it's segregated in a special interest-bearing account. In fact, each NVC deal has its own account; we don't commingle funds. *Never.* If one deal goes sour, we lose only the money in that deal; all the other bank accounts are untouchable. Anyway, I use only NVC money until the closing. If, for any reason, the deal doesn't go, I take the licking; you get your money back."

"But we can't take our money back now, can we?" Marvin Guralnik asked. The needle-nosed dentist sounded even more worried than usual. "I read the papers you gave us. No backing out until the closing is officially canceled."

Leave it to the twitch. How he could be a dentist, working to such tiny tolerances with his jitters, was beyond me. I should've known when I first saw him on the golf course. There has to be something wrong with a man who always—I mean *always*—scores an exact ninety-six. "That's right," I said. "The money has to be under my control, otherwise I can't function."

"But you're—that is, Warren—is working on the case, isn't he?" Iris Guralnik asked. "With your help? Trying to find the murderer, to clear Bill Carey of suspicion?" Marvin gave his wife a *look*.

146

"We're doing our best, Iris, but there's no guarantee we'll succeed. As a matter of fact, with less than three days left, I have to tell you it doesn't look good. Which is why I called this meeting. Anyone who wants his money back now can have it, regardless of what the papers say."

Iris jumped up. "That's pointless, Ed. Three days before? What do we gain? If we take our money out now, you'll find someone to take our place, won't you? Then there'll never be room for us to go with you again."

"Probably," I said politely. With Iris in the picture, I'd never get rid of Marvin Guralnik as an investor. "Depends on the size of the deal and if anyone else drops out."

"We're staying till the end," Iris said firmly, and sat down. Marvin put his hand on her arm and whispered in her ear. Iris shook her head angrily.

"Anyone want to leave the limited partnership now?" I looked around.

"Do your best, Ed," Leonard Vogel said. "We'll all go along with you. If you win, we all win; if you lose, only you lose. Who could complain?"

"I'm not an idiot," I said. "I take the up-front risks, but if we win I get a bigger return per dollar than you do."

"So who's arguing?" Lenny asked. He stood up to go and the others followed.

All except Iris. "Take the car home," she told Marvin. "I want to have a talk with Ed. Now." He started to object, but she shut him up. "Just *do* it."

We went to the same Howard Johnson's where we had our first talk during the Kassel case. From the parking lot to when we got into the booth, Iris didn't say a word to me. When the waitress came, she ordered just a low-fat yogurt. "I had supper already," she explained.

I hadn't had supper yet, so I ordered a hamburger with everything and french fries. "What are you trying to do, Ed?" Iris asked. "Make trouble? I thought you wanted Lee and Warren to get married this fall."

"If not sooner," I said. "What trouble?"

"The only thing holding Warren back is his uncertainty—the feeling that he's still dependent on you, that he's not a man in his own right."

"And you think I'm . . . ? You're crazy, Iris. I'm doing the exact opposite, building him up in every way. I tell everybody he's handling the Brodsky case. I let him handle the bank work, relations with the executives, everything, and he does a good job. He's a real asset to the business."

"So's the guy who sweeps the floor. You *let* him? What's this 'let him' business? Who makes the important decisions? Whose idea was it to call a meeting of the limited partners and offer to give them their money back? Is this the way you show your confidence that he'll solve the case?"

"What do you want me to do, Iris? Lie? Hold out on my investors?"

"Nothing, that's what I want you to do. Who'd want to leave just to get his money back two days earlier?"

"Your husband did."

"Marvin didn't understand you were doing it to undermine Warren, to show him you were still the big boss."

"Me? Undermine my own son?"

"Not consciously, but it's there. And you'd better stop it, Ed, otherwise . . ."

"Otherwise what? You threatening me, Iris?"

"You're threatening yourself, Ed. You keep this up and you know what? No grandchildren. None. Zero."

That really got to me. "You sure?"

"You may know the building business, Ed, and the venture capital business, but from psychology, you don't know shit. Like the way you play golf. Bang the ball as hard as you can and hope it goes straight."

"You got it all wrong, Iris. I'm figuring every little

detail, trying to find out where every suspect was to the nearest second, making a pattern. You think that's easy?"

"What does Warren think about it?"

"He doesn't; too busy working on motives."

"And you're not? Motive is the most important thing. I spend all my professional life working on motives, getting people to see what their motives really are."

"Sure, when it's there. What if it isn't?"

"No motive?" She couldn't believe I said that. "In a *murder*? What the hell's wrong with you, Ed?"

"I don't mean *no* motive. Everybody disliked Barney, but that's no reason to kill a guy. Not for a normal person."

"Then maybe one of the suspects isn't normal."

"Nah, I know them all. They're normal."

"Then maybe you don't really *know* them. Why don't you start working on that? With Warren? Tell Warren you finally saw the light, that you're now sure the way to find the killer is to find his motive. That'll make Warren happy, restore his confidence, and find the killer for you."

"Then he'll propose to Lee?"

"Proposing is sexist. They just agree that they should commit themselves to an official long-term relationship."

"But they have grandchildren, don't they?"

"*They* have children; *we* have the grandchildren."

"You sure?"

"Trust me."

"I liked the old way better, Iris. More romantic."

"So did I, Ed, but things change. People change. Twenty years from now Warren and Lee will be looking at their kids and wondering what's wrong with them, that they want romance in their literature, music, sex, dance. In their lives. It'll be the perfect revenge for us."

"I should live to see it happen."

"Stop eating greasy hamburgers and fries, and maybe you'll make it."

I had to get her off that subject, and I also remembered something. "I won't have time for our golf game tomorrow morning. Probably not Friday either. Call Jerry Fein and see if he can get somebody else to play with him."

"That's not a good idea, Ed, to give up the game. With all you have on your mind, you need the relaxation."

"Relaxation? Golf with you? Wouldn't it be easier if I just deposited a check in your account three times a week?"

"Not for me. Half the fun is watching you turn blue when you hit a perfect three-hundred-yard drive right into the water of the adjoining hole."

"Maybe if you kept your mouth shut when I'm driving . . . ?"

"Maybe if you stopped trying to kill the ball and started playing the game the way it should be played . . . ?"

She always gets the last word. Iris can't resist nagging. Even when she's right. Maybe motive was the way to go, but how do you get a suspect in a murder case to tell you his motive? If I asked them to take inkblot tests, you think they wouldn't get a little suspicious? So even if I wanted to work on their motives, assuming there were any, how could I find out what they were? Hire a detective agency to investigate each one? By Thursday 3 P.M.? With today being Tuesday? Tonight, I mean? Maybe the reason I didn't want to go the motive route was that I already had a suspect with a good motive. The best. Sex and money. And revenge. And hate. Yeah, motives I had plenty, but only for the wrong guy.

24

I could see the light under Warren's bedroom door when I got home, so even though I wasn't sure whether he was studying for his orals or thinking about motives—guaranteed he wasn't working on NVC business—I knocked.

Warren was sitting at his desk, but he only had a yellow pad in front of him. Studying he wasn't, and working on NVC papers he wasn't either. "Motives?" I asked.

"I've been sitting here since after supper, and I can't come up with a single one that could apply to this situation."

I sat down on the big black recliner. "I haven't gotten anywhere trying to figure out who could've or would've or should've, anyone who positively did or who positively didn't. They all might've, so if we find the guy who had a reason to do it, that guy's gotta be the killer. So you were right, the only way to find the killer is to find the motive."

"But there is no motive, Dad. Not for this murder."

"No motive for a *murder*?" Iris thinks I don't listen to

151

her, but I do, sometimes. "A random killing in a steam room?"

"I didn't say it was random; just that I can't think of a reason to kill Mr. Brodsky. I don't care what Mr. Hoffman said about irritations adding up to an explosion. He's right about that, but explosions are unexpected. This was a carefully planned murder, perfectly executed right under the noses of several people who all knew each other. Including me. Nobody shouted, nobody frothed at the mouth, nobody threatened Mr. Brodsky; none of the typical signs of somebody going crazy. It's driving *me* crazy."

I tried to calm him down. "Why don't we look at it your way, with backward logic? Instead of trying to find who had the motive, let's list a bunch of motives and try to see who each one could apply to."

"You think I haven't done that?"

"Maybe with me . . . ?" He hesitated. "What could it hurt?"

"Okay," he said, practically sneering, like if he couldn't solve the problem, how could his poor old ignorant father. Hah! Education he had over me, sure, but life experience? I could spot him cards and spades and still take him over the hurdles. "We'll start with sex."

"Sex? *Barney?*"

"Sure. People kill over sex. A very strong motive."

"Cross off sex. I don't see Barney fooling around with any of the wives of our suspects. To be more exact, I don't see any of the wives fooling around with Barney."

"Or their daughters?"

"Double that for the daughters."

"Just trying to be comprehensive. Money?"

"A suspect wanted money from Barney? Forget it. None of them is exactly poor; in addition to what they gotta have put away elsewhere, each one has at least two million invested with Carl Lerman. And even if one of them wanted more money, how would killing Barney make money for him?"

152

"There's one suspect who fits, Dad. Bill Carey. It would be pointless for Mr. Brodsky to leave any money to Maurice or Ellen Edel, or even to Gene. Aside from his charities, the bulk of Mr. Brodsky's estate would probably go to his grandchildren. So if Mr. Brodsky died, Sharon would get a third of the estate. After Bill married her he'd have all the money he'd ever need."

"First, Warren, let me teach you about life. You learn to read character in the building business damn fast, or you don't last, and I don't read Bill as a killer. Second, he isn't a damn fool either. I'm sure Barney put a clause in his will that if Bill married Sharon, her share of the estate would go to some charity or be split between Gene's kids, so there'd be no point in killing Barney for money."

"How about marriage? The biggest obstacle was Mr. Brodsky. With him gone, Sharon and Bill could get married."

"Even with Barney in the way, they could elope and get married in a civil ceremony. Why the emphasis on Bill? I thought you agreed he didn't do it?"

"I do, Dad, but I have to consider every possibility."

"Not this one; Bill didn't do it. What's the next one?"

"Hate. Nobody liked Mr. Brodsky, but nobody hated him."

"That we know of, but there had to be somebody. Maybe in the past? You think they all told us the whole truth?"

"Not about something that might make them look bad, but in the time we have left . . . ? It's Tuesday night; how can we check the pasts of five suspects by Thursday afternoon?"

"So we'll skip hate for the while, but I'm not dropping the idea. What's next on your list?"

"Revenge, but that's similar to hate. Insanity?"

"These guys are as sane as I am. Hide craziness in the club for all these years? Somebody would notice."

"That's what I assumed. Blackmail?"

"Somebody blackmailing Barney? Then why kill him?"

"To keep him from going to the police and charging the blackmailer with extortion. But maybe Mr. Brodsky was blackmailing the killer."

"That's possible, but why? For the money? Doubtful. For the pleasure? Like his needling? Then it wouldn't be blackmail. The threat in blackmail is that you're going to expose the victim to the police, to the papers, TV, whatever. Once you've done that, you can't blackmail him any more. It's not like the needling Hoffman and the others told us about, what Palmieri said. That had to be about something the victim was ashamed of, but not something he could be blackmailed for. Anyway, blackmail comes under the same category as hate and revenge; we don't have time to check back to find out who has something to be blackmailed about. Any more motives?"

"Showing off. To do something right under the noses of the audience, to show how much smarter you are than they are."

"It fits the conditions; why else kill Barney in the steam room with a bunch of people watching your every move? But you're risking twenty-five-to-life if you're caught, and that could take a lot of fun out of the game."

"The risk might make it even more interesting."

"For someone who's crazy. Maybe one of them is insane and he's hidden it all these years; I just don't believe it. Besides, all these guys are smart, very smart, and everybody already knows that. George Rubin, in fact, is considered an electronics genius."

"Now you see why I said there was no motive?"

"What about the gossip Palmieri told us about? The stuff Barney kept needling the suspects about?"

"Interesting, but impossible to prove, so who would kill over it? If Mr. Brodsky could prove that Mr. Greenleaf had bribed a surrogate, do you think he would have left it at that? He'd have turned Mr. Greenleaf over to the D.A.

154

If it was provable, would Mr. Greenleaf have stood for the needling all these months, or would he have killed Mr. Brodsky long ago? I'm a trained philosopher, Dad; I've considered everything. So as I said, there's no motive to work with."

Except for Bill Carey's. I thought it would boost Warren's confidence and help solve the case to analyze the motives, but the way it turned out, Carey looked even worse than before. So did Warren. In his present mood, there was no way he was going to marry Lee this fall, much less have grandchildren. I'd be lucky if he didn't quit NVC and turn into a professor on me. I'd have to find the murderer fast, and not just to save Bill Carey. But how?

No sense thinking about it now. It was late, and I was tired. Sometimes when I had a problem, I'd sleep on it. With no distractions, my brain would come up with a solution by the next morning.

It would've worked too, if I'd been able to sleep.

25

There was no point staring at the ceiling, so I got out of bed and went into the kitchen to eat. Warren was already there, half finished. Just juice, coffee, and a croissant. Practically no protein. This case was getting to him. "You couldn't sleep either?" I asked.

"After you've gone over the same ground the tenth time," he said, "and nothing new comes up, it's time to quit."

"A Baer never quits."

"I didn't mean quit for good, Dad. What I meant was to put my mind on something else for a while so that when I got back to the problem, I could approach it from a fresh angle."

"That's different. What're you going to do?"

"Go to the office, catch up on my work, and put the murder completely out of my mind."

"What about the gym? Today's Wednesday, time for your regular workout."

"I'm not in the mood for exercise today."

"You look like you're not in the mood for anything today. Once you start loafing you'll get in the habit and, before you know it, you'll stop working out altogether."

156

"Okay, I'll go to gym before I go to the office. I have to talk to Bill anyway, tell him what Sharon said. She can't call; afraid someone will pick up the phone and listen in."

"So what does she want to tell Bill? That she loves him and wants to elope the day after she graduates?"

"How'd you know?" he asked. I shrugged. When you're my age, you *know*. "She also wants him to come to the house today to pay his respects to her parents."

Normally I would've told Warren what to say, but with all Iris had been pounding at me, I asked, "What do you think?"

"Bill should go to the Edels' house to show his sympathy, bring up nothing, but if her mother asks him, tell the truth about how he feels and what he intends."

"And about eloping?"

"I'm against that. Not only is Sharon an only child, but with a formal wedding, a full Jewish ceremony, it'll be like accepting Bill into the family. It'll give all the relatives a chance to get to know Bill, see what a good guy he is, and Mrs. Edel will have the pleasure of seeing Sharon married."

"Setting up a formal wedding—with the Edels it'll be a big one—takes months. That'll give Bill time to find a rabbi who'll help him convert, the way he wanted, or one who'll marry them in a religious ceremony if Bill doesn't convert."

"You approve?" He seemed a little surprised.

"Absolutely. And I have another suggestion. Tell Bill not to bring to the house what everyone else does. Half of them will bring bought fancy food, and the other half will bring their specialty gourmet dishes. Nobody in the family will eat much of either. At a time like this, what they need is real *haimish* food, Jewish soul food, to sustain the body and lift the spirit. *Cholent*."

"What's *cholent*?"

"You don't remember? Maybe you were too little. It's dried lima beans, soaked overnight. Add onion, garlic, *schmaltz*, chicken, duck, lamb, *gedempfte fleisch*, leftovers. Cook till it's almost dry, then bake for a day. If you

157

were Orthodox—and everybody was, those days—you couldn't cook on *Shabbes* and the baker couldn't work, so you put the pot into the baker's oven overnight. It was the heart of the *Shabbes* night supper."

"Sounds like cassoulet to me."

"Cassoulet is *nothing*, absolutely tasteless, compared to *cholent*. And such small portions they serve in restaurants, you could starve from *two* portions. *Cholent* you eat until you can't get up from the table. If Bill brings *cholent*, it'll be a symbol of his willingness to become part of the family, whether he converts or not, and Maurice Edel will love him."

"Where do you buy *cholent*?"

"You don't buy *cholent*; you make it. With love. When Violet comes, I'll tell her how. And what it's for."

"But it won't be ready till tomorrow. Just when you tell Bill that we're not going to close the Lerman deal."

"It'll help soften the blow. In fact, if the Edels talk with Bill about his plans, they might even invite him to eat with them. To eat *cholent*. It'll make him feel better." And then it struck me. What was I saying? That I was giving up? Never. "We've got to stop talking like this, like we're not going to solve the case. We *are* going to solve it, and I know how. Don't go to gym now. Instead, meet me in the gym at twelve. We'll take a good workout together—that'll clear your mind—then a little steam. No, no steam. I don't feel like going into the steam room ever again. Or at least till we find the murderer. We'll relax a few minutes in the whirlpool and then we'll have lunch at the club. At two o'clock. My regular table. I'll make the reservation."

He looked at me suspiciously. "Are you going to get drunk again, Dad? That won't necessarily work twice."

"Drunk? Me? Never. I don't drink; you know that. What I'm going to do this time is get *you* drunk."

He just looked at me. Some people don't appreciate original thinking.

26

After Warren left, I ate a good solid breakfast, full of protein, which I was going to need to fuel some heavy thinking: a pot roast sandwich, left over from last night when I didn't come home for supper; solidified bean soup that I didn't bother heating because it's delicious cold—full of fiber and very healthy—especially when you add Tabasco and garlic powder; and two cups of cocoa, hot, because it soothes the nerves at the same time it helps the digestion. Then I went up to my bedroom and lay down on the recliner to think; God forbid Violet should catch me in the living room when I'm supposed to be at work, out of her way. You'd think she'd be glad I used up some leftovers, but she doesn't trust my judgment on food. She wants me to wait until she comes in to make me hot cereal; by her, hot cocoa doesn't count.

When I woke up it was almost twelve; didn't even have time to shave. Well, I could always shave in the gym; better than having Warren worry what happened to me. I don't like razors, but Carey doesn't allow anything electrical in the wet area, even though all the outlets are ground-fault-interruptor receptacles; supposed to be absolutely safe.

Warren was already working out when I came into the gym. I waved to let him know I was there and went into the heavy lifting area; it'll be a long time before he's as strong as the old man. I was feeling real good: The weights felt like feathers and I hardly worked up a sweat. This had to be on account of the high-protein breakfast I had and the routine I use. Bob Pasternak, one of my investors, is a cardiologist, and he says that at my age I should avoid strain as much as possible, all kinds, but if you don't keep up the level of your workout you're going to drop down and down until you have no strength left. So I do heavy exercises, but after each set, I do a supine breather with light dumbbells to stretch the chest and oxygenate the blood. Really works too. Brings the pulse rate down fast and takes away the tired feeling.

Warren and I finished about the same time. We changed into our swim trunks, took our big towels and shampoo, and went into the wet area. The main shower room was pretty busy and I don't like being splashed by the cold-shower heroes while I'm hot, so Warren and I put our stuff on the towel shelves and checked the small shower room. It was empty, so Warren took the near shower and I took the far one on the other side. I don't lather up until my final shower; soap removes the oils your skin needs to protect it from the chlorine. Basically, what I'm trying to do is rinse off any sweat and warm up the system for when I go into the whirlpool, so I start hot, make it a little hotter, still more hotter, and move fast, right into the pool area.

Warren started to go into the near whirlpool, but I grabbed him. "You want to cook me alive?" I asked.

"It's only three degrees hotter than the other one."

"That three degrees is just enough to boil the meat off my bones," I explained, and led him to the next one. We stepped down onto the first step, waited a few seconds to get used to the temperature, then down onto the second step and waited, and so on until we were all the way in. I went into my favorite corner, where I could get jets massaging my spine from two sides at once, leaned my head back against the tile rim, and closed my eyes. It felt so good, so relaxing, I could've stayed there an hour. "I should've made massage appointments for us," I told Warren. "Sorry. Maybe after we shower, we can find two masseurs and get a half-hour rubdown."

"We don't have the time," Warren said. "Our lunch is set for two o'clock, you said. The one where you're going to get me drunk so I can solve the case subconsciously."

"I never said drunk," I protested. "You know how I feel about losing control. All I want is to loosen some of your inhibitions. Let you think freely."

"I really don't need alcohol for that, Dad; I'm trained to think freely, with no preconceptions or prejudices."

"Yeah, but we haven't gotten anywhere so far." Again I spoke too fast; I could see him tighten up. "Look, I didn't mean it that way, Warren; we've gotten very far in very little time. It's only two days—would you believe it?—since Barney was killed. I think we've learned a lot. We probably know all we need to know to solve the case; we just don't see it clearly, haven't put the pieces of the jigsaw puzzle together yet to make a clear picture. Give it an honest try."

He sighed. "I'll do it, Dad, but it really seems silly."

"Trust me." I turned my head to look at the clock. "We've been in here four minutes. One more minute and we'll get out; dangerous to stay in this temperature too long."

161

Warren was sitting at the table when I got into the dining room; I needed an extra few minutes to shave. Cut myself twice, even though my bristles had been softened by the heat. Why Sid Hoffman shaved with a razor every morning was beyond me, especially with his poor eyesight.

"Give Warren a very cold double martini," I told Clarence, "easy on the vermouth, and no olive. Just seltzer for me. Start with a shrimp cocktail, broiled well-trimmed lamb chops, baked beefsteak tomatoes and mozzarella, and for me chocolate mousse. Warren can have a double armagnac. And bring him a double martini between each course."

Clarence just looked at me. "You know better than that, Mr. Baer," he said. "Mr. Warren's not used to drinking."

"I know that, Clarence; thanks for your concern, but he's not driving. I'm deliberately trying to get him relaxed."

Clarence looked doubtful. "I don't know, Mr. Baer; he don't heft much. You want him laying down or sitting up?"

"Talking and thinking, but good and loose."

"Then you better leave it to me, Mr. Baer. The brandy is definitely out. If you let me decide how many martinis . . . ?"

"I'll trust your judgment, Clarence."

He smiled and left. Won again. As usual.

Two double martinis was all it took. Warren had a stupid grin on his face, but he was still upright and able to talk. Babble. Philosophical babble. Which might've been interesting to his friends at school, but was totally useless

162

for solving the case. Every time I brought up the murder, he went off into "What Is Life?" or "What Is Death?" or "What Is Justice?" stuff like that. You wouldn't believe how many different ways there are to answer even one of those questions. Each answer made a lot of sense until Warren came up with his "but on the other hand" or "viewed from a different perspective" or "assuming a narrower referent" and everything that sounded so reasonable five minutes before was now pure horseshit. In a philosophical sense.

As for getting him down to specifics, like who murdered Barney Brodsky, forget it. Philosophers don't want to give answers to simple little questions like that; what they want is to find answers to questions that have no answers, so they'll hold for all times and all places. I think that, secretly, they're all looking for ways to become God or, if they can't get that, to understand Him. Nice work if you're a hermit, or a professor, but not too good for getting a handle on this case by tomorrow, three o'clock.

I'd have to do it all by myself. As usual.

27

"What're you doing to my boy?" Violet yelled when I brought Warren home. "Teaching him to be drunk?"

"Relax, Violet," I said. "Just an experiment that didn't work. He only had two drinks."

"That's what they all say. *Only.*" She took Warren from me. "I'm gonna put him to bed; cover him good. Be quiet and don't wake him till tomorrow. And don't go in the living room; I ain't finished yet."

"But the cleaning crew was here yesterday."

"Them!" She sniffed. "Waste of money. You can go to your room; that's clean now. And stop leaving your underwear on the floor."

No sense arguing. Days like this, you can't win. I went upstairs, kicked my shoes off, and pushed all the way back on the recliner, ready to do some really heavy thinking.

I woke up at five; not getting any sleep the night before will do that to you. God, another day shot and nothing to show for it. Just when I was really willing to figure out motives. I kept trying, in spite of my gut feeling that the key was who was where when, but it didn't help. What we needed was a pro. Not Palmieri—cops aren't suited for this kind of case—but an Ellery Queen, a Nero Wolfe, an Alexander Magnus Gold, somebody with the kind of brain that could just look at the problem and see the answer right away. And not even the whole problem; just the motive part. If I knew who had to kill Barney, the rest I could figure out later.

An inspiration: I leaned over, picked up the phone, and called Iris Guralnik at her office. The machine answered first ring: "Dr. Guralnik is busy now. Please leave your name, your phone number, and the time of your call. You will be called back when she is free."

Five to six she called me. "You finally realized," Iris said, gloating, "that there are so many things wrong with your golf game, you had to call my office for a consultation?"

"Don't *noodge* me, Iris," I said. "I got enough problems without you. I have to talk to you."

"You mean real problems? You want to consult me *professionally*?"

"Why not? That way you have to listen; no wisecracks."

"Okay, give me a moment." I could hear paper rustling, then she came back on. "Next Thursday, two sharp."

"You don't understand; it has to be now."

"An emergency? For real?"

"Goddammit, Iris, would I call your office otherwise?"

"I was going to make supper for Marvin, but if you really need help, come right now. I'll call Marvin and tell him to grab some Chinese near his office."

"He's working tonight? I thought all dentists took Wednesdays off."

165

"We need the money."

"You still don't have enough in the wedding fund? What're you going to do, rent the Taj Mahal?"

"It's not the wedding fund, Ed; it's you. Every couple of months you come up with a new deal we have to invest in."

"Have to? It would kill you to miss one deal?"

"In a sense, yes. Marvin doesn't get a pension, you know, or stock options; all we have is what we make. And I want him to retire soon; I can see the work is killing him."

"Still, with two good incomes . . ."

"Every penny I makes goes into NVC. You're keeping us broke with those terrific deals you cook up."

"Another year, and they'll start paying off big."

"I hope. Now I have to tell you something. You come to the office, I charge you; consulting is how I make my living."

"Me? But we're going to be *mishpocheh* soon. This fall."

"Here's how it works, Ed. You come to my house for dinner, and you're in the mood for caviar, I'll buy you a hundred bucks worth and hope you enjoy it. You want golf instruction, I'll give you all you want, no—"

"I don't want help with my golf," I broke in. "In fact, I'll pay you to not help me."

"Don't interrupt, Ed," she said, "I'm trying to make a point. But when you come to my office, that's my profession. So, until you go to a friend who's a butcher and ask him for a dozen porterhouse steaks free, you don't ask me for free psychological consultations. And I'll tell you something else, Ed; when you don't pay, you don't listen."

"Okay, whatever you say. I'll be—"

"Unless it's about Warren and Lee. Then we can talk like potential *mishpocheh*. Until they're married; after that, you pay the normal ten percent extra for in-laws."

"It affects them, but it's not about them. Now can I come over?"

"So come already. And to make you feel better, everything I'll bill you for goes into the wedding fund."

I leaned back in the leather recliner and Iris sat sideways from me on a smaller chair with a wide arm, so she could write in her steno book.

"It's more relaxing this way," Iris said. "Doesn't look like I'm interrogating you. And if you want to look at me directly, all you have to do is shift your *tuchis*. Now, what's on your mind?"

"The murder. I have to decide about going ahead with the gym deal by tomorrow afternoon. If Bill's in the clear, we go, but if he's still a prime suspect, we don't."

"At the meeting you said you didn't think he'd done it."

"I still don't, but as long as he's a suspect . . ."

"Who do you think did do it?"

"One of the other five: Lerman, Greenleaf, Hoffman, Rubin, or Kaner. The trouble is, none of them had a motive."

"Then why do you think one of them did it?"

"If it wasn't one of them, it had to be Carey or Warren."

"That's ass-backward reasoning, Ed. How sure are you?"

"Absolutely positive."

"Then you're wrong when you say none of them had a motive. At least one of them did have a motive. The killer."

"That's what Warren said. I should've listened to him."

"I told you to listen to what Warren says, but you

167

don't listen to me either. So what motives are there for murder?"

"Warren and I went through that already: sex, money, hate, revenge, insanity, blackmail, showing off. Everything."

"You're going about this wrong, Ed; trying to fit a normal motive to an abnormal situation in a straightforward way. Have you tried Warren's way of backward thinking?"

"I don't know how to think backward; I just know logic. But Warren tried it, and he didn't get anywhere either."

"You're not Warren, and his backward thinking wouldn't be the same as yours." Iris hesitated, then said, "Usually I don't give direction to a client, especially this early in a case, but with the time pressure, and what I already know about you, I'd like to suggest something." She stopped.

I waited. Finally I said, "So? Go ahead."

"I was waiting for you to argue. The way you do exactly the opposite of what I tell you to do on the golf course. I don't want to mess things up by bringing out your usual reaction to my trying to be helpful."

"This is different, Iris. I asked for it and I'm paying for it. So talk, already."

She smiled. "See? I told you. If they pay, they listen. Okay. Take what you've been doing about motives, trying to fit a motive to each suspect. Now reverse it."

"Fit a suspect to each motive? No good. Warren and I already tried that. Doesn't work."

"Instead of a complete reversal, a ninety-degree turn."

"What the hell's a ninety-degree turn for motives?"

"When you're yelling, Ed, you're not thinking. Try thinking for a few minutes instead. With your mouth shut."

This is what Iris calls not giving direction too early in

168

a case? Of course: It's not direction, it's giving orders. And, I guess, with Iris and me, it's not like she's working with a complete stranger, so it's not really early in the case. And I don't think she considers me a case. Not in the usual sense. She better not.

Ninety degrees. What the hell was ninety degrees when it came to doing something? Backward thinking I could understand, sort of. It's directly opposite to . . . That had to be it. If backward thinking is one hundred eighty degrees from regular logic, then ninety degrees must mean halfway between forward and backward. Instead of looking for the motive a suspect had, the regular way, or trying to fit a motive to a suspect, the backward way, what I had to do was . . .

I knew about Barney needling the five suspects and, from what Palmieri had told me, I had a good idea what the needling was about. Sure it was gossip, but if several people knew about it, like Palmieri said, there must've been something to it. And guaranteed it wasn't as unimportant as the suspects made out, otherwise they would've just told Palmieri all the details instead of clamming up. So if I acted like I had proof the gossip was accurate, and was even worse than what Palmieri had told me, important enough to kill Barney for . . .

Perfect. No problem. Well, yes, there was a problem. Five problems. If it didn't work I'd end up with the most important men in the club hating me, maybe suing me, God knows what. Maybe even trying to kill me. I mean, whoever killed Barney, he wasn't going to let me accuse him in public. Or tell the police he was the killer. The moment he knew I knew, I'd have to watch my back night and day. My front too; this killer was smart. It was too late in the day to do it now, to do it properly. Better to think about it a while, figure out how to accomplish . . .

It'd have to be first thing tomorrow morning. Another problem: how to bring Warren into it. To boost his morale, like Iris wanted, Warren had to be the one to find the murderer. On the other hand, there's no way I was going to put Warren in danger. With my life, yes, I'll take risks. But to take a chance that a killer, a genius killer like the one who knocked off Barney, would go after my son? Never. The first way, if I succeeded, I'd get my grandchildren, true, but I also stood a good chance of sitting *shivah*, God forbid, for my only son and ending up with no son as well as no grandchildren. No choice, I'd have to do it myself and figure out how to encourage Warren another time.

I got up fast, that's how excited I felt and how anxious I was to get started figuring out the ninety-degree way for each suspect. I went to Iris and kissed her on the forehead. "Thanks, Iris," I said, and I meant it. "You're pretty good at consulting. I know exactly what to do; I just hope I can get it done in time." I checked my watch. "Okay, send me the bill personally, not to the office. Fifteen minutes' worth."

"Professionals charge by the hour," she said. "A forty-five minute hour. And, in this case, double for overtime."

"On second thought," I said, "send the bill to my office. This consultation was so we could close the Carey gym deal. And if we do, it's going to be charged to that company so, as a limited partner, you're going to pick up part of the expense." Anytime a psychologist can outsmart me . . .

I took off for home fast. I needed supper and I was good and sleepy too; less than five hours' sleep in the last twenty-four. Troubled sleep, at that. When your mind is as active as mine, you need lots of protein. And calm, deep sleep. I just hoped Violet would be gone when I got home; more nagging I didn't need.

28

Thursday morning, D-Day, when I woke up, I had my problem solved. All five problems: how to approach each of the suspects with my ninety-degree technique for finding the murderer. One that fitted my personality and the way I liked to get things done: the direct attack. And I could do it right away; just had to wait till after nine. There was still some pot roast left, and some cold bean soup, so I had a good breakfast to get ready for the rough day ahead.

Warren came down just as I finished washing the dishes—God forbid Violet should catch me eating solid food in the morning—so I made him coffee, toasted a bagel, which has more nutrition than a croissant, and put out some chive cream cheese. He didn't look as happy as a kid his age should on a nice morning, so I didn't bring up the case; let him relax a little longer and work out his own ideas. I'd use my terrific idea on finding who had the motive to commit murder, and if I uncovered anything, I'd give it to Warren so he could take the credit.

"I've been thinking about the case," he said, as I squeezed him two oranges. "I want to ask you something."

171

"You don't need permission, Warren; I'm your father."

"We're not going to close this case by three o'clock today, are we, Dad?"

"Well, you never know." If I told him my idea, it might influence his thinking. Then we'd both be working along one line rather than each one using his own talents to come up with a different way of solving the problem. In case my way didn't work. Although I was sure it would. "Something could happen when you least expect it."

"It's not very likely, is it? I need more time for the pattern to take shape, and I can't do it with that deadline facing me. I'm used to having lots of time to analyze a problem and to synthesize a solution. Time without pressure."

In the venture capital business, he'd have to learn to think under pressure and come up with the right answers fast, but he was young yet. "What do you have in mind?"

"Don't call the bank today to cancel the closing."

"Are you serious, Warren? Do you know how much that'd cost? *Us*, not our investors? There'll be the lawyers and the bank officials and everybody involved, all sitting around waiting for us, and then I call and say 'Sorry, I changed my mind.' A fortune. Not to mention our reputation."

"It won't cost all that much. If we decide not to go ahead with the loans, whether it's today or tomorrow, the two percent commitment fee will be gone anyway. That's the bulk of the money, and it'll cover the cost of the bank employees. The rest, say two hours' fees for the lawyers and title people, can't be all that much. A couple of thousand dollars at most. We've had a good year; NVC can afford it."

"And what about Lerman's time? And his projections?"

"He'll be getting hundreds of thousands of dollars' worth of improvements to the mall for free, to induce another gym company to take the lease at a higher rent."

Warren was right, thinking like a real financier. For a couple of grand more we'd buy a half day of time, which might let us solve the case and save a hefty commitment

172

fee. Also, while my approach was solid, it depended on all five suspects being available when I went to their offices. I'd be surer of getting my work done if I didn't have to finish it by, say, noon today. In addition, finding the guy with the motive was only part one. There was still the problem of proving to Palmieri that the guy with the motive was the murderer. I'd worry about that when I completed part one, but every hour helped. "That makes good sense, Warren," I said.

He smiled, relieved. Iris would've been proud of me.

As long as I was going to use shock tactics, I wouldn't call for any appointments—too easy to put me off for a day on the phone—I'd just show up on their doorsteps. Joel Kaner I'd have to talk to by phone; to go to New York I didn't have time. Rubin, Hoffman, and Lerman would be in practically all the time, so the first one I went to was Arnold Greenleaf.

Since he was supposed to be there by a quarter to nine, I was outside his office door at eight-thirty. Arnold was right on time, unlocking the office door himself. His secretary probably came at nine, which was all to the good, since what I had to say to Arnold might cause heavy screaming, and witnesses I didn't need. He was a little surprised to see me, but asked me in anyway. "I don't have much time," he said, "but if it's important, I can make room for you late this afternoon. Business or pleasure?"

"It's about the murder. The police didn't find anything in Barney's clothes. They checked his professional diary for the past couple of weeks; still nothing. But Gene let me go over his father's calendar. Way back I found some notes. Wouldn't mean anything to a cop, but to me . . . He had a code name for you: Lincoln. Because you're tall and thin, I guess, and you have a plain, cheap-looking old-fashioned office."

173

"You're sure he was referring to me?"

"It checks with what people remember he used to needle you about. They didn't understand what he said, but they remembered some key words. If the cops start digging, they'll be able to put the whole story together too. Right now I'm the only one who knows what Barney was needling you about."

Arnold wasn't shocked, or if he was, he hid it well. "If you felt it was that important, you could've asked me. Not that I want everyone to know, but it's not the worst thing in the world either."

That threw me. Even though I had the general picture from what Palmieri had told me, I had spent a lot of time figuring what each one of the five had to have done that jibed with his situation and his personality, things that he would kill to keep quiet, that would be perfect motives for murder.

Barney just hinted at what terrible things each one had done, so he could torture his victims for a long time. It was also how he kept them loyal on the board of directors. So it was blackmail after all, though not for money. Each of the suspects had to live with the fear that, some day, Barney would accuse him publicly, in plain English, and ruin his life. Yet here was Arnold Greenleaf taking it like it wasn't all that terrible. Something wasn't kosher. "If you would've told me," I asked, "why didn't you?"

"Why should I?" He looked annoyed, but not scared. "It wasn't true, it wasn't all that important, and I'm not proud that anyone could think that of me. It could also have made trouble for me. *You* know, now? Okay. But why should I have volunteered anything?"

"It could've gotten you disbarred, maybe sent to jail."

"Jail? Disbarred? Never. You're a layman, Ed; you don't understand how these things work."

"It's not so different from the building line. You said it wasn't easy dealing with the bureaucracy unless you knew your way around. That means to get in good with the clerks, give them gifts, slip them a twenty once in a

174

while. You buy season tickets to all the sports events and give them to your friends in the departments you deal with, tell them you can't go to the game and it's a shame to waste the tickets."

"It's the only way to exist with bureaucrats," Greenleaf said. "Saves the clients money too; my time costs a lot more than a ticket to a ball game or a bottle of perfume. And I never ask for, nor would I get, anything I'm not supposed to have; all it does is accomplish what I'm supposed to have done for me in the time it really should take instead of in months. Big deal."

"Yeah?" He wasn't getting mad, which meant I wasn't getting close enough to the bone. "That ain't all. How about the donations to the political clubs and contributions to judges' reelection campaigns? How about some really heavy contributions to the surrogates, the ones that name you administrator or executor of estates, especially when somebody dies without leaving a will? You said it yourself, some of your business comes in that way."

"So what? If you checked, you'd see that the lawyers who do business here usually give the legal limit to all campaigns, regardless of party; you never know who's going to win. And we all donate heavily to our own party; that's par for the course. It's not the kind of thing I'd like in the headlines, but it's no crime."

He was too cool; had to be hiding something, something I hadn't mentioned yet. "That may be," I said, "but there was one thing in Barney's notes that I wasn't sure I understood. Now I do. If it becomes public, you're dead." When Palmieri told us the gossip was that Greenleaf had a surrogate in his pocket . . . That had to be it. "You bribed a surrogate, Arnold. Probably with cash; hard to trace, but an investigation will prove it. That's what Barney really had on you. And that's why you killed him."

He sighed. "If you really have any evidence of that, Ed, you're supposed to turn it over to the police. I don't relish the idea of an investigation; just being investigated

175

itself would hurt me. I'd sue you, and I'd win every penny you have. Not because I want to, but because I'd need it; you'd be putting me out of business. Not only that, the surrogate you name will sue you too, for ten times as much as I would. And the party, the elected officials, the appointed ones too, would put you on their shit lists. You can't believe how many ways you're breaking the law, or some regulation, just by being alive. You'd not only be out of money and out of business, you'd find it impossible to stay in the county."

He got up. I had to get up too; this was more than I'd bargained for. "If you want to go to Palmieri with that crap," Greenleaf said, "go ahead. That is, if you think he'll act on scribbled and not-too-detailed notes. But be aware of the consequences. And if there's any fairness in your heart, think of what you'll be doing to me, without any reason, all based on a misinterpretation." He led me to the door. "One more thing, Ed. You seem to be under some pressure to close this case. I don't know why you don't leave it to the police, but that's your craziness. What you just did wasn't funny. And it certainly wasn't warranted. So before you talk to me again, I expect an apology. Not in public; just here in my office, where you accused me. Okay?"

The door closed behind me. Struck out. He as much as admitted I was right about schmearing the clerks, but unless he was a better actor than I gave him credit for, I was wrong on the bribing of the surrogate. At least there was some motive, but only if Barney had been willing to go public with his accusations of low-level bribery of government workers, which there was no way of proving. But was that a motive for murder? I had to be missing something. Or else Arnold Greenleaf was completely innocent. Maybe not completely, but as innocent as a lawyer could be. Or a builder. Or anybody, in a world where the bureaucrats had you by the nuts.

176

29

Sid Hoffman was next. Kaner had lost a whole day on Monday and was probably still up to his ass in alligators, so the later I talked to him the more likely I could get in ten consecutive minutes of conversation. Rubin and Lerman? Them you wouldn't bother first thing in the morning when the day's decisions had to be made and the progress of the day's work adjusted to fit. This early, Hoffman was probably not too busy; the people who buy Mercedeses need time to dress right for the important activity of the day.

I was wrong. Hoffman's secretary told me he was in the service department, making his daily check of that section. Another reason he was the biggest dealer on the Island. Most businesses act like the deal is over when the sale is closed. Not Sid. He knew that they remember the price once, but lousy service stays with you a long time. I picked up a magazine. It was a good half hour before Sid came back; clearly it wasn't just a quick look-in for him.

He asked if I wanted to see the latest of the latest, but I told him I had to talk to him urgently and privately, so he took me into his office, closed the door, and told his secretary not to disturb him for fifteen minutes unless it was a customer with a complaint. "That takes precedence over everything, Ed," he said. "I hope you understand."

I understood, and told him the same story about Barney's notes I had told Arnold. Sid didn't seem too bothered either. Maybe I was crazy. If somebody had come up to me and said he knew all about my crimes and my sins—and I've led a pretty clean life for a guy who'd been in the building business thirty years—I'd turn blue and start worrying. Not these guys. Maybe their morality was different from mine. A scandal that a man would've considered suicide for thirty years ago today was an opportunity to see how much he could get for a personal confession on TV in complete dirty detail.

"The first thing I want to ask, Sid," I asked, "is if what Barney's notes said is true."

"What exactly did Barney's notes say?" he asked back.

I didn't really expect him to fall down and confess the minute I acted like I knew he was the murderer, like they do in TV mysteries. "It was about your fooling around. Here you are, with some very beautiful young women working for you, intelligent, competent women, perfectly dressed, making a good living, and dependent on you for that living. Surrounded by women like that all day long, who could blame you? You're a handsome guy, Sid, tall and built like a Mr. America, still under fifty, with all your hair, and at the age when some men think that if they don't do it now, they'll never have another chance, that life is slipping away. The age when they divorce their wives and marry girls younger than their own daughters."

"Did it ever occur to you, Ed," he came back, "that Barney was making this up? That he saw the situation exactly the way you're describing it and, without a bit of evidence, put together a story that sounds like it could be true, even though it's absolutely not?"

"Of course it did. But tell me, you never took one of

178

your saleswomen out to dinner at night? At a fancy restaurant not in this neighborhood? And had some drinks together?"

"I do it all the time. Once a week I take one of my people to a fancy restaurant. It's on the South Shore, so I don't bump into anyone I know, especially a yenta who'll go running to my wife and upset her. If a saleswoman wants wine, she gets wine. Or champagne or Perrier or Coke, her choice. I take out all my people, in rotation, men as well as women, including the head of the service department. Does that make me gay too? We talk about business and things that affect the business, like morale. I find out what's bugging them, not just in the shop but at home too, try to help with their problems. I give them tips on selling and service and how to handle customers; good as they are, there's always something to learn. And good as I am, I find out from them ways to improve the operation. You think I'm successful by accident?"

"But what happens afterward, Sid?"

"We go home. In separate cars. What else?"

Time to take a chance. "That late at night?"

It worked. He got red. "Sometimes it takes longer than other times; we stay as long as is necessary."

"So why did you let Barney's needling bother you, if you're that innocent?"

"It went on and on. Sooner or later somebody might understand what Barney was hinting at. Sooner or later somebody would take the stories home to my wife. I don't let anything interfere with my home. Or my marriage. Nothing."

"Would you kill Barney for that?"

"Is that what you're getting at, Ed? Kill? Okay, yes, I would, if it was a choice between my wife and anybody. *Anybody*. My wife comes first. But it wasn't. Everybody knew what Barney was, and if my wife heard anything that had come through Barney Brodsky, she knew enough to ignore it."

"There were indications in the notes that Barney had records, dates and places. Could those have been motels?"

"I don't care what those notes said. I never in my life went to a motel with anybody but my own wife. Look, I worked like a dog to build up this business to where it is; you think I'd risk it all just to get laid? You don't shit where you eat, Ed; that's Rule Number One."

"You've never been tempted?"

"Sure; who hasn't? But I never did."

"If the dates and places in the notes refer to homes . . . ?"

"You can get addresses out of the phone book. And every Wednesday is when I take one of my employees out to dinner, so you could write down the dates a year in advance. We usually go to one of two restaurants, French or seafood, so that doesn't mean anything either. Anybody could put together a record like that; it depends on how you look at it."

"Most people would look at it the way Barney did. A divorce lawyer could easily make a good case of it."

"Where'd you get that divorce business? From Barney?"

"Where else? Maybe he saw himself as an Iago, trying to make trouble. If he had, what would you have done?"

"Same as you would've done, Ed, if he pulled a trick like that with you and Thelma. Excuse me for bringing her up; no offense intended. I would've busted his head for him; I don't care how old he was."

"Not strangled him?"

"That's not my style, Ed, just like it isn't yours."

"Did you tell all this stuff to Palmieri?"

"All what stuff? Barney's bullshit? Hell, no. Why should I? To have that crap on record?"

"I may have to, tomorrow."

"Have to what? Tell the police what you told me? You better not, Ed. You upset my wife, I'll have to set the record straight and sue the shit out of you. You want to turn those notes over to Palmieri, okay, I can't stop you. Legally you probably have to, so go ahead and do it. But keep your interpretations to yourself."

"Yeah, that's how I'll handle it. I'm not trying to make trouble for you at home, Sid; but I got to do what's right."

"Sure." He got up to his full height, towered over me, even though I'm above average. "But make sure you know what's right, Ed. It ain't always what's written in the rule book."

I left, and sat in my car for a while. It had struck me, though neither Sid nor Arnold had made the threat, that the smart thing for the killer to do would be to knock me off and make sure that no one, particularly Sergeant Palmieri, saw those notes. And if the guy who beat my brains in with a baseball bat didn't find those notes on my dead body, it would be very hard for me to explain that there were no notes, that I had made it all up, that I had figured out what Barney's records had to say and acted like that was what Barney wrote. What the killer'd have to do is assume that I had left the notes with Warren and proceed to take his bat to Warren's head. Not only would there be no Baer grandchildren, there wouldn't be any Baers left either.

30

Since Gold Coast Mercedes was halfway to Rubinetics, I figured I might as well go to there next. A minute after I spoke to the receptionist, Rubin's secretary came out. George was in a staff meeting and would be tied up until eleven, but if I waited he could see me then. I told her it was a personal matter and, since she knew me from last year when we were dickering about NVC financing the Rubinetics expansion, she said she'd try to get me an uninterrupted fifteen minutes.

I made myself comfortable in one of the hard, straight-backed chairs in the reception room and picked up an electronics magazine to read. I don't understand electronics, but I do have an engineering background—I almost got a degree—so I can read semitechnical articles. I try to keep up with the latest in technology but, even so, I was amazed at how far we'd come since I went to school.

George was not in a good mood when I went into his office. His shirt was damp under the arms and his usually neatly combed hair looked like he'd been running his hands through it. His desk was piled high with paper, a sign he'd been letting things ride while he attacked his most pressing problems. I knew he was under a lot of pressure, but showing that to me was not the best way for the head of a company to act. He had to be showing it to his associates too, and that was death for a business. "What's so goddamn important," he snapped, "that you have to bother me twice in one week?"

"If you think I'm such a big bother," I snapped back, "that you don't want to have a chance to answer, I can leave right now and you can talk to the police instead of to me."

"Answer what, Ed? Don't beat around the bush."

"Barncy left some notes I got hold of. About why he was needling you. It's a lot more serious than simple needling."

"Barney was full of crap. If he was so sure he was right, why the hell didn't he act on it?"

"Because he was killed, that's why. Which points the finger straight at you."

"You think I killed him? That's bullshit. He didn't have a leg to stand on, and he knew it."

"Barney was a lawyer, George, a good lawyer. You think he wouldn't check with a top patent attorney before he took the case? You think they didn't order at least two thorough patent searches before he even spoke to you?"

George turned blue. "That transducer is mine, Ed." He sounded desperate. "I invented it. All by myself. It's a completely new principle, never been *known* before, yet so simple a high-school kid could understand it. My claims are so broad that they cover practically *anything* that's moved by electricity. I didn't copy somebody else's ideas and I didn't infringe on any patent. I'm smart enough not to need to."

"That's not what Barney wrote."

"I don't care what he wrote. You think my patent attorneys didn't do a thorough search? One? Hell, they did three. Not just in transducers, in allied fields too. There's nothing in the literature like it. Nothing!"

"Sometimes something shows up in a completely different field. No searcher looks at every patent in the world; it's impossible. All he can do is check what seems to have a bearing, what seems to have some overlap. If a patent's been issued in a completely different field, like a toy or something, and the principle that's the basis for your transducer is described, your patent is worthless."

He began shouting. "It's not. It's valid; completely original. Anyone tries to claim infringement, he's got a fight on his hands."

"Which means *you've* got a fight on your hands. A fight that could cost you more money than you've got, more time, more energy. It would take away from your work here and, for all practical purposes, force you to close your business, even if your patent holds. There are people who attack vulnerable patents solely on the chance they'll collect for the nuisance value of their claims. You can't afford to fight them."

"Whatever Barney had"—George cooled down swiftly, began speaking normally—"couldn't have been a hell of a lot at best. Why would anyone with a real claim of infringement go to Barney Brodsky? Barney wasn't a patent attorney. Whoever his client was, he had to have gone to a legitimate patent attorney first, maybe more than one, and been turned down. I know I invented the controlled electric drive transducer."

"The point is that, for whatever reason, Barney took the case. That he let you know, generally, through hints and whispers, what it was about. That he was attacking the only thing that kept Rubinetics afloat, considering all the money you've taken out of the company for your personal investments. Whether the claim was valid or not is not the issue. Whether Barney took the case because he believed in its validity or not is irrelevant. Barney was preparing a suit that could destroy your business, and you with it. As

184

the police will see it, you had the best motive to kill him. Sort of self-defense, to stop him from killing you."

"I'm an engineer, Ed, not a killer. I solve problems with a computer, not by violence. A few months ago we spent a lot of time together, and you got to know me pretty well. Do you think I'd kill anybody, even a bastard like Barney Brodsky, for any reason? Even to save my business?"

"In terms of personality, George, no I don't. And if I was asked, I'd say the same about any of the other people involved. Still, one of you did it."

He looked completely beaten down. "Look, Ed, do us both a favor. Before you give the notes to the police, check them carefully against my patent. My secretary'll give you a copy. You've had some engineering training. If you think there's any reason for the suit, that there's any basis at all for an infringement claim, then see a patent attorney you trust. At my expense. Anyone you pick. Then if you find something, give the notes to the police, everything you have. But if there's no basis, bury them. Don't destroy a good company for nothing, just on the word of a vicious old man like Barney."

I knew what he was saying. It was "Don't destroy *me*, don't kill *me*, unless you're sure beyond a reasonable doubt." Just like in a criminal trial. I felt like crying, but I had to say it. "You've got the picture wrong, George. I don't need a copy of your patent. It isn't whether or not the suit Barney was going to file was valid; it's did *you* think he was going to destroy Rubinetics? And destroy you? The way it looks to me right now, you did think that. Which gives you a very good motive to commit murder. Whether you did or not, that's for the police to decide."

He lifted his head. "You're going to Palmieri now?"

"No," I said. "I have a couple of other suspects to talk to first. After I do that, I'll give the police what I think they need for the case. No more and no less. I'm not going to do anything to hurt you, or to hurt anyone else, unless

185

I think you're the murderer. But if I think you're the killer, I'll tell the police everything I know."

I left fast and quietly. I'm not stupid; I knew exactly what I was doing. If George was the murderer, I was setting myself up to be killed. Given the little I really knew, given that I had no notes by Barney Brodsky, given that I had to protect Warren, how else was I going to catch the killer?

31

I changed my mind about phoning Joel Kaner. In person you can see things—like George Rubin's reaction when I mentioned patents—so, much as I hated to go to New York, I'd have to drive in and catch Joel. Also, on the phone, it's easy to say "I'm tied up; see you tomorrow." For me there was no tomorrow; now that I'd opened the can of worms, I had to find the killer today, or else. Or else he'd find me? *That* I didn't particularly care for. So I'd talk to Carl Lerman now and leave Joel Kaner for last. Who knows how bad the traffic would be? Good, it positively wouldn't be.

I figured I'd catch Lerman just at lunchtime. Probably he ate in the trailer with the phone in his ear—I'd done it that way myself, in the bad old days when I was working for a living—and I'd never be able to get two consecutive sentences out of him. Best would be if I could take him to a nearby restaurant. Anyplace, as long as it was away from the job.

Carl didn't want to leave the jobsite, so he told his super to order us each a corned beef on rye and a diet soda, and we went to the rental agent's trailer that had just been set up near the entrance to the site. Lerman had to be as anxious to get away from the headaches as I was to get him away. The trailer was still bare inside, just a couple of chairs and a desk. Later it would be furnished luxuriously, to impress the potential renters that this was going to be the most fabulous mall on the Island. I liked it the way it was; gave a no-nonsense feel to the interrogation. And it was better than a restaurant; we could talk in absolute privacy. Carl could even scream, if he wanted to.

I started with the opening I had perfected with the others; that I had gotten hold of Barney's notes and that they had described, vaguely but unmistakably, the terrible crimes that Carl Lerman had committed.

"Me?" Carl asked. "At my age and position? Crimes? Barney put that kind of crap in writing?"

"He didn't go into detail; more like a memorandum. To remind him what to needle you about."

"For that Barney didn't need reminding, Ed. He enjoyed annoying men who were still productive. Because he wasn't."

"Didn't that bother you, the constant irritation?"

"Sure it bothered me, but I didn't show it. With guys like that, if they see it bothers you, it just encourages them. Besides, he did it so that nobody who heard could know what he was talking about. So why come to me about it?"

"I'm trying to find who had a motive to kill him."

"And you picked me?" His voice was mild, a bad sign for someone built like him. Or like me. Same thing, practically.

"Not just you. Everybody who was in the wet area at the time of the murder. I have to check them all out."

Lerman let his breath out slowly, got his voice back to normal. "Let me tell you a couple of stories, Ed; might teach you something. I don't know if they're true—probably not—but they make the point. There's this big Holly-

188

wood producer. A guy comes into his office and throws a bunch of photographs on his desk, pictures of the producer in bed with two beautiful young starlets. Getting ready to blackmail the producer. Doesn't say anything. The producer looks over the pictures and says 'I'll take a dozen of each, eight by tens, glossy.' The guy who was going to blackmail him walks away."

"You think I'm here to blackmail you, Carl?"

"Don't know yet. You can talk after I tell you the next story, also probably not true. About a builder, one of the biggest and best. Some politicians who wanted to make the headlines so they should be reelected held an investigation into the builder's practices. They subpoena his books and call him up as a witness. Going over the builder's numbers, one of them asks him what a two-million-dollar figure, listed under Miscellaneous, was for. 'Bribes,' the builder answers. Real loud. Big uproar, the session is recessed, and the builder isn't asked any more questions. You know why. They were afraid that he'd be just as honest about who the bribes were for and once you start investigating one politician, who knows who's going to make a deal and turn in the others."

"I assure you, Carl, I'm not the least bit interested in blackmail or in making trouble for anybody."

"Then why are you here and why are you talking about Barney's bullshit notes that describe my crimes?" He shook his head in wonder. "My *crimes*? What crimes?"

"Like what you said before. Bribes. Zoning boards, building inspectors, politicians."

"Did he give dates, places, *names*?"

"Not that I could make out."

"What I figured. Guesswork. Bullshit. And this kind of crap is supposed to be my motive for killing him?"

I should've known better. Builders, who are used to facing the problems that are normal to the business, aren't easily bulldozed. I sure as hell wasn't, in my day, and Carl Lerman was what I would have been ten years later if I had been so stupid as to stay in the lousyconstruction-business. And he had learned a few things in those ten years. "I have to check everything, Carl" was my weak answer.

"I never in my life did anything crooked, Ed. Illegal, maybe, just like you did a hundred times; you have to, in this business, no way to avoid it. What did you do when one inspector told you a certain thing was against regulations, and another said you absolutely had to do it? And that each one would stop the job if you didn't obey him? What did you do when some shithead, who had just moved into the neighborhood, started a campaign not to allow any more building in the village so as to maintain the rustic atmosphere, even though the zoning laws said you could? What did you do when some assholes decided that instead of lowering the cost of their bureaucrats, they'd pass a regulation that anyone who built in their village had to provide a fully equipped park for them? Huh? What did you yourself do?"

"What had to be done. Same as you probably did."

"Damn right. And if somebody accused—*accused*—you of doing these things, *unspecified* things, not even openly, but just hints, would you kill him?"

"Of course not."

"Well, neither did I," he said triumphantly. "Case closed. Now will you drop the bullshit? Do you want to eat with me like a civilized human being, or do you want to haul your ass out of here? Or maybe I should ask myself, do I want to break bread with a criminal like you?"

There was only one thing to say, so I said it. "Does your lunch man know enough to bring plenty of sour pickles?"

That broke Carl up. "Tell me, Ed," he asked, "did you talk to the others the same way?"

"Just about. I haven't seen Kaner yet; I'll do that later, drive into New York. If there's anything you need to have done in midtown, maybe I can do it for you after I finish with Joel. I haven't forgotten how to be a builder, and I didn't need you to remind me."

"It didn't hurt either, that I reminded you. Thanks for the offer, but I don't need anything right now, especially in New York. I do all my business on the Island now, it's much easier. You got any hot prospects for the murder?"

"Not really. Everybody has the same kind of motive you have. It's there, but it's nothing to kill somebody over."

"You still convinced it was one of us?"

"I don't see who else it could be, do you?"

"Bill Carey. I understand he's the one Palmieri favors. So let me ask you something else. What if he's arrested?"

"He won't be. There's no evidence."

"There's evidence against *me*? You're questioning him like you're questioning me?"

"I already know his motive."

"It's the best one, isn't it, Ed?" I didn't answer. "What you're trying to do is prove he didn't do it."

I had nothing to say. There was no point in trying to con Carl Lerman. He was as smart as I was, with ten years more experience.

"Are we still on for the closing tomorrow?" Carl asked.

"Still on."

"What happens if Carey's arrested tomorrow morning?"

"I won't be associated with a killer. Or someone I suspect is a killer."

"It'll cost you to pull out at the last minute, Ed."

"Only money."

"That's what I thought you'd say. It'll be a pleasure doing business with you, Ed. On some other deal. You want to call tomorrow off?"

"Would you give up now, in my shoes?"

"I never give up."

"Neither do I, Carl."

The guy came with the sandwiches. The pickles smelled good, but I had to force myself to eat.

32

The Long Island Expressway is the world's longest parking lot, and weaving in and out didn't help. Each nail-chewing extra minute of the trip put me that closer to the pile-up at the tunnel and reduced my chances of catching Joel Kaner when he could see me, and brought me that much closer to the rush hour on the way home. When I finally got through the Queens-Midtown tunnel and found a parking garage that wasn't full, I was not in a good mood.

Kaner's office was as I expected: modern furniture in dark colors, with etchings of old English buildings on the walls; giving the impression of conservative dependability. The receptionist was attractive and business-friendly. After checking with Joel's secretary, she told me Mr. Kaner would see me in a half hour and, as long as I was waiting, could she bring me some coffee. I asked for hot chocolate and a chocolate doughnut. She apologized for not having the chocolate doughnut but offered a cheese danish, and my respect for Joel went up a notch. For the cost of a few hundred bucks a year, you give a visitor the feeling that

Kaner goes out of his way to make you happy. Not a good sign if I was going to squeeze a motive out of him. On my next murder case—God forbid there should be one— maybe I'd get lucky and deal with dopes instead of smart businessmen.

Joel was wearing the most expensive, but conservative, everything the uniform required, and was clearly trying to hide that he was in a hurry and hadn't wanted to see me in the first place, so I got right down to business. I gave him my spiel about Brodsky's notes and said, "What Barney was insinuating was that you fooled around with the books."

"Not insinuating," Joel said. "More like teasing."

"He was hinting he'd go public with what he knew."

"There was nothing to know, so why should I care if he went public or private or wrote notes to himself?"

"Your reputation is what you sell. If that goes, you're dead. Is one accountant that much better than another?"

"You think that gives me a reason to kill him?"

"Motive, the police call it. Means and opportunity you all had, but your motive is the best."

"Opportunity? I was the first one out of the showers."

"Once in the small shower room, nobody in the big room could see you. Instead of turning left into a shower, you turned right into the steam room. Two minutes to kill Barney, you peek out of the door, nobody's watching, so you take a quick shower and go into the whirlpool."

"You could make up the same story for any of the others. And your motive stinks. Accountants don't fool around with books; we get the information from our clients. In fact, we usually put a disclaimer on our work that what we did is based on information given to us by the client."

"Every once in a while I read in the papers that a big accounting firm is being investigated for issuing misleading documents, depreciation, net worth, things like that."

"There's a difference between accountants; some are

smarter and work harder. The average accountant just follows the clearest regulations; I look for legal ways to help my clients keep a little of their hard-earned profits."

"By cheating the government?"

"You can't cheat the government. Most of those cases come about because the IRS wants publicity or wants to scare the industry into not pushing the limits of the regulations. There's always some federal attorney who's looking to make a name for himself, even with a weak case."

"What about the accountants who were accused of inflating the value of companies prior to takeovers, that forced the leveraged buyout guys to issue more junk bonds than they had originally planned on, so they couldn't make the debt service payments? Good accounting practices or crimes?"

"I don't know enough about those specific cases to say whether they were good or not, but they weren't crimes. When a major client asks you to produce figures that show the worth of his company is a certain amount, you have to take advantage of everything that's in your favor. Accounting isn't exactly the dry, clear-cut arithmetic most people think it is; judgment is very important."

Now I knew I had him. "Statements like that, they require an audit, don't they?"

He bit his lip. "Usually." A lot shorter answer than the ones he'd been snowing me with before.

"In an audit you don't take the client's word, do you? You have to dig out the facts? Fully backed up?"

"That's the proper procedure."

"Barney indicated there was one company that you did an audit on where you used what's politely called creative accounting. For which somebody could go to jail."

"What company?"

"He wasn't specific; do you want to be investigated?"

"Nobody wants to be investigated. What do you want?"

"Talk to me. I'm not the least bit interested in your

194

business or your professional ethics. Convince me that what Barney found out about had nothing to do with his death, and I destroy the notes and keep my mouth shut."

The air seemed to go out of him. "I don't know how to convince you, Ed, that what you're talking about had nothing to do with the murder. If I tell you what I know, I want your word that . . ." He shook his head. "What good would that do? You either believe me or you don't."

"Try me."

"It was some time back. A young company, a really good company, had grown very fast and outgrown its capabilities and capital. It needed money fast and was negotiating a merger with a big company. It had a lot of solid receivables, but no liquidity, and a big debt service. The president of the company was a good manager but a financial idiot. He didn't ask me for anything; I did it on my own. I didn't get a big fee either, but I made sure the books showed the company was a little better than the audit warranted. It turned out well, thank God, as I was sure it would; if it hadn't, I might have been in the papers too, even though I'm not a criminal. The topper is, the merged company dropped me as accountant and stayed with the firm that handled the bigger company's books. How Barney found out about it, I'll never know."

Exactly what I suspected. "So you did have a motive to kill Barney."

His face got red. "If I had fooled the big company, if the merger had turned bad, maybe I could be blamed to some extent. But it turned out well. Nobody hangs you for things that benefit them. So I had no motive to kill Barney. If he knew all the details, which I doubt, he could've disclosed them and embarrassed me a little, but that's all. In fact, he might even have done me some good that way. Some companies want an accountant who's able to solve their problems."

What he said made sense. Assuming it was true. A man who'd cook the books, even for—as he claimed—a good cause, wouldn't necessarily tell the truth, and certainly not the whole truth, if it could land him in trouble. And even if Joel's story was completely true, couldn't there have been *another* deal that he forgot to mention, where he came off as a really crooked accountant? Who had done something he could go to jail for? Cops know the technique. You stop a guy for not signaling a left turn and, if he's got a kilo of cocaine in his trunk, he's not going to argue the ticket.

I left, worn out from the day's work, just in time to hit the rush hour. Everybody trying to leave New York at the same time is a lot worse than people trickling in. I had a guaranteed two-hour trip home and a quarter tank of gas, which could easily leave me dry if there was a *real* holdup, like some morons slowing down to watch a guy change a tire.

The worst part was, I'd accomplished nothing. I had five half-assed motives for the murder, but what I had really wanted was that one of my guesses would be right and all the others wrong, so that the murderer would stand out. Confess. Attack me. *Something.* I had killed my last day and still had the same number of suspects as before.

33

By the time I got home it was almost time for supper so, after I washed up, I sat down at the kitchen table to wait for Warren to join me. Violet wants us to eat in the dining room, formally, but to me the kitchen is a homier place. It's also a lot easier on Violet's feet. She doesn't complain, but I notice. "How'd the *cholent* come out?" I asked her.

"Easy," she said. "Poor black people been cooking like that for a hundred years."

"Yeah, I guess all poor people have a dish that's mostly beans with whatever's around thrown in. Now that you know how to make it, I wouldn't mind if you served it once a week."

"I always knew how to make that, Mr. Baer. Just like a dried-out Brunswick stew, with more garlic and less onions. We never had duck either; just put in whatever was left over. When's Mr. Carey gonna pick it up?"

"He didn't yet? I thought he'd take it to the Edels this afternoon when there weren't too many other people around."

197

"You want to bring *beans* to rich people?"

"Maurice wasn't always rich. He'll love it, guaranteed. In times of trouble, it's very comforting to eat what your mother used to make."

"Yeah, good idea. I'm gonna make a Brunswick stew next time my girls come to visit. Do them all a lot of good; remind them where they come from. *And* their husbands."

Warren came in, looking all worn out, and not from heavy exercise either. Violet might not have known every little thing that was going on the past few days, but she had sharp eyes and a grandmother's instinct for getting to the heart of the matter right away. The first dish was a thick split-pea soup with lots of garlic croutons. I didn't say anything until the soup was finished, then I asked Warren, "I thought Bill was going to take the *cholent* over to Sharon's house today?"

"I advised him to wait till tomorrow," Warren said, "after everything was settled one way or the other. If he went there today he wouldn't know what to say to Sharon."

"He thinks Sharon wouldn't marry him if he was broke? Sharon's not like that."

"I know, but he wouldn't marry Sharon if he was broke."

"That's twice as stupid. The greatest happiness a young couple can have is when they're building a life together."

He gave me a look. "Even when one of them's in jail?"

"That's not going to happen. The worst problem we had was that Bill was the only one with a motive. Well, I've got news for you. First of all, you were right about working on the motive; that's the way to solve the case."

"You know who did it?" His eyes got big. "Really?"

I shook my head. Violet was at the stove, ready to serve the boiled beef with horseradish sauce and roast potatoes, but she knew this was not the right time. "No, but I found out that all our suspects had motives to kill Barney Brodsky. Not as strong as Bill's, but something." I gave

198

Warren an almost word-for-word report on what I had done. Then Violet served.

We didn't talk for a while; that's the greatest compliment you can give a cook as good as Violet. Then Warren said, "Does that mean we can close with the bank tomorrow?"

"If it was only our own money at risk, I'd say yes. But with our investors' money we have to be very conservative."

Warren thought for a moment, then said, "Fair enough. Then let's close the deal with our own money."

"No way," I said. "We took the limited partners' money on the basis that they'd share in the venture. If we give them their money back and take the whole deal ourselves, we're reneging on our agreement. What would it look like if we give the money back and a year from now the gym is a terrific success? That we let them in only on regular deals and keep the best stuff for ourselves? Besides, we can't afford to do it alone." I waved his objection aside. "I know we have enough cash available over what's set aside for the new deals we're considering, but suppose someone else comes along, someone with a really good venture he's been working on for years. What do we say? That normally we'd finance him, but since we put all our cash into a friend's business, we can't help him?"

Warren clenched his jaw. "I'll use my personal money."

"Same argument as before, with two more problems. What if Bill finds out? You think you'd be able to remain friends in such an unbalanced relationship? With NVC, it's business; with you financing it, it's friendship. Business and friendship you should never mix. How would Bill feel if the business failed? It's one thing if a company goes into business with the expectation that it'll succeed and understands that it might fail. But for a friend to put in a lot of money would put such pressure on the poor guy, he'd start thinking in terms of not failing rather than in terms of succeeding. A guaranteed recipe for failure."

"Then what should we do?"

"Think. Analyze. You do it backward, I'll do it forward. We have a lot of new information; let's put it into our computers and see what comes up."

"Before tomorrow morning at ten o'clock?"

"Baers never give up." I hadn't forgotten that Palmieri wanted me to call him to report on what I'd learned today, little as it was, but I wanted to think things over first.

34

I had two cups of coffee after supper to make sure I wouldn't fall asleep—it was tonight or never—and still my head kept dropping down. Slow analysis is not for me. You need a quick instinctive decision that'll be right almost every time, that's my meat. I was successful in the building business where you're always operating in real time, and a day's overhead can run you tens of thousands, so you better be right 99 plus percent of the time. But this kind of slowly examining the facts is not my way.

I have a feel for space, so I closed my eyes and visualized the murder scene: who came in, who went where, who could see what, and it all fit, like one of those French bedroom farces where there are ten doors, and the wife comes in just as the maid goes out and the lover is hiding under the bed and the mistress is in the closet and . . . I couldn't find anything wrong with the way each suspect described what he did, even though one of them had to be lying.

Then the motives. Each suspect had given the right answers: Barney was wrong or he didn't care if Barney went public, or he couldn't be hurt much by what Barney said, or Barney didn't have proof. But if it wasn't so bad, why was Barney killed? One of them was lying and the liar was the killer, but who was the liar? I hated to admit it, but when it came to motives, Iris was the expert, so I reached for the phone to call her, and that second the phone rang.

It was Iris. "I have to talk to you," she whispered.

"So talk," I said.

"Not on the phone; Marvin will be back in a minute. Meet me in the club. In the pool room. Twenty minutes." She hung up.

All of a sudden Iris is keeping secrets from Marvin? At nine o'clock at night? Usually she did anything she wanted, that's how bulldozed Marvin was; now she was worried he'd find out? And what did she want from me? Advice? Iris *gave* advice, not took it. Besides, I always had the feeling she thought I wasn't really very smart, so why me? Well, whatever it was, I needed her to figure out who was lying, and if she wanted anything from me, she'd have to tell me how to find the liar. I didn't have the time to fool around any more; ten o'clock tomorrow morning was *it*.

I got to the club fast, took a quick shower, turning it to hot at the end so I'd be used to getting into the whirlpool, and went into the pool area. Iris was already waiting for me in the first whirlpool, the hot one, looking like she was wondering what the hell took me so long. I motioned to her to go with me to the second whirlpool. She didn't argue, just came out and followed me. I went in slowly, to get used to the heat, while she, having just come from a hotter pool, was able to go right in. First time I ever saw her in a bathing suit. She didn't look too bad either. Chunky, yes, but solid, not fat. Huge oversize bust, but still not too bad. "Why here?" I asked.

"We can be seen here in public at night and no one can make a big deal of it. And we can talk privately; the noise of the whirlpool will keep anybody from hearing. It's a perfect excuse to go out without Marvin."

"What reason did you give him? The place is almost deserted; practically nobody comes here this late."

"I pulled my back on the golf course yesterday, and I need the heat and the water massage to relax it. In fact, I really did make a massage appointment for a half hour from now, just so you could leave before me."

"Why all the secrecy, Iris? What's going on?"

"Lee called me. She's flying home tomorrow night for the weekend. To see Sharon Edel, lend her support. But Marvin and I have this weekend in New York that I arranged months ago because Marvin has to take some time off or get a nervous breakdown. It's one of those hotel deals where we get a special rate. We see three shows, hit a couple of museums, eat terrific meals in good restaurants, all different cuisines. So we can't pick Lee up at the airport."

"That's the problem? Don't worry, I'll pick her up."

She glared at me. "What's the matter with you, Ed; losing your memory? You can't pick Lee up either because you're going on this weekend with us."

"I am? Me? You never told me a thing—"

"Of course I did; with the pressure of business, and the murder, you forgot. Just like Marvin. Men!"

"Come on, Iris; I have a perfect memory. You never said a word about—"

"Are you getting stupid in your old age, Ed? *You* are not going to pick Lee up. Warren has to."

Then it was clear. "Aha! So why didn't you say so in the first place. When did you make the reservations?"

"One minute after Lee called me."

"Okay, understandable. Sneaky, but understandable. But why do I have to go with you?"

"You know, Ed," she said, still irritated with me, "sometimes I wonder if you're worth all the trouble I take training you. You want Warren and Lee to go to a motel?"

"A motel? Of course not. What has that . . . ? You want them to . . . ? In your house?"

"Or in yours. For the whole weekend. If you're at home, Warren will feel he has to come home too. This way, they won't have any pressures on them. They can relax in familiar surroundings, be together a whole weekend."

"But you're encouraging—"

"They don't need encouragement, Ed. What they need is peace and quiet and freedom from responsibilities and obligations. By themselves. Like a honeymoon."

I thought about it, for the first time. And much as I hated to say it, Iris was right. But I wanted to make sure. "They're positively going to get married this fall?"

"Guaranteed. I've started talking to the rabbi and looking for a hall. Quietly, so keep your big mouth shut."

"And Lee still wants a big family?"

"More than ever."

"Three and three? Maybe even four girls?"

"You'll take what you get, Ed, and love it."

"I'll pray. But why do I have to go with you and Marvin? You want me to disappear, I can go someplace by myself."

"Because if you don't come with us, Marvin might decide to call it off so he can see Lee two days sooner. With you involved, I can tell him we don't want to disappoint you."

Another thought struck me. "Look, Iris, don't take this wrong. But am I supposed to share a suite with you and Marvin? You want two men with you at the same time?"

"Is that so bad? I'm such dull company?"

"No. Yes. Not dull. *Definitely* not dull. But I'm not . . . It's not even a year since . . ."

"Stop sweating, Ed; I told you once, I'll let you know when you're ready. And whom to start dating. And don't worry about your virtue. I'm not a prude, you know, but I don't play trios either. Not that I wouldn't enjoy having two men escorting me, but you don't particularly like Marvin.

At dinner, you wouldn't say a word to him, just talk to me. I don't need him feeling left out; I want him to have a good time too. So you'll be escorting Dottie Lesser."

"Dottie Lesser? But I took her to dinner at your house last year. If I go out with her again, she might think—"

"Yeah, twice in six months. What a dashing lover you are. Sweep a girl right off her feet."

"We'd be together in the same hotel? A whole week-end?"

"You can lock yourself in your room. But would it be so terrible if she knocked on your door? She's nice."

"I wouldn't know what to say, how to act. I don't really want to . . . I don't know how to . . ."

"When you're ready, it'll all come back to you; like riding a bicycle. Just act natural: Do what you'd normally do, say what you'd normally say. Just don't say anything to hurt Dottie. She isn't over it either."

"Either? Me? I'm in perfect shape, Iris. I run a business, I get along with Warren most of the time, I go to gym regularly, play golf three times a week, enjoy myself. So what's with the either?"

"Everything's absolutely perfect with you?"

"Sure. Almost. Except, when I'm alone at night, I keep thinking of Thelma."

"You don't have to stop thinking of Thelma, but you shouldn't stop living either. One of these days, come to me professionally. I mean that."

"I'd feel funny . . . Maybe I will, Iris, but not right now. Give me time."

"You decide when. Okay, then, we're all set? We'll pick you up at your house at six. Bring a tux, just in case."

"Yeah, but I want to drive. The way Marvin drives . . ."

"He'll take it as an insult. I'll drive."

"Never; you drive like a cowboy."

"I drive, Ed; don't argue."

"If you drive, I sit in the back."

"Natch. With Dottie. You can even hold hands if you're scared. Do you both some good." She glanced at the wall clock and started to get out of the whirlpool. "I've got to get ready for my massage."

"Wait. I have to talk to you. About motives. The murder. I spent all day today working on it."

She came back, reluctantly. "Okay, but make it fast."

I reported, as accurately as I could, everything I'd heard today. "My problem is, everything I accused them of was guesswork, what I figured out about each one, where I thought he'd be vulnerable."

"As it turned out, you were right. Five out of five? I don't get results like that very often."

"Yeah, but these were pretty obvious, once I started looking for motives. I was hoping to uncover one motive. Instead, all of them had some reason to kill Barney. Not very good reasons either; none of them seemed too worried about being found out. A couple of them even said I was obligated to turn Barney's notes over to Palmieri."

"That might have been bravado. Did you expect one of them to offer to bribe you not to tell the police? That would be a clear indication that he was the killer."

"But what do I do next?"

She thought for a moment, then said, "Do what you'd do if you found only one suspect with a motive; that's the kind of thing you're good at. Assume that each suspect's the murderer; that he killed Barney for the reasons you know. Consider everything you've found out, and see if it all fits with him as the murderer. Then do the same thing with each of the others, one by one. By the time you've finished, you'll know who the killer is."

"But that could take me all night."

"You got anything better to do, Ed?" She smiled like a cat and got out of the whirlpool.

I followed her. She was right, as usual; I had nothing better to do. But she didn't have to enjoy that.

35

Warren was in the living room looking mopey, defeated. At his age? Kids today don't have the stamina. I'd have to cheer him up, then give him something productive to do. "I need you to do Iris and Marvin a favor," I said. "I forgot to tell you before, but Lee Guralnik is flying in from school tomorrow night to sit with Sharon. There's no one to pick her up so I volunteered you, okay? Where and when you can get from Iris tomorrow morning. Or tonight; it's still early."

"Sure," he said, brightening up right away. "Happy to. But why can't her parents?"

"We—and they—have a long-standing date to go out together, to go to New York for a weekend. Tomorrow night to Sunday night. See three hit shows, eat at good restaurants, the works. For rest and relaxation. Everything's all set; reservations all made, can't be changed."

"You and the Guralniks?"

"I'm escorting Dottie Lesser." His face changed. "Don't get the wrong idea, Warren; it's just to even out the table."

"That's all right, Dad; I don't mind."

Mind? I'm a big boy; I can't go out with girls now? I got to ask my son for permission? It was too complicated to explain. Besides, if I started explaining, I'd get stuck in a whole mess of contradictions that were built into the Iris Guralnik secret plot that wouldn't've been there if she'd let me arrange everything. Engineers automatically set things up so that there are no loose ends and no internal inconsistencies. Which reminded me.

There was no point in mentioning Iris again; the less her name came up tonight, the less Warren would try to find holes in what I told him. "All our suspects," I said, "had the means and the opportunity, and now we know they all had motives too, sort of, so nobody stands out as the murderer. We still have tonight left so why not take each suspect by himself, as if he, and only he, had a motive. Make a scenario that shows he's the murderer. Compare the results. The one with the best scenario, he's the killer."

"That's an old trick, Dad. Occam's razor. The explanation that requires the least assumption is best."

And I thought Iris had invented it. "Old or not, I'm going to my room to work on it. If I get something before eleven, I'll come to you to discuss it and you can try to tear it apart."

He nodded. Bad sign. Unless his mind was on Lee Guralnik. Then it was a good sign. Things were in a hell of a state, when I couldn't tell good from bad. "And you do the same," I added, "if you come with anything. Okay?"

He nodded again. Useless. I'd have to do it all myself. As usual.

I'd been going crazy trying to do what Iris told me, when I realized that my mind was not focusing on what it

208

should. Then I realized what the problem was. Everything I knew about what had happened in the wet area was secondhand, either from what Warren had said or from what the suspects had told me. What the suspects said I couldn't trust. Warren I could trust but, let's face it, he wasn't me. I can look at a set of plans and the first thing I'd notice was where the architect had screwed up. I could walk on a construction job I'd never seen before and my eye would go immediately to where some jerk had made a cross connection or a sloppy weld. Doris used to complain, before we had the computer, that she'd type a perfect spec and I'd zero in on a typo on the last page.

What I needed was to see the scene of the crime myself, with all the suspects in place. A reenactment of the crime, just like in the mystery books I used to read when I had the time. Then I'd know in a flash what didn't fit. Or see it. Or hear. Whatever. The only trouble was, how could I get the suspects to cooperate? *Cooperate?* Hell, I'd be lucky if they just hung up on me.

But I knew who could make them do it. If I approached him right, that is. Palmieri. Whom I had forgotten to call to report on the suspects' motives. Maybe if I told him I was busy analyzing . . . ? And it was close to eleven. Well, he couldn't kill me over the phone. I dialed his home number.

He sounded sleepy, then mad. "I got a life too, Baer; I'm not a cop twenty-four hours a day."

I gave him everything I had heard today. "See, they all had good motives to kill Barney Brodsky."

"Lousy motives," he said. "If you knew this at four o'clock, you should've called me from New York. Maybe I could've done something earlier."

"I was busy analyzing—"

"Too late. I'm pulling in Carey tomorrow morning."

"You're arresting him?"

"Going over a few points. Depending what he says, I may have to arrest him."

"You have no idea the trouble it'll make if you arrest him tomorrow."

"You got no idea the pressure I'm under."

I was desperate. "Maybe if we reenacted the crime while you were watching, we could see—"

"Are you nuts, Baer? You been seeing too many TV shows lately. I got to get five civilians, big taxpayers, together in one room, tell 'em one of 'em's a murderer, and make 'em go through the motions to show which one it is? One phone call, just one, from one of their lawyers, just one, and I'd be lucky if they only made me turn in my badge."

"But that's the only way. I'm sure that if—"

"Don't you listen, Baer? Your being sure ain't worth shit to a D.A. What you want a cop can't do. Even if you found the guy that way—which I doubt you could—the evidence—which I doubt you'd get—wouldn't be admissible. So forget it. I'm going to sleep now. But I'll do this for you. Before I pull in Carey I'll take your statement and interrogate the suspects again, ask 'em why they didn't tell me all this before, and see if I can catch one in a lie. That's if they admit they said what you say they said. Which I doubt too. Geez, Baer, bribing a surrogate, paying off politicians, screwing the help, cooking books . . . You got any idea what size can of worms you're opening?" He sighed. "Go to bed, Baer. Come see me tomorrow at ten. Bye."

See him at ten? *Ten?* The closing at the bank was set for *ten.* If I didn't have this all wrapped up by nine— eight-thirty would be even better—there'd be no closing. It'd cost NVC thousands, no bank would ever trust me again, Carl Lerman would tell everyone I'd lost my marbles, Bill Carey'd go down the tubes, Sharon Edel's heart would break, I'd look like an idiot, and worst of all, Warren would have broken his promise to Bill to clear him by Friday. Which would ruin Warren's self-confidence and

210

kill his spirit and insure that he'd never marry Lee Guralnik and that I'd never have any grandchildren.

"Wait." I was desperate. "I have an idea. We don't have to tell them anything; we'll just *be* there. It can't be illegal for us to just be there. One of them—I forget who—said that what they did on Monday was what they do every weekday, no change. We just observe, see what happens, see if anything's different. See if every one of them really had the opportunity, or if only one of them did. See if the pattern of the movements, the lines of sight, are exactly as they described it. As Warren saw it. What could it hurt?"

Palmieri was quiet for a few seconds. "Just observe? It's not a bad idea, Baer. Our hanging around, *my* hanging around, watching, maybe it'll rattle the killer so he does something, says something, I can use. What it can hurt is, it'll kill an hour for me."

"It might also get you the killer. You'll get all the credit, okay? See you in the upstairs lobby at seven-thirty. And bring your swim trunks and rubber sandals. You can use my locker. And one of my bath towels." The old man still had the touch.

36

At ten to eight, Sergeant Palmieri, Warren, and I, wearing swim trunks and rubber-thong sandals, were standing in the big shower room, just behind the stone bench nearest the entrance, where we would be out of the way of anyone coming in. Our towels were on the shelves at the far end of the room and Warren wasn't wearing his glasses, so it would be just like when he was there at the time of the murder. The entrance to the steam room was clearly visible from where we were standing, but we couldn't see into the little shower room. Or into the sauna or the sun room either, but we could see their doors clearly too. As soon as we had come into the wet area, Warren reached into the steam room and turned the thermostat all the way up, so conditions would be just like when Barney was murdered. I kept checking my watch every few seconds, wondering why everyone was moving so slowly.

"There's no way to be sure," I told Palmieri, "but Barney could've come in at this time."

"Doesn't matter," he said. "According to what I figured out, Mr. Brodsky could've come at almost any time and not be noticed. What's important is when could the killer have gotten into the steam room?"

A minute later Joel Kaner came in, wearing blue swim trunks. He took a quick surprised look at us and, with just a slight hesitation, kept on walking to the towel shelves. He put his towel on the top shelf and went into the small shower room. I couldn't see what he was doing from where we were, but I could hear the noise of the shower. "Kaner could've gone into the steam room instead of the shower," I said, "turned up the steam so he couldn't be seen, waited for Barney to come in and lie down, and killed him. Kaner could even have turned on the shower—so people would think he was taking a shower—before he went into the steam room. When he came out, he could've slipped across the aisle and turned off the shower, so whoever heard that would think he was finished taking his shower."

Palmieri just grunted.

"He could even have stayed in the steam room at normal temperature," I added, "and, when Barney came in, told him it was okay to turn the heat all the way up."

Kaner finished his shower and we could see him going into the pool area. Ramon came in, carrying his bucket full of cleaning stuff and dragging his hose. He hooked it up to a hose bibb near us and began spraying water on the walls at our end of the room. Sid Hoffman came in naked—had a terrific build for a man his age; any age—put his towel on a shelf, and went into the shower cubicle at the other end from us and Ramon. Sid's water was hot—I could see it steaming—and Sid kept washing his face with heavy lather.

"Ten steps and he's in the steam room," I said, "and no one would notice. Or else Barney could've come in at this time. If he did, it means Joel can't be the killer."

"Not necessarily," Palmieri said. "Mr. Kaner could've

213

come back from the pool. It's only a few steps to the steam room and no one would see him."

"I don't think so," Warren said. "We didn't ask, but the lifeguard would've told us if Mr. Kaner went out and came back again. Depends when the lifeguard got there."

"It would've been easy," I said, "for Kaner if Barney had come in just after he did. Kaner could've kept an eye on the steam room door and gone in directly from the showers."

Bill Carey walked in, dressed in a gray sweat suit. He stopped when he saw us, but I waved him to keep going. "Just do what you normally do," I said. He turned right to peek into the sauna and the sun room, came back, took a quick look around the big shower room, and walked to the small shower room. There he took another quick look around and went into the steam room. "That's when he could've killed Mr. Brodsky," Palmieri said, "and nobody would've seen it." Bill came out of the steam room after a minute, his suit damp all over, and went into the pool area.

Sid Hoffman finished showering and softening his beard. He walked quickly over to the towel shelf, unwrapped his towel and took out his shaving kit, wrapped the towel around his waist, lathered up carefully, and began shaving. Carl Lerman came in, put his towel on a shelf, and went into the same shower Hoffman had just come out of.

"No one would've seen Carl either," I said, "if he just walked into the steam room right now."

Palmieri didn't answer. His eyes were on the sweep-second-hand clock on the wall. "All of this was just a couple of minutes, so far," he said, "and did you notice how long it seemed to take?"

"That's because we're concentrating," Warren said. "Subjective time can be very slow or very fast."

"Yeah, but what I was thinking," Palmieri said, "is what a D.A. would say when I tell him everything that

214

happened and that it all took place in a couple of minutes. He'd never buy it, never be able to explain it to a jury."

"Are you saying," I asked, "that even if we catch the murderer, he can't be convicted on account of a jury not being able to believe how quickly the murder took place with a bunch of people watching?"

"That's the last part of my troubles, Baer," Palmieri said. "First we got to catch the rabbit."

George Rubin came in, carrying his towel and walking fast. Didn't even notice us. He started for the pool, then seemed to change his mind and went into the sauna. "He's got a lot on his mind," I told Warren. "I hope his business survives." Just then, Bill Carey came out of the pool area and went out the exit door of the wet area.

George Rubin slipped out of the sauna and into the sun room next door. Carl Lerman finished showering and went into the sauna.

A few seconds later Arnold Greenleaf, wearing tan swim trunks, came in, moving fast. He headed straight for the small shower room, took a quick look at us in passing and nodded, put his towel on a shelf, and turned left when he got into the little shower room. A few seconds later we could hear the shower going. "Greenleaf could've gone into the steam room before he went into the pool," I told Palmieri.

"It could still be any one of them," Palmieri said.

George Rubin came out of the sauna and went into the sun room. Carl Lerman went into the sauna.

A minute later Greenleaf went into the pool area. "This is when I came in," Warren said. "By this time, Mr. Brodsky was already dead." Warren had a frown of concentration on his face. "I think I know who the murderer is. Give me a little time to think it out." He sat down on the stone bench and stared into space. Time dragged for me.

George Rubin came out of the sun room and Carl

Lerman went into the sun room. Warren didn't seem to notice.

Warren seemed to come to a decision. "Yes," he said, standing up. "I'm sure."

"Who is it?" Palmieri asked.

"I can't prove it, but if I talk to them all . . ." He turned to Palmieri. "Get them all together. Now. Maybe the shock . . . ? In front of his friends . . . ? Before they separate?"

Palmieri grabbed me. "Go to the quiet lounge. Get Bill Carey in here. Then get Kaner and Greenleaf." I took off.

It felt great. The Baers had done it again. But what about not being able to prove it? If you can't prove it, what good is it? Did Warren think one of these intelligent, sophisticated, wealthy men, all professionals and heads of companies, would just fold? Confess? Like on TV? Never. If they hadn't gone into shock when I hit them with their motives, there was no way any of them would confess to Warren's philosophical logic. Well, maybe that's where I'd come in. Just like the last time. There was still work for the old man to do. Thinking like a philosopher is great, as far as it goes. But sooner or later, a philosopher needs a practical man. An Ed Baer. *The* Ed Baer.

37

The six suspects—Bill Carey included —were leaning against the walls and sinktops watching the three of us: me, Warren, and Palmieri. They were not happy. Bitching out loud, in fact. George Rubin was the loudest, pointing out that it was a crucial time in his business, that he objected strongly to this high-handed interference with his schedule, etc., etc., etc. The others weren't saying it out loud, but I could tell they all felt the same way.

That didn't faze Palmieri one bit; he must've gone through something like this a thousand times in his life. Like, for instance, the past Monday morning, when I had tried to talk him out of questioning Warren without a lawyer. If Ed Baer hadn't scared him, no way was this bunch going to do it.

"If you don't want to spend about fifteen minutes here"—he glanced at Warren, who nodded—"just talking informally, listening to what Warren Baer has to say—and I don't know what he's going to say—I can listen to him by myself. I think it'd be worth your while to stay, but you

217

don't have to. After I hear what Warren tells me, if I think it's appropriate, I can arrange to have each one of you driven, courtesy of the Nassau County Police, down to my office and we can talk there. With a stenographer present. A *police* stenographer. Any takers?" He looked around. None of them said a word. "Good. What Warren says is not official. You don't have to answer or say anything or do anything, and you can leave whenever you want to, but that doesn't mean I won't be listening and won't use the information if I think it has any bearing on the Brodsky case. Warren?"

All eyes turned to Warren. "Practically everything I saw today," he said in his typical lecturing style, "agrees with what you gentlemen told us: that you all follow essentially the same routine every weekday morning that you followed today and that you followed on the morning Mr. Brodsky was killed. Practically everything all of you did today was exactly as you described your movements to Sergeant Palmieri and as you told my father and me when we spoke with you, with only minor variations that seemed to have no bearing on the murder."

"Then what the hell are we being kept here for?" George Rubin asked. "I have to go now."

"I'll try to be quick," Warren said. "Isn't it worth another few minutes to learn who killed Mr. Brodsky?"

George settled back against the sinks. "Another few minutes? To learn . . . ? Okay."

Warren continued. "One small difference was that Mr. Greenleaf didn't have his towel wrapped around his waist when he went into the pool area, the way it was when I saw him on the morning Mr. Brodsky was killed. Today he put his towel on the shelf before he went into the small shower room."

"That's what I usually do, Warren," Greenleaf said. "It's almost automatic, as I pass the shelves."

"But this past Monday you took the towel into the small shower room with you."

"Possibly, if I'd been thinking about some problem I had that day. We're all a little absentminded at times."

"And where do you put the towel if you don't put it on the shelf? There are no shelves in the small shower room."

"I hang it on the near partition. To keep it from getting wet, I use the far shower on the other side."

"That's reasonable, Mr. Greenleaf, but wouldn't it be just as reasonable to go back two steps and put it on the shelf next to the entry?"

"I'm usually in a hurry in the morning, Warren, and just keep moving fast without thinking."

"Again, perfectly reasonable, but if you wanted to keep your towel dry, why did you wrap it around your wet body when you went into the pool area?"

"Force of habit, I guess. I don't always do things logically when I'm rushing."

I was beginning to see where Warren was heading, but I didn't understand how all this could prove anything. Suspicious, yes, but enough for an arrest? Never.

"Rushing? Yes. Mr. Kaner said you rushed into the whirlpool. What he actually said was that you, quote, 'threw the towel on a chair and zipped right in' unquote."

"I said I was in a hurry." Greenleaf was clearly trying to keep his voice calm, but he was clearly getting irritated.

"You went into the hotter of the two whirlpools, Mr. Greenleaf. When my father goes into the cooler whirlpool he usually stands on each step for several seconds to get his body accustomed to the increased temperature."

"Your father is ten years older than I am. I don't mind the heat. I like it, in fact."

"My father takes a hot shower before he goes into the *cooler* whirlpool, and turns it up even hotter at the end, to reduce the shock of the increased temperature in the whirlpool." Warren's voice grew harder. "You told us you took a shower to *cool* off," Warren said. "And then you *zipped* into the hotter whirlpool? I suggest there's another explanation for all of your actions that Monday morning."

Greenleaf just shrugged. He was going to play it cool, and there was nothing I could do about it. What I could see of what Warren had wouldn't be enough even for Palmieri, much less a D.A.

"You had decided to kill Mr. Brodsky at the first opportunity," Warren said, "in a setting and situation where, even if someone discovered your motive, everyone else there had an equally good motive, equally good means, and an equally good opportunity. The steam room. What would have been an impossible situation for anyone outside this little group of people was a perfect situation for you. Here were four of your associates who had also suffered under Mr. Brodsky's needling and threats of disclosure, and, above all, there was Bill Carey, who had the most to gain by Mr. Brodsky's death. Even if you made a mistake, or something unforeseen happened—such as my coming into the wet area in time to notice the towel around your waist—there were still five other suspects who were as vulnerable as you are. Further, if I hadn't come in when I did, the murder wouldn't have been discovered until after nine, and all the memories of who was where would have been extremely vague. Worthless, in fact."

"As an attorney," Greenleaf said, not quite as coolly as before, "I should advise you that what you've said is actionable, and I fully intend to bring suit against you as soon as I finish hearing you out."

Warren ignored that; I hoped he knew what he was doing. The other five, and Palmieri, were hanging on his every word. "You waited in the locker room, Mr. Greenleaf, until you saw Mr. Brodsky go into the wet area. Giving him a minute's lead, you followed. But when you got into the small shower room, you didn't take a shower; you went right into the steam room."

"The lifeguard won't let you into the pool unless you've taken a shower."

"The lifeguard won't let you in unless you're *wet*, and you were soaking wet from being in that super-hot steam room. You didn't put your towel on a shelf, and you didn't hang it over a shower partition, because you had to take it into the steam room with you. Why? Because you're not a killer by nature. You didn't want to strangle Mr. Brodsky with your bare hands. Not only might he have bitten you, but the touch might have revolted you, made it too personal, caused you to hesitate, to change your mind. That would have been disastrous for you. Mr. Brodsky would now have attempted murder to charge you with, which was a lot worse than claiming you bribed a public official. You needed something, a barrier between you and death, to separate you from your victim. Ergo, the towel. Once in the steam room, you quietly climbed up to the top tile shelf, suddenly sat on Mr. Brodsky's abdomen to drive out the air, held the folded towel over his nose and mouth, and in a minute or two he was dead."

Greenleaf smiled, and I could swear it was a genuine smile. "You're now accusing me, in front of all these witnesses, of murder as well as bribing a public official? I suggest you stop while you can."

Warren didn't stop. Philosophers don't stop when they think they have *the* truth. "I didn't accuse you of bribery, Mr. Brodsky did, but that's a side issue. You couldn't go out into the main shower room after the murder to put the towel on a shelf—someone might see you, wonder about it, and mention it to the police. It would've looked odd to carry the towel into the whirlpool area when you could have put it on a shelf on the way in, and you couldn't afford to have any attention directed toward you, so you wrapped the towel around your waist. And since you had just come from a much hotter steam room, you had no trouble 'zipping' right into the hot whirlpool."

"Are you finished?" Greenleaf asked.

"Isn't that enough?" Warren asked.

221

Greenleaf turned to Palmieri. "Do you want to arrest me, Sergeant, on the basis of what you just heard?"

"I'll want to look into things a little more," Palmieri said, "and talk to you again. I may also want to look into that accusation of bribery too."

I knew what that meant. Warren had come up with an ingenious solution to the case, and it had to be right, but there was nothing in it to take to a jury. We were going to get the ass sued off us, and we'd be lucky to keep the gold in our teeth. On top of that, Warren would be humiliated. In court. In front of everybody. He'd lose his confidence and he'd never get married, and I'd never have any granddaughters. NVC was gone too. Unless I did something. What I needed was a miracle. What miracle, I didn't know, but something like in TV, when the cavalry comes galloping up at the last second. And it had to be something I'd be able to recognize and not ignore.

Like what Warren had figured out. Once he explained the towel business, it was obvious why Greenleaf had the towel around his waist and why he zipped into the hot whirlpool. And the reason he didn't turn blue when I accused him of bribing a surrogate was because he *hadn't* bribed a surrogate. Once you see it, it's obvious. What he had really done was—was—*obvious*. Obvious? Sure it was. Of course it was. What it was, was . . .

"I have something to say," I told Palmieri, and took center stage. "When I went around the second time, talking to the other gentlemen here"—I swept my hand around the circle—"I told them that I had found some notes Brodsky had written that described the things he'd been needling them about. That wasn't exactly true; there were no such notes."

There was a release of relieved breath all around the circle. "You mean," George Rubin asked, "there was no patent infringement suit Barney was working on? That you gave me heart failure for *nothing*? You lied, you son of a

222

bitch?" He looked ready to kill me right in front of Palmieri.

I ignored that; I'd straighten things out with George tomorrow. Or rather, Monday, after I came back from my vacation in New York. "Barney's needling was about things anyone could've accused all of you of. He picked these things simply by doing what I had done: by seeing where you were most vulnerable, listening to gossip and rumors, and making up the obvious stories. None of what Barney needled you guys about was true, probably. And if it wasn't, there was no reason for any of you to kill him, no *motive*. To stop a little needling, or even a lot, you don't have to commit murder; you can just walk away, remove yourself. But one of you did kill Barney, therefore there had to be a *real* motive for the killer. To accuse, say, Greenleaf of bribing a high official is crazy. Something like that would be almost impossible to prove. Barney might have needled Greenleaf about bribery, at first, but when he came to something that was accurate and checkable, *accurate and checkable*, that was a different story. And it had to be something that would get Greenleaf not only disbarred but sent to jail for. No ifs. Something Greenleaf *had* to kill Barney for."

"Are you trying to add to the claims I'm going to make?" Greenleaf asked. He still sounded cool, but the look on his face told me I was on the right track.

"Sure. Sue me for this too," I said. "Barney had been sending you clients, old friends of his, particularly for their estate work. Some small stuff, some not so small, none of it really big, and over the years it totaled up to a lot of dough. You commingled the funds, Greenleaf; put them all in one account."

"There's nothing wrong with that," Greenleaf said. "The old-fashioned way is to keep a separate bank account for each client, which becomes very unwieldy, especially if you have a large number of clients, as I do. What we all

223

do today is keep everything in one fiduciary account and keep accurate records as to how much is earned by each client, his annual totals, and how much is taxable." It was humid, but none of the others had sweat on their foreheads.

"In my business," I said, "I do it the old-fashioned way. It's cleaner. There's nothing wrong with doing it your way, if you can keep all the accounts straight. But when I was in your office, your *old-fashioned* office, I noticed something. That is, I didn't notice something: a computer. Without a computer you'd spend half your life keeping track of every little . . . Here's the way I figured it. You kept your accounts, professional and personal, in Barney's bank, the one where he was a director. He probably insisted on it, being the type he was, otherwise he'd have his friends trust their money to another lawyer. You made a mistake or something, or one of Barney's friends complained he didn't get as much return on his money as he had figured on, so Barney took a look at your account. Or maybe he looked just out of curiosity. At any rate, he checked your accounts, personal as well as professional. And discovered something."

"I don't have to listen to this crap." Greenleaf was getting red, his skinny neck swelling.

"You can go, but I'm going to keep talking," I said. He didn't go. "The way I figure, a few weeks ago Barney found that a big lump of money had been taken out of the fiduciary account. Six hundred thousand dollars. The money that you used to buy a share of the Lerman Mall. And Barney decided to play with you for a while, make you sweat good, before he exposed you. So his needling was now about stealing from the trust accounts instead of bribing politicians. And you knew that he wouldn't wait too long before exposing you publicly. So you had to kill him."

The other four members sort of shrank away from Greenleaf a little. Not obviously, but it was there. "Some attorneys," Greenleaf said, "borrow from funds they're holding." He had to admit it; it would take only five minutes for the bank to show that the money had been withdrawn on the day he paid Lerman for the mall share. "In my files, you'll find a note for the money, backed by the mall share as security. All I did was to exchange one type of security for another. Good as gold. In my judgment that was a prudent investment. Go show it wasn't."

"That's pretty clever, Greenleaf," I said, "but I doubt that would've protected you from criminal action if Barney and his friends pushed it. Certainly it would lose you all your clients. And you couldn't have backed the six hundred thousand you 'borrowed' with a mall share because the shares weren't distributed until some time later. And there's a hell of a lot of difference between the liquidity and security of a mall share and cash. You stole that money, period. I'll bet you've made a pattern of this, from the time that Carl Lerman started syndicating his jobs, five, six years ago. By now you must've 'borrowed' close to two million to invest in Lerman's projects."

"There's nothing wrong in what I did."

"Yes, there is. You never asked any of your clients if you could borrow the money, did you? Or even told them? Taking someone else's money—especially fiduciary funds—without permission is stealing, I don't care how many pieces of paper you put in its place. And since projects like Carl's pay off as tax losses the first few years, before they start producing a cash return, you haven't put back a hell of a lot of the money you took; probably used some of your other income to fake a return on your clients' investments. And not a very good return either; a one-man office like yours doesn't bring in a hell of a big income."

"All this has nothing to do with what we're here for."

"It's a motive for your killing Barney."

"Bullshit," he exploded. "First there's Warren's weak conjectures about a way I could have killed Barney, all based on my having a towel around my waist. You could

225

put together an equally worthless pattern about any of us here, and it doesn't mean a thing. Then you guessed I had a motive, that Barney was threatening me, that I bribed a surrogate. That was yesterday. Today it's a perfectly legal action I performed. What'll it be tomorrow? And these two weak guesses add up to me being a murderer? Sergeant Palmieri is here. You see him pulling out the handcuffs? No? Because he knows there's no evidence, that the same guesswork could be applied to anybody here."

I had another inspiration. "You want evidence? Okay, here's evidence." I turned to Bill Carey. "How do you store your bath towels?"

"We store all linens by type, on skids, ready to load on the laundry truck. A skid for each day, so I can walk into the laundry rooms and, with one look, see what our pattern of use is."

"Bath towels on their own skid? Monday bath towels on the Monday bath towel skid?"

"That's what I just said. They're laid on the skid in the order they come in at the desk. When one comes in, the linen man punches the number into a computer—it's not a whole computer; just a terminal—so my bookkeeper can bill for the extra. For your spa fee, you get three of each item per week; all extra items are charged for."

"Yes, fine, very efficient." When it comes to his own specialty, nobody gives short answers. "So you can pull Greenleaf's towel easily, the one he used Monday morning?"

"It has to be very near the bottom, on the Monday skid. All lined up with the locker number in the lower right-hand corner."

I turned to Palmieri. "When Greenleaf held the towel over Barney's face, he got Barney's sweat, saliva, tears, mucus, maybe even bits of skin or hair, on it. All from Barney. When Greenleaf put the towel around his waist, he got his own sweat on it. He wasn't wet from a shower; he was covered with sweat from being in a hot steam

226

room. He got more of his sweat on the towel when he wiped himself too, though he probably used the other side of the towel. Maybe even bits of his own skin and hair. You can match the samples directly or check the DNA. With everything else, is that enough evidence?"

"If there's anything on the towel," Greenleaf yelled, "it could've been wiped off from an adjacent towel when it was put on the skid. Brodsky's, for one."

"Are you admitting, sir, that there are some of Mr. Brodsky's tissues or body secretions on your towel?" Palmieri asked, superpolitely. "If there are, it's not from Mr. Brodsky's towel. That wasn't put on the skid; it was taken for evidence." There was no answer. "And if anything was wiped off on your towel from an adjacent towel—assuming the towels next to yours belong to somebody in this room—the amount has to be a tiny fraction of what's on your towel."

Greenleaf turned white, jerking his head left and right, his eyes looking for a loophole. There wasn't any, and he knew it. Palmieri swung into action. "Mr. Carey, I want you over there personally, in the linen room. Right now. Watching the Monday bath towel skid. Don't let anyone touch it or the bath towels either. I'm going to call in my technical team, and I'll be right there with you."

"I want a lawyer," Arnold Greenleaf said.

38

Warren and I were in the second whirl-pool, relaxing. At least I was relaxing; Warren still looked upset. I had insisted we come here right after the big denunciation scene, when I noticed how beaten down Warren looked.

I could understand that. It's one thing when you solve a difficult philosophical problem on paper; there's a satisfaction, a feeling of triumph, of doing a good job that maybe nobody else in the world could have done. But when you've solved a real murder case, where real people have been killed, where other real people, friends, could have had their lives ruined, or worse, and the only way you could do it is the way you did do it, by ruining another person's life, by *destroying* a man's life and that of his innocent family, a man you know—even if he's a murderer—then it doesn't feel so wonderful any more.

But the heat and the massage weren't working. Warren still looked mixed up, unhappy, confused. And he hadn't said a word to me in five minutes. I kept not staring at him, deliberately; God forbid he should think I was try-

228

ing to pressure him. He didn't want to talk? Okay, so we wouldn't talk. Finally he said, without looking at me, "I really messed that up, didn't I?"

"Messed it up?" I couldn't believe this. "Are you kidding? You're the one who solved the case. It couldn't've been done without you. You saved Bill Carey. You saved Sharon Edel. You saved all the others the shame of having people think they might've been murderers. You gave Palmieri a big boost in the department. You saved us the money it would've cost us not to close the gym deal today; they'll give you a standing ovation when we go to the bank later. You saved a good project for our investors. There isn't a person involved in this that doesn't owe you. Including me."

It was like he hadn't heard a word I'd said. "I went off half cocked. I didn't think it through. All I was interested in was in showing how smart I was by setting up a train of logic based on one little thing I had noticed. If it wasn't for you, Mr. Greenleaf would have gotten away with it, with murder, and he would have sued us. And won. A lot of money, maybe everything we have. The business too, which you worked so hard to build up."

"All I did was follow up on what you figured out. Simple logic, the way you always tried to teach me. If I hadn't done it, you think Palmieri wouldn't've? He's a cop; he knows how to do those things. Maybe he was ready to let Greenleaf walk around a little longer while he made his case, but he sure as hell would've started checking him out in depth. He would've found out about the bank account, the withdrawal, the investment in the mall. It would've stared him in the face, like it did to me."

"Yes, but four hours later the towel would have been on its way to the laundry."

"That towel wouldn't've gone anywhere. That's the kind of evidence the police love. As soon as you mentioned that Greenleaf used his towel to kill Barney, Palmieri was already figuring on getting that towel into the police lab. That's routine for him."

"I still couldn't have done it without you, Dad."

"Maybe. I don't mind getting compliments from you. But look at it another way. Nobody could've done it without *you*."

He brightened up a little. "Well, I guess we have to keep on working as a team, then."

That's what I was waiting to hear. Just as good as hearing him say "I love you, Dad." In fact, that's exactly what it was. I hesitated, not wanting to make any mistakes. Kids sometimes take things wrong, not the way they're intended, especially if you're trying to say something good. Normally I would've asked Thelma first before I said a word—she always knew when was the right time for everything—but now it was up to me alone. On the other hand, it seemed the perfect time to do it, so I said it. "Warren, do you value my opinion? I don't mean about business, I mean about important things."

He looked at me strangely; like he couldn't figure out what I was getting at. "Yes, Dad, very much."

That was a good sign, so I took the chance. "This may be the kiss of death, Warren—I know how children feel when their parents interfere in their personal life—but I think Lee Guralnik is a wonderful girl and you're at the age now when you might be thinking of settling down and I trust your judgment and my opinion shouldn't count in this a bit but if you picked Lee it would make me very happy." I hadn't intended to go that far, but once I got started the words just kept pouring out.

He just looked at me. God, if I had killed the whole thing, if I ended up without any grandchildren, if Iris found out I said *anything* . . . "I thought you didn't approve of Lee; that she wasn't smart enough."

"Not approve? Me? Where'd you get that idea? Sure she's smart enough. A three-point-five average from Bennington is bad? And she's an absolute doll. I love her even more than Sharon. I just hope you like her."

"I do, but don't you dislike her mother?"

"Iris? Only on the golf course. Actually, I spoke to Iris a couple of times about the Brodsky case—every day, to be honest—and she was very helpful. Would I go to New York with her and Marvin if I disliked them?"

"I wondered about that."

"No, really; it's okay. You're all set to pick up Lee tonight?"

"I'll call Mrs. Guralnik for the time and place right after the closing." He looked up at the clock. "Shouldn't we go to the office now, get the papers ready?"

It was go-for-broke time. "Actually, Warren, I have a favor to ask you. I'm a little tired right now. All this tension over the case, and worrying about Bill Carey and if the deal would go through, and concern over Sharon . . . I'm still a little upset about Arnold Greenleaf—I've known him for years, and his wife too—and I'm not as young as I used to be, not as resilient. Maybe you'd . . . ? Would you mind handling the whole closing yourself while I took it easy for today?"

"Me? All by myself?" A moment of shock, then a glow of happiness. "You'd trust me to handle our biggest closing? By myself?"

"Who else? Go now, so you won't get there out of breath." He practically jumped out of the whirlpool.

I leaned back. Irv Waxman, who'd done a hundred closings, would be there to handle the legal end, so I had nothing to worry about. And Warren looked so good, so happy, so confident, I knew he'd do everything perfectly. On top of that, he was smart too, real smart. Thelma's genes, of course, but with a little of mine too. I leaned my head back on the tile and relaxed, really relaxed, for the first time in a week, and started picking out names for the grandchildren. Boys' names too.